W9-BRI-244

"So you'll be staying longer, then," Will said

"Do you have a problem with that?" Cassie asked.

He smiled wryly. "I could."

Her body tightened. She looked at him, trying to read his intent. "What exactly are you saying?"

He shifted his long frame. "I'm sayin' it could get interestin'." Then after a pause, he added, "I mean you—tryin' to untangle Uncle Ray and Granddad."

The way he looked, the way he moved was having a strange effect on Cassie's knees. "Untangle?" she murmured.

"This has all been goin' on for a long time. You're gonna need somebody to give you a history lesson."

"I come from Love, remember?"

"It's family history I'm talkin' about, not town."

She should just leave, but she couldn't make herself move. Something was happening here, something that went well beyond the words he was actually saying.

"Are you volunteering?" she asked.

Dear Reader,

Writing *Love, Texas* was such a joy for me because it reflects the best that I believe Texas has to offer the world—its wonderful people. Particularly those who live in the many small towns throughout the Lone Star State. I hope you enjoy reading about some of them.

Ginger Chambers

LOVE, TEXAS
Ginger Chambers

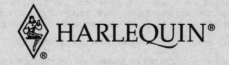

HARLEQUIN®

TORONTO • NEW YORK • LONDON
AMSTERDAM • PARIS • SYDNEY • HAMBURG
STOCKHOLM • ATHENS • TOKYO • MILAN • MADRID
PRAGUE • WARSAW • BUDAPEST • AUCKLAND

If you purchased this book without a cover you should be aware
that this book is stolen property. It was reported as "unsold and
destroyed" to the publisher, and neither the author nor the
publisher has received any payment for this "stripped book."

ISBN 0-373-75068-4

LOVE, TEXAS

Copyright © 2005 by Ginger Chambers.

All rights reserved. Except for use in any review, the reproduction or
utilization of this work in whole or in part in any form by any electronic,
mechanical or other means, now known or hereafter invented, including
xerography, photocopying and recording, or in any information storage
or retrieval system, is forbidden without the written permission of the
publisher, Harlequin Enterprises Limited, 225 Duncan Mill Road,
Don Mills, Ontario M3B 3K9, Canada.

All characters in this book have no existence outside the imagination of
the author and have no relation whatsoever to anyone bearing the same
name or names. They are not even distantly inspired by any individual
known or unknown to the author, and all incidents are pure invention.

This edition published by arrangement with Harlequin Books S.A.

® and TM are trademarks of the publisher. Trademarks indicated with
® are registered in the United States Patent and Trademark Office, the
Canadian Trade Marks Office and in other countries.

www.eHarlequin.com

Printed in U.S.A.

To my family—each and every one.
And especially to Steve, my love.

Books by Ginger Chambers

HARLEQUIN AMERICAN ROMANCE

Don't miss any of our special offers. Write to us at the
following address for information on our newest releases.

Harlequin Reader Service
U.S.: 3010 Walden Ave., P.O. Box 1325, Buffalo, NY 14269
Canadian: P.O. Box 609, Fort Erie, Ont. L2A 5X3

Chapter One

Love, Texas, had changed. Housing in the small Central Texas town now reached the water tower on the east side, new businesses had sprouted up here and there, trees along Main Street that Cassie remembered as puny saplings were now tall enough to menace utility wires.

But when she arrived at the Four Corners—the intersection where Main Street was cut by Pecan—nothing seemed to have changed at all. The ten years she'd been away might not have happened. Once again she could be her miserable young self, desperate to escape but unable to until she turned eighteen. At Swanson's Garage the same old-style gasoline pumps waited for customers under the same rickety canopy. The Salon of Beauty still sported the same eye-popping candy-pink front door and green-and-white striped window awnings. Handy Grocery & Hardware's oversize plate-glass windows were plastered with what could be the same garish sale banners. And from the number of pickup trucks and cars crowded into the parking lot on the remaining corner, Reva's Café still claimed the prize as the area's most popular eating place.

Old feelings of panic rose up to engulf her, lightening her head, shortening her breath—forcing her to pull the car onto the side of the road. Only the solid feel of the steering wheel kept her from fully giving in as she fought to regain control.

She had to remember—those ten years *had* passed. She *had* escaped. She was twenty-eight now, assured of herself, with a job she loved and a wonderful apartment in Houston. She wasn't the Cassie Edwards the people of Love, Texas, thought they knew so well. She'd changed. She wasn't the same person she used to be.

As the grip of panic eased, Cassie made herself look again at her surroundings, and this time she could see that there *were* differences. The old rusted-out wrecker, long an eyesore at Swanson's, had been uprooted from its spot and the weeds around it cut. The salon now boasted a regulation sidewalk to the front door instead of irregular stepping blocks. Handy's had a different—

A horn tooted behind her, alerting her to the fact that her car was blocking the path into the café parking lot. Instinctively, she glanced in the rearview mirror and with relief found she didn't recognize the driver. As quickly as she could, she pulled back onto Main and continued on her way.

Cassie didn't let herself think about what had just happened until a few blocks later when the road reverted to state highway and she left the town proper behind. Naturally, she'd felt some trepidation about returning to the town where, despite the tender emotionalism of its name, she'd known so little love. But she hadn't expected that the past could still hold such sway over her, could affect her to the point where she had to battle for control. Pointed looks, uncomfortable silences, strained conversations…yes. But not—

She brought a halt to that line of thought. She'd come here to do a job—to negotiate a land deal—just as she'd successfully negotiated other land deals across the state. Love, Texas, was no different. Get here, get the needed signatures, then get out…fast! That was the plan she'd constructed in Houston and that was the plan she would follow. No matter what.

Another flutter of panic tried to assert itself as her thoughts moved reflexively to her mother, but she quickly beat it down. She'd known all along that she'd have to see her. She couldn't be in town and not stop by. But the visit would be brief and the last thing she'd do before starting back to Houston.

The saving grace was that her boss, James T. "Jimmy" Michaels, had insisted that she stay outside of town on the Taylor ranch. He'd even booked one of the guestrooms the family advertised in a small vacation guide. Leave it to Jimmy to ferret out every pertinent bit of information concerning a deal he was interested in. On the hunt, few things escaped his notice.

Cassie had never been to the ranch, but she remembered the Taylors. Both sets of Taylors. The ones living in the country and the ones living in town. She'd had little interaction with either branch, though, just as she'd had little interaction with the rest of the populace. At least, not interaction of a positive nature. It was hard to grow up the town kook's daughter.

Cassie shook the thought away and instead concentrated on watching for the turnoff to the Taylor ranch. She knew it to be about seven miles beyond the town's western limit, where rolling limestone hills took the place of flatter land. When she spotted the turnoff she slowed to make it. Then she continued along the two-lane blacktop road until she reached a single set of railroad tracks where she stopped the car. From that vantage, she looked back at the roughly one-hundred-yards-deep and five-hundred-yards-long strip of fenced-off land that lay between the tracks and the highway. The narrow ten acres was a part of the Taylor ranch even if separated from the main acreage by the railroad right-of-way. How would the family react when she presented them with Jimmy's proposal to buy it?

Jimmy's research showed that, like many ranchers, the ranch Taylors could use the money. They were in debt to the bank and after some setbacks other debts were piling up. It had even reached the point that toward the end of last year they'd opened their home to strangers. The town Taylors, on the other hand, had no particular financial need. But Jimmy's research, as well as her own knowledge, gave her other avenues of approach.

The car bumped over the tracks and Cassie continued her journey, paralleling another line of tightly strung barbed wire that enclosed groupings of grazing Black Angus cattle. The working fence ran for about a mile before being replaced by a rustic rock fencing that decorated either side of a wide metal gate, on which the ranch's name, the Circle Bar-T, was proudly proclaimed in a circle of black wrought iron.

A sprawling two-story white frame house with a wrap-around porch sat a distance down a graded drive, the rugged landscape around it softened with flowers and more delicate greenery. A windmill stood off to one side, its blades curiously still in the breeze. Tucked close beside the windmill was a thriving vegetable garden. And in the background, she could see weathered outbuildings. In all, the ranch was a setting sure to please any visitor who hungered for a bucolic vacation.

After hopping out of the car to swing open the gate, Cassie steered the way up the drive and went over in her mind how she'd approach the family. She'd wait until after dinner that evening, while they were all still gathered around the table. Then she'd tell them who she represented and what Jimmy—

"Hey!"

Someone—a man—shouted.

Cassie looked around but couldn't see him, until movement drew her attention to the windmill, where a slim jeans-clad man in a long-sleeved shirt and a bone-colored hat was climbing down the metal frame. Once he'd taken the last step to the ground he headed directly toward her, and he didn't look pleased.

In reaction, Cassie stamped on the brakes, spraying gravel in all directions. She hadn't been going that fast, but the brakes locked, the tires slid and—tell *that* to the man striding purposefully toward her! If he hadn't looked pleased before, he looked even less pleased now.

Her first instinct in Houston would be to slam the car into reverse and get the heck out of there. Strangers couldn't be trusted, particularly hostile strangers. But she quashed the impulse. Because she wasn't in Houston, and, as he drew nearer, she recognized that this man was not a stranger.

She stepped out of the car to await his arrival. She'd had a thing for Will Taylor since she'd first started to notice boys. He'd been older, eighteen to her twelve. Trim and athletic with thick blond hair and eyes the same blue as the Texas sky, he was handsome in the way that made a girl's heart quicken if he so much as looked at her. And he was smart—he was always winning prizes in school. And nice—nice to everyone. But even if he had noticed her in the same way that she'd noticed him back then, there'd been a gulf between them far wider than the difference in their ages. She was Bonnie Edwards's daughter. And that was enough.

Little about Will Taylor had changed during the intervening years. When he halted in front of her and removed his work-stained hat, she saw that he still had the same thick blond hair, the same blue eyes, the same clean-cut features. He was older, of course, in his midthirties, but the wear of time and experience had only increased his handsomeness, lending him a rugged maturity that he hadn't had before.

Cassie's heart sped up, even as she tried to steady it.

"You forgot somethin', ma'am," he drawled in a husky baritone, his relaxed manner at odds with the taut line of his mouth. "You didn't close the gate. In these parts if you open a gate, you need to close it." His eyes made a quick assessment of her person. "You the visitor we're expectin' today? We thought you were a man."

Cassie thought to lighten the moment with a small attempt at humor. "Well, obviously I'm not, but I am the visitor."

Her attempt fell flat.

"Just remember to close the gates," he reiterated. "And another thing—don't drive so fast. In here—" he indicated the fenced area in which they stood that included the drive, the house, the windmill and the outbuildings "—barbed wire does a pretty good job of keepin' the larger livestock out. But we have smaller animals around that could get hurt. So you need to be careful."

The reality of her "speeding" was debatable, but Cassie already knew the hard-and-fast rule about gates. She'd just forgotten.

"All right," she agreed.

Will Taylor continued to look at her. Was he starting to remember her, too? He hadn't up to now. But then she'd changed far more than he had during her years away. The dark brown, almost black, hair she used to wear hanging straight to her waist was now short and layered, feathering her face. She wore makeup and nice clothes where before, as a teenager, she had done neither. Back then, if she could have faded into the walls whenever she was forced to be with people, she would have. The biggest difference in her today, though, was the way she carried herself, the way she presented herself. She had confidence now. In herself, in her abilities. She—

He broke into her thoughts. "Just go knock on the front door. My mom's expectin' you." Then, with a little nod, he stuffed his hat back on his head and started back to the windmill.

Cassie stared after him. Not exactly an auspicious beginning. But it was a beginning.

She returned to the gate on foot, closed it as instructed, and returned to the car. Then accelerating slowly forward, she parked beside a battered blue pickup already in place at the right side of the house, mounted the two steps onto the wide front porch and knocked on the frame of the screen door.

The pungent odor of cooking tomatoes tickled Cassie's nose as she waited. When there was no response, she knocked again, only harder. She peered through the screen and even called out. But the inside of the house remained silent.

Two old-fashioned rocking chairs and several well-used cane chairs waited for occupants on the porch, and a partially completed jigsaw puzzle was laid out on a table. There was no sign of life, though, until a good-sized gray cat with a snowy-white blaze on its chest and equally white-tipped paws glided silently around the curve of the porch. The cat stopped in front of the first rocker, made a graceful leap onto the thin seat cushion, settled, and then looked up at her with jewel-like eyes.

"Do you know where Mrs. Taylor is?" Cassie asked.

The cat blinked and turned its head, unconcerned.

Cassie tried the door again. Still nothing.

Vexed, she released a breath and weighed her options. She could cross to the windmill and ask Will for help—which, if he was already back up on top, would entail him coming down again—an occurrence she doubted would go over very well. Or, her better option, she could begin a search on her own. If, afterward, she still couldn't find the woman, she'd sit in the rocking chair next to the cat and wait. Mrs. Taylor had to turn up sometime.

The screen door behind her pushed open and a tall woman in her midfifties, silver-blond hair pulled back from her face and her eyes the same sky color as her son's, stood in the entrance. Sylvia Taylor. She was much as Cassie remembered her—the same handsome features with an array of laugh lines crinkling the corners of her eyes. The lines might be more deeply etched than they used to be and she might be carrying a few extra pounds on her once-trim frame, but the changes looked good on her.

The woman was the first to recover from her own start of surprise. "Oh! You must be C. A. Edwards. Silly me. I thought you were a man! Oh, come in…come in," she said warmly as she drew Cassie inside. "A man made your reservation, so I assumed—" She laughed at her mistake as she ushered Cassie through the entry and into a comfortable living room. "I should be old enough to know better than to assume things, shouldn't I? I'd just stepped outside for a few minutes to do somethin', when I heard you knock. I got here as fast as I could, but—did you have to knock more than once? If you did, I apologize." She drew a breath, then began what had to be her usual greeting to guests. "Welcome to the Circle Bar-T. We want you to feel at home and enjoy your stay with us. We don't force our guests to do anything they don't want to. If your plan is to rest and enjoy the beautiful countryside, we'll provide whatever you need to help you do that." Her eyes twinkled. "Up to and includin' leavin' you alone. If you want more of a ranch experience, like our advertisement says, we'll provide that, too. Same goes for anything in between. I'm the cook, so if there's somethin' you don't want in the food department, let me know." She paused, but when Cassie remained silent, she continued, "Your luggage is still in your car, right? I'll have Will—he's my son—get it in for you shortly. All around, I think you'll find us Taylors a pretty friendly bunch."

At the finish of her spiel, she reached for the kitchen towel hung over one shoulder as if to wipe her fingers before offering Cassie her hand, but the simple act must have sparked a memory because she sent a distressed look toward the rear of the house and exclaimed, "Oh, my heavens! I forgot! I was just finishin' up with some canning, and I need to—please…you'll have to excuse me." She hurried out of sight.

Cassie used the unexpected time alone to more closely inspect the area around her. It was a nice room, not huge but large enough for a good-sized family to relax and entertain in. The furnishings might be a little worn but they were well cared for— a pair of long overstuffed couches, several comfortable chairs, a well-used recliner positioned perfectly toward an older-model television set. A colorful crocheted afghan was draped over the arm of one of the couches, a braided rug brightened one section of the bare wood floor. An old-style pedestal lamp stood in the corner nearest the recliner, while a pair of more modern lamps with fluted shades occupied each end table. The walls were decorated with pictures of what must be family members along with knickknacks and books on a couple of narrow shelves. Overall, the area spoke of familial warmth and comfort, but it was easy to tell that little money had been spent on it recently.

She was just settling into one of the chairs when there was a loud pop of shattered glass and a cry.

Cassie jumped to her feet and hurried toward the sound.

At first, she wasn't sure what was tomato and what was blood as she looked at the woman standing amid an explosion of red. The lower portion of Sylvia Taylor's dress, her legs, her shoes, the nearby floor and cabinet faces—all were wet with what could have been either. "Are you hurt?" she asked.

"I…don't think so."

Cassie grabbed a dishcloth from the counter and started forward. "You shouldn't move. Broken glass is everywhere."

She'd taken only a few careful steps herself when boots pounded up to the back screen door, it flew open and Will Taylor charged inside.

Quickly assessing the situation, he gave a stronger echo of Cassie's earlier warning, "Don't move, Mom!" Then his attention switched to Cassie. "And you…you need to get back." When she didn't respond right away, he added tersely, *"Now."*

"Will, she was just tryin' to help."

Will's blue eyes flicked to Cassie as he went to collect a broom from a corner closet. "The last thing we need right now is for a guest to get hurt. So the best way she can help is by stayin' out of the way."

Without a word, Cassie set the dishcloth back on the counter and retraced her steps to the living room.

"WILL, THAT WAS INEXCUSABLE!" Sylvia Taylor scolded her son as he began to clear a pathway through the debris. "She's our guest."

"She was gettin' in the way."

"She was just tryin' to help, that's all. And you—"

Will drew a breath. He knew he'd overreacted, but hearing his mother's cry just as he was about to remount the windmill had unsettled him. It didn't take a lot these days to make him think the worst.

"She's a visitor," his mother continued, "and you promised that you'd be friendly to our visitors. Which you have been, up to now. Why would you—when you know—"

Will paused in his sweeping. "I thought somethin' bad had happened to you. So I—it just kinda spilled out. You want me to apologize to her?"

His mother held his questioning gaze, then her face softened into a smile. "Would that be so hard?"

Will grinned. "Depends."

"I'll settle for you bein' nicer to her while she's here."

"I'll do my best," he promised and, giving a final sweep

to the last pieces of tomato goo and broken glass, said, "Here, that gets the worst of it. You can step out now."

Released, his mother passed safely to a clear area by the counter. "My heavens, what a mess!" she exclaimed, looking back. And, despite his protest, after cleaning what she could of the tomato residue from her skirt, she set to work beside him, scooping up the piles to be disposed of and then taking them outside.

"I can get it from here," she said as she went to the closet for the mop.

Will tipped his head toward the living room. "You should get changed…the guest."

His mother looked torn. "I don't want to leave you with this."

Will took the mop from her. "All that's left are the counter fronts and the floor, then it's done."

"Still—"

"She's probably gettin' bored by now."

That got his mother moving and he was left alone to finish the job.

When his mother had first presented the idea of taking in paying guests late last fall, he'd been dead set against it. So had his granddad. They raised cattle. It was what they did. They and the past generations of Taylors before them, since the first had come to Texas, had grazed cattle on this land, cared for them and sold them at market. They didn't cater to tourists—which was what his mother had proposed. But despite their protests, she'd done it, determined to bring in any extra money she could to help replenish the ranch's rapidly shrinking coffers. At first, visitors had come in dribs and drabs, and then increased to where there seemed to be someone in the house's spare room for a day or two almost every week. And Will had found himself being forced to be amenable to strangers on the property, though it still went against the grain.

For the most part, the visitors had been easy enough to deal with. A ride on a horse, an accompanied look at a few cows. Mostly they wanted to go for nature walks or take photographs or just lie around and eat his mother's good meals. The majority had been little trouble. His degree of involvement hadn't interfered all that much with his regular chores. A couple had created headaches, though. One had wandered into a pasture she'd been told not to enter and, leaving the gate open, let a number of the cattle inside it wander into the neighboring pasture he was resting so the grasses could replenish. He'd had to waste part of an afternoon to round them all up again and put them back where they belonged. Another visitor had gotten lost and that had taken several hours to put right. He shook his head at the memory.

His thoughts went to their latest visitor. He'd been hard on her earlier, too, when she'd left the front gate open. But he'd just settled into the snake-of-a-job that windmill repair was and there she'd come, up the drive pretty as you please, the gate wide open. Turned out *she* was pretty, too. Which for some reason irritated him even more.

He wrung out the mop and set it outside to dry. Then he decided that before he got back to work, he'd better go through and offer to bring in the visitor's luggage.

How long had she been at the Taylor ranch? Cassie wondered as she resumed her place in the living room chair. Fifteen, maybe twenty minutes? And in that short time she'd already managed to rack up three black marks against herself in Will Taylor's eyes. Never mind that only one—leaving the gate open—was truly valid. She was here to persuade the Taylors, not annoy them—not any of them. What would Jimmy say if he knew, she wondered, and she instantly had the answer. He'd say, *Buck up, girl, you're just gettin' started. Be patient. Be positive. Now, get to it!* Which was precisely what she'd do.

Jimmy had done more to bring her out of her emotional shell than any other person in her life. He'd gotten her to see that she had as much to offer the world as the next person. She was twenty-two when she'd first gone to work at his small office on the west side of Houston, the four years since leaving Love having brought her little personal change. She'd no longer felt trapped, but she'd remained quiet, introverted, unwilling to call attention to herself. All negative attributes that were impossible to retain around Jimmy. A swashbuckling land speculator, he was one of those bigger-than-life individuals who is wildly successful because he takes chances other people won't. Not to mention being brashly, humorously very much his own person, because that was him to his core. He had more than enough self-confidence for ten people. And he happily spread the knack to everyone near him.

A murmur of voices continued in the kitchen, along with intermittent running water and the screen door opening and closing several times. Until, finally, Sylvia Taylor tiptoed barefoot to stand in the wide living room doorway. Though the worst of the tomato bits had been removed from her skirt and legs, she still hunched forward with the wet portion of her skirt gathered in one hand so as not to spread wayward drips.

"I don't know if this dress'll ever be the same," she said ruefully, smiling. "I was movin' the quart bottles that'd already cooled over to the table so I could put the hot bottles from the pressure cooker in their place…when one of 'em just slipped through my fingers and *crash*. What a mess!"

"At least you weren't burned," Cassie said.

Sylvia's answer was wry. "No, just hurt my pride." She

glanced back toward the kitchen and a frown creased her brow. "Will's finishin' up in there. Just what he needed today—*more* work." She sighed. "I'll go get changed, and then show you to your room. It won't take me long, but if you'd like a glass of sweet tea while you wait, there's some in the fridge. Help yourself, or ask Will to get it for you."

"Thank you," Cassie murmured.

Yet Sylvia Taylor didn't move away. "You should know," she added quietly, "Will didn't mean anything by what he said just now. He's a good boy. Sometimes he's just, well, sometimes he has more heaped on his plate than he can handle. I hope you won't hold it against him."

Cassie shook her head. "No. No, I won't."

"He didn't mean to be so sharp."

"I'm sure he didn't," Cassie assured her. "He was worried about you."

Sylvia Taylor gave her a long considering look, then nodded and moved away.

Cassie fingered through a stack of magazines on the end table, selected one and started to thumb through it. She'd stay out of the kitchen, thank you very much. She didn't want to chance racking up any more black marks! Only, try as she might to concentrate on the magazine's glossy pages, she couldn't. Sylvia Taylor's long look kept creeping into her consciousness, reminding her of another time when the woman had looked at her in a similar way.

Throughout Cassie's years in the small town, she and Sylvia Taylor had done little more than occasionally pass each other in doorways or stand in the same checkout line in a store. As was her habit then with people, Cassie had busied herself looking at something else—anything else—to avoid making eye contact. Except once. The time—the *last* time— her mother had dragged Cassie with her to a town function.

It had been a parent-teacher association meeting at her middle school, and Bonnie, of course, had stood to advocate some inane idea that no one in town would ever think of backing. It was impossible to remember *which* inane idea because there had been so many.

At thirteen, Cassie had felt nothing but intense shame as her mother had carried on about the reasons her idea would be so wonderful for the children of Love and for their parents as well. She'd sensed, even though she'd been too mortified to look, the impatient, irritated, disgusted glares of the people sitting around them. She'd wanted to crawl into a hole. But her mother had been blithely unaware and continued to talk even after the association president asked her to relinquish the floor. Cassie had fully expected someone to come force her mother into her seat and tell her to shut up. But no one had, so the torture continued…until Sylvia Taylor, from her seat at the front table among the association's elected officers, had gently interrupted her mother's flow of words to suggest that the board look into the matter and have a report ready for the next meeting. She'd even thanked Bonnie for bringing the matter to their attention! Bonnie had sat down, then, smiling beatifically, reached over to squeeze Cassie's icy-cold hand as if she somehow shared in the victory. It was then that Cassie had looked up and found Sylvia Taylor gazing, not at her mother, but at *her.* And though she hadn't been able to fathom the message in the woman's eyes during the long seconds her gaze had been held captive, she'd not seen derision or disgust in them either. As quick as possible, she'd looked away, her cheeks blooming even redder in confused embarrassment.

Cassie sat rubbing her forehead, her elbow propped on the arm of the chair, when she suddenly became aware that Will Taylor had come to stand in the doorway and that he was watching her. Almost guiltily, she sprang to her feet.

"Okay," he said after a long moment, "kitchen's all set. If you give me your keys, I'll bring your luggage in."

Cassie retrieved the keys from her purse and handed them over. "I have only one suitcase," she said.

"You travel light."

"I'm only here for a few days."

"Some folks seem to think they need a different outfit for each hour of each day."

Silence fell between them. He seemed to be making more of an effort to be friendly, to be polite. While the two of them were alone in the kitchen, had his mother reminded him that she was a paying guest in their home? Cassie had yet to detect any sign of recognition in either of them. As far as she could tell, she continued to be a stranger to them.

Will tossed her key ring in his hand a couple of times before saying, "I'll be right back."

Seconds later the front door closed behind him, leaving Cassie to release a pent-up breath. She didn't like being watched, especially when she wasn't aware of it. She also didn't like the way her schoolgirl crush on Will Taylor still seemed to have the power to unsettle her. He was a different person now. She was a different person. And it wasn't as if there'd ever been anything between them in the first place.

The front door opened and Will, lifting her suitcase, motioned with it up the stairs. "I'll take this on up. You wait here. Mom always likes to be the one to show folks around."

"That, I do," Sylvia inserted from the top landing. "You come on up, too," she told Cassie. "I'm ready for you." She brushed the skirt of the pastel-print dress she'd changed into.

Cassie purposely lagged behind Will as he made his way upstairs. As he passed his mother, the woman patted his shoulder before smiling at Cassie who was about to catch up.

"We could've put you in our newly renovated bunkhouse," Sylvia Taylor said, "but a family of four is comin' tomorrow—a mom, a dad and two kids—so I thought you might like to be up here in the room we used to use for our guests. The folks who've stayed in it before have always said they love feelin' a part of the family. Hope you will, too."

The women followed Will into the first doorway. Cassie saw that the guest bedroom's decor matched what she'd seen so far of the house—warm, comfortable, well cared for, but aged even in its neatness. A double bed was covered by a handmade quilt, a tall chest of drawers stood against one wall. A lamp and a writing desk were next to the window, the desk doing dual service as a bedside table.

"This room doesn't have a separate bathroom, I'm afraid," Sylvia said. "So that means we share the one down the hall."

Will, who'd already hoisted Cassie's suitcase onto the bed, stood with his hands resting casually on his lean hips. "Well, if that's all you ladies need, I'll be off," he said. "That windmill's still givin' me trouble. I need to get back to it."

"Let me know if I can help," Sylvia Taylor urged.

Will nodded and was almost out the door before Cassie remembered *her* manners.

"Thank you for bringing in my bag," she said.

He paused, gave her one of those indecipherable looks that he seemed to have inherited from his mother, then murmured, "No problem," before continuing on his way.

Cassie's heart had sped up again the instant he'd turned to look at her. She tightened her lips, irritated with herself for having let it happen again.

Sylvia Taylor moved about the room, needlessly smoothing the quilt and adjusting the curtains. "If you need more hangers just let me know. That goes for an extra blanket, as well. It can be cool some nights still. It also works best if you slide your suitcase under the bed after you unpack. Gets it out of the way." Then glancing around, she summed up, "Room's not very luxurious, but I hope you'll enjoy it. Just like you'll enjoy all your vacation at the Circle Bar-T."

"I'm sure I will," Cassie murmured.

They moved into the hall.

"The bathroom's down there—" Sylvia Taylor motioned toward the end of the hall "—linen closet's inside. Will's room and my room are along that way, too. Which brings up somethin' you need to know. The bathroom door always stays open unless it's in use. That way we don't have any 'accidental' meetin's. Will's granddad's room is on the bottom floor," she added as they started downstairs. "He's in his seventies and was startin' to have trouble gettin' up and down the stairs, so we moved him to where his 'gettin' around' would be a lot easier." She paused to glance at Cassie, her blue eyes filled with mischief. "He also snores like a buzz saw, so nights are a lot quieter up here now. We couldn't inflict *that* on a guest. You'll meet him later…you won't be able to avoid it!" Then as she started down again, she mused, "You know, what with everything that's been happenin', I don't believe we've introduced ourselves properly. I'm Sylvia Taylor…call me Sylvia. Everyone does. And you—you don't go by your initials, do you?"

The time had come, ahead of Cassie's plan but she wouldn't deceive the Taylors by lying. "No, my name's Cassandra…Cassie for short."

"Ahh, that's a very pretty name," Sylvia said, turning again as she reached the lower level. "*Cassandra*. Cassandra Edwards. Cassie—" Her eyes widened as she put the two names together. "*Cassie Edwards!*" she exclaimed. "Little Cassie!"

Sylvia Taylor was a good six inches taller than Cassie's five foot two. In order to meet the older woman's gaze on an equal level, Cassie refrained from taking the last step.

"All grown up," she confirmed.

Sylvia frowned. "But why would you stay at the ranch when your mother's house is—?"

"Because I have a business matter to discuss with your family," Cassie broke in.

"But—" Sylvia repeated, only to stop when suspicion replaced puzzlement. "What kind of business matter?"

Cassie took the last step. "Something I hope you and your family will welcome. I'm here to tender an offer, Mrs. Taylor. But I prefer to wait until I can present it to all of you."

"Call me Sylvia," the woman murmured automatically. "I think you should, don't you? Our other guests I don't know from Adam call me Sylvia." Her gaze swept slowly over Cassie. "You've changed," she concluded when she was done.

"Yes, I have," Cassie agreed, and with a confident smile added, "Sylvia."

Chapter Two

"Will."

His mother's voice sounded odd to him. Will glanced at her as he took the last step from the windmill's metal frame to the ground.

"What's up?" he asked, tipping back his Resistol to wipe the perspiration from his brow. "I was just comin' in for a break. Finally got that part to work right." He looked up and was satisfied by the slowly turning blades and the sound of water gurgling through the pipe into the fat metal cistern a few feet away. He returned his attention to his mother. She looked kinda odd, too. Like something was wrong.

"That girl," his mother said, "that young woman. She's—"

He frowned when she broke off. "What's she done now?"

"Will…those initials—C. A. Edwards. She's Cassie…Cassie Edwards."

His mother seemed to think the name would ring a bell with him, but Will couldn't place it. It was somewhat familiar, but—

"Cassie Edwards, Will, from Love. Bonnie Edwards's daughter? Surely you remember her. She was younger than you, but you had to have seen her. Her mother was always draggin' little Cassie around with her. I felt sorry for the girl. Dressed in those hippie clothes like her mom. She didn't look happy."

"I remember her now," Will said flatly.

He remembered her, all right. Not so much in her earlier life, but later, when she was starting to leave childhood behind. His most vivid recollection came from the time he'd gone into town for something late in the summer before he'd left for college and had come up on a few of the local boys giving her a hard time outside the post office. She'd been a mousy little thing back then, all long dark hair and big dark eyes. He'd stopped what was going on and had a word with the boys—boys, hell, a couple of 'em were as old as he was! But he'd doubted it would do much good. She was a juicy target for bullies. Rarely looking at people, seldom saying a word. When he'd turned back, intending to offer her some sort of solace, she'd been gone. It probably would have been another waste of words, though, falling hollow on her ears. Still, the way she'd looked that afternoon had stayed with him for the next few weeks. Her defenselessness, her alarm, her misery…and, for just a moment, a spark of something in her eyes that he couldn't put a name to. Then he'd left for A&M and gotten busy with his courses and college life. A few years after that his dad had died in a ranch accident and he'd come back to run the Circle Bar-T. Bonnie Edwards was still around town, but he never saw the daughter. Later, someone had mentioned that the daughter had moved away. He remembered wishing her well in his thoughts. Then he'd forgotten about her, having plenty of problems of his own to deal with.

"She says she's here to make us an offer."

His mother's words jerked him from the past. "What kind of offer?"

She shrugged. "She says she'll tell us at dinner. She must

mean supper, considerin' what time 'a day it is. She's…different, Will. And I'm not just talkin' about losin' most of her accent or referrin' to things the way most big-city people do."

"What did Granddad say?"

"I haven't told him yet."

To ease his mother's apprehension, he teased lightly, "Who knows? Maybe this'll be good news. At least that would be somethin' of a change."

She wasn't ready to be cheered. Instead, she fell back on the phrase she used almost automatically these days as the family faced unknown prospects for the future. "Whatever happens, we'll be fine."

As usual, Will pretended to believe her. Then, setting his hat back to the proper low angle over his forehead, he bent to collect his tools. "I think we should tell Granddad," he said as he straightened. "Warn him about who she is and what she wants."

"Me, too," his mother agreed.

"He awake from his siesta yet?"

"Should be."

"Then let's go do it."

Side by side, they started for the house.

WILL HEARD HIS GRANDFATHER before he spotted him. The old man was in full form under the shade tree behind the house, his woolly white head bobbing as he hobbled around in front of his companion and gestured with his arms, telling one of his tales. Their visitor was sitting on one of the old kitchen chairs his mother used for outside work. Once Robbie Taylor had finally succumbed to the idea that the Circle Bar-T would be taking in paying guests, he had appointed himself official "ranch character." And he now had a great time playing up to the visitors, which was a good thing because it kept him from brooding so much about not being able to work the ranch like he used to. At the moment, though, Will could only watch the show with growing impatience. He'd wanted to get to his grandfather first, before the old man made a fool of himself in front of an ex-local, particularly an ex-local with an ulterior motive.

"'At's the way it was, I swear!" Robbie guffawed as he slapped the rolled brim of his favorite hat on his thigh. "'At ole horse took off and prob'ly made it to Kansas City 'fore he stopped to look back!"

The old man had yet to notice that the two of them were drawing near and, from the way he was positioning his rangy body, he was about to launch into another story. But *she'd* noticed, and the amused smile that had been curving her lips disappeared as she stiffened slightly, and then stilled.

Will studied her. He could see now that she was a grown-up version of the child-woman he'd last seen all those years ago, but, as his mother had said, she'd changed. She had to know that his mother had told him who she was…yet she didn't seem to care. She didn't draw away as her younger self would have done. She didn't cast her eyes away. Instead, she awaited their arrival with a quiet dignity she'd never possessed before. Definitely, a very different Cassie Edwards.

Robbie Taylor swiveled to see what she was looking at, and a wide grin creased his weathered features as he saw them. The many years of hard ranch work had gnarled the man, leaving him with arthritic hands and knees, and a spine that protested all too frequently. Yet he'd railed at having to be relieved of all but the lightest of his lifelong responsibilities. "I'm an old critter, but not that old!" he'd protested. "I can still do things!" Only he couldn't, not the things he wanted, or the way he wanted. Instead, he'd found that exaggerating his infirmities added to his "ranch character" persona and amused the guests who seemed to love his humor and his stories.

Robbie quickly sensed that something was wrong. "Will?" he questioned.

"Granddad," Will said, "we need to go inside."

Robbie sent a weather eye to the sky. "Don't see no storm clouds gatherin'."

At Will's continuing steady look, the old man glanced uneasily toward his companion, saw that her expression matched the graveness of his grandson and Sylvia, and agreed. "All right, I guess we'll mosey ourselves on in then. After you, ma'am." He politely extended his arm for their guest to precede them into the house, but behind her back he shot Will a look that said, what in heck's goin' on?

Will gave his head a little shake.

Robbie transferred his silent demand to his daughter-in-law, but she only murmured, "Come on, Dad," and, tucking her arm through his, urged him toward the back screen door.

Once they were in the kitchen, Will motioned for everyone to sit at the table. The two women took chairs across from each other, while Robbie assumed his usual position at the head and Will himself settled at the foot. Both men removed their hats and set them to one side.

"Awright," Robbie said, shooting a determined look at each of them from beneath his bushy brows. "When's somebody gonna let me in on what's happenin'? 'Specially since the rest 'a ya already seem to know."

Sylvia tipped her head toward the visitor. "Dad, this is Cassie Edwards. *Love's* Cassie Edwards. Bonnie Edwards's—"

"Mr. Taylor," Cassie interrupted, directing her words to the older man. "I've been sent by my employer, James T. Michaels of Michaels Enterprises in Houston, to make an offer—

a very nice offer—for the strip of land you and your brother own between the highway and the railroad track."

After he absorbed the information, Will waited for his grandfather to explode. It didn't take long.

"But that's the Old Home Place!" Robbie burst out, shocked. "Where the first Taylors that came to Texas built their house! We ain't about to sell it! It wouldn't be right!"

Cassie didn't seem ruffled by his adamant refusal. "An extremely nice offer, Mr. Taylor," she embellished. "The contract is upstairs. If you'll excuse me, I'll get it."

"The Old Home Place!" Robbie repeated incredulously as their visitor's footsteps receded down the hall.

"It's out of the question," Will agreed.

Sylvia hesitated. "But…it would solve a whole mess of problems if we did sell it."

His grandfather sputtered indignantly, but Will had to admit, if only to himself, that the same thought had popped into his mind before he'd discarded it. "We can't do it, Mom," he stated firmly.

"'A course we can't!" Robbie railed. "It's a sacred trust! What's it been? A hundred and twenty…no, a hundred and twenty-*two* years since the first Taylors came here with nothin' more than a horse, a wagon and the clothes on their backs! We can't even *think* of sellin' that land!"

"It's either that…or we could lose it all," Sylvia said softly.

Robbie set his jaw. "We can't do it. *I* won't do it."

"Dad," Sylvia continued, "I know what the Home Place means to you…and to Will. It means the same to me! But if the alternative's worse—"

Robbie shook his head, denying everything she'd said.

Will was torn. He understood the strong emotions fueling his grandfather's stubbornness. One day—far into the distant future, he hoped—the ranch and its heritage would pass to

him to protect. Five generations of Taylor men and women
had worked their hearts out on this land. Been born on it, suffered for it, some had died on it. But he was also enough of
a realist to recognize the truth of his mother's argument. If
things didn't get better—

But they *were* getting better. The three-year drought the
area had been suffering had broken late last summer, feed
prices were down a little—they were still way too high, but
somewhat lower—there was hope the spring calves would
bring higher prices in the fall, and his mother's plan was actually starting to pay off. Not big-time yet, but enough to
make renovations to the bunkhouse, which gave them more
space for guests. With more guests, there'd be more profits.
Then if he could get a new hunting lease worked out in time
to replace the one they'd lost…and *keep* things going with the
herd and the equipment and everything else… He had to support his grandfather in this. There wasn't any other way. The
Home Place was the Home Place. They'd just have to keep
battling on. It's what Taylors did.

He drew a breath, about to disclose his thoughts, when
Cassie Edwards reentered the room.

Robbie Taylor was waiting for her, and before she could
even sit down he stated obstinately, "Nope, we won't do it!"

She slipped into her chair anyway and suggested, "Possibly you should see this before you make a final decision. All
of you should read it and discuss it. Take your time. There's
no rush." She flipped open the document, folded it to a specific page and slid it to Robbie. "This is the amount Mr.
Michaels is prepared to pay you. He'll pay an equal amount
to your brother."

The old man's eyes widened as he read the number, but he
gave no other response before scooting the contract back to
her and refolding his arms.

Will felt his mother's hand creep into his under the table. Her fingers were cool and trembling lightly. He closed his own around them and the trembling stopped.

"I'll leave the contract with you anyway," Cassie Edwards said. "Again, I'm in no rush. You can give me your final decision tomorrow. In the meantime, I'll be glad to answer any questions you might have." She waited, looking at each one in turn. When no one said anything she stood up. "What time did you say dinner is, Mrs. Taylor?"

"Noontime, Cassie. You know that," Sylvia chided softly. "*Supper's* at six."

Cassie gave a half smile. "I'll be here," she said.

As she passed beside Will's chair, he caught and held her gaze. Though there was no alarm or misery in her dark eyes, for a second he thought he saw a shadow of that old illusive spark that he'd been unable to put a name to in the past. And he still couldn't say what it was. Or even if it had truly been there. The afternoon had been strange all around...maybe he was starting to imagine things.

His eyes followed her as she moved into the hall—her head up, her back straight.

She sure was different.

WHILE THE FAMILY CONTEMPLATED the offer she'd put before them, Cassie unpacked the clothes she'd brought with her for her allotted three-day stay, hanging some in the closet and placing the remainder in a single drawer of the chest. Jimmy had taught her that a positive inner confidence created its own success, and over the past few years since she'd started to act as his agent, she never made plans to extend a negotiation for any longer than the amount of time she'd set for it in the beginning. If she thought the task would take a week to accomplish, she brought a week's worth of clothes. If, as in this case, her plan called for at most a few days, she packed lightly. It was a philosophy that had yet to be challenged, and she doubted that it would be here. Not judging by the way Robbie Taylor's eyes had widened the instant he'd seen the amount of money on offer. The man might be stubborn, but common sense would win out in the end. The family needed the money. She had been surprised to learn that the strip of land held such significance for the Taylors, though—a fact Jimmy's research had failed to uncover.

It was the other half of the equation, Robbie Taylor's twin, who could present a greater challenge. At 76, Ray Taylor was still very much a man of finance, the head of his local business empire. Not only had he built Handy Grocery & Hardware store from a small shop on the corner of Main and Pecan into the thriving concern it was today, he and his family had branched out into several other small businesses around town. Though he likely had less of an attachment to the ranch and what turned out to be the Old Home Place than his twin, having made the town his home for the majority of his life, from a business standpoint he would prove harder to negotiate with. In her favor, though, a lucrative deal for something that he, in all likelihood, rarely thought about could interest him. She just had to present it to him in the right way. And she also had a secret weapon—Jimmy's authorization to increase the money amount by several levels in order to cinch the deal. Of course, whatever the final agreement was for one brother would apply to the other, both having equal ownership.

Cassie sank onto the edge of the bed. This was the point where, despite her positive inner confidence, an attack of nerves usually launched a thousand butterflies in her stomach. Jimmy had such faith in her; she didn't want to let him down. As if on cue, the butterflies appeared and she dealt with them as she usually did—by telling herself that they were a good omen she needed in order to keep her edge. Then she always did something active, like taking a walk, going out to dinner, seeing a movie....

Only here her situation was different from any she'd ever encountered. She'd always been on her own before, staying at a hotel or motel close to the negotiation site. She rarely met with the principals for more than a couple of hours at a time, and never stayed in their company nonstop. Being so intimate a part of the Taylor household at the ranch was an aspect she hadn't considered before. All she'd been concerned with was that she wouldn't have to stay in town and be prey to—

She moved restlessly about the room. No, she wouldn't think about that again now. She would concentrate on her professional position. So, she'd had a rockier than usual start in this instance; she was back on track now. And tomorrow morning she'd arrange a meeting with Ray Taylor for later in the day. After that she'd—

The image of Will Taylor as he'd sat watching her walk past his chair pushed all other thoughts aside. She'd felt so...*exposed* under his steady gaze. It was as if he could see right through her. See how difficult coming back to Love was for her. See how, as a fanciful preteen, she'd viewed him as her knight in shining armor after he'd rescued her outside the post office—well, knight in boots, faded work shirt and worn jeans. Her cheeks warmed at the fanciful recollection.

No! That was an even worse thing to think about than what she'd rejected moments before!

Cassie dug out the book she'd brought with her, but couldn't lose herself in its story.

She paced the tiny confines of her room, but soon tired of that.

She needed more—more space, more freedom and something that would totally occupy her mind.

MOVEMENT OUTSIDE the kitchen window caught Will's eye. *Cassie* was walking away from the house, heading toward the windmill. He hadn't heard her leave, so she must have let herself out very quietly. His eyes narrowed as he wondered what she was up to, and if it would be a good idea for him to follow her.

He pushed away from the table. "I should be gettin' back to work," he said.

"Whatever it is, it'll keep!" Robbie decreed.

Will was starting to lose patience. "Granddad, we're just goin' around in circles and it's gettin' us nowhere. I have things to do."

"Nothin's more important than this!"

"But you aren't goin' to change your mind."

"Don't tell me what I will or won't do!" Robbie snapped back.

Will was about to answer just as sharply when his mother leaned forward to look intently at his grandfather.

"You mean…you might be willin' to change it?" she asked.

Robbie shifted in his chair, his arthritic hands clasped on the table. "I never said that."

"But you're startin' to see some sense in what I've been sayin'."

Robbie shrugged, his bushy eyebrows twitching.

At this unexpected drift toward concession, Will's mother turned to him in a silent plea for support.

Will heaved a deep sigh and scooted his chair back into place. This time he'd speak his mind.

"Purely as a business proposition we'd be crazy not to grab this money with both hands. But—" he added quickly as his grandfather started to swell up again "—that strip of land's a major part of our heritage. What Mom's sayin', though, is that the rest of the ranch is also a major heritage. Possibly even more of one. We haven't been usin' that land out by the highway for much, Granddad. And that house Ida and Nelson Taylor built back when they first got here…it burned down sometime before the turn of the century. By then, they'd already abandoned it themselves and moved closer to where we are now. Then your daddy tore that house down after he inherited and used most of the wood and such to build on this spot. You and Uncle Ray were born here, then you made improvements, my daddy made more and I've made a few…until we sit as we are today. That's an awful lot of *heritage.*"

"It's the principle 'a the thing," Robbie defended gruffly. "How'd those earlier Taylors feel about me bein' the one to sell it?"

"Nelson and Ida sold a section when they needed to back in the twenties," Will replied. "They'd probably tell you you'd be a fool not to do it."

"You're sure 'a that?" his grandfather demanded. "And that section they let go of wasn't the Home Place. It was out in the far reaches."

"I'm not sure. I'm just guessin'…but you are, too. Do what you think's right, Granddad. We'll keep on workin'. I'm willin', Mom's willin'. But we're gonna need some luck comin' our way before the end of the year, and that's somethin' we've been missin' a lot of around here lately."

"We have to face facts, Dad," Sylvia said, then added softly, "I don't want Will workin' himself to death like my Johnny did. And I know you don't want that for him either." She stilled Will's protest with a brief lift of her hand.

"'A course not!" Robbie snapped. "But you've been sayin' all along that we'll be fine."

A small silence followed. Then his mother asked, "What

if we could get the price up? That man Cassie works for…he's sent her a long way to show us this." She tapped the contract. "We could at least try. See what happens."

Robbie frowned. "I still don't like it."

"Won't you at least think about it?" Sylvia asked.

Robbie glanced at Will.

Will was quick to respond. "I don't mind hard work, Granddad. You know that. Don't let me be a part of the issue."

Robbie pushed himself up and out of his chair. "Awright, I'll think on it," he said. Then he walked slowly outside and plopped himself down in the chair under the shade tree, where he always claimed he went for his "thinks." Usually, he took naps there, but today Will doubted that he would sleep.

Will, too, got up to leave, but his mother caught hold of his arm. "I meant what I said, Will," she said seriously. "I don't want you followin' in your daddy's footsteps by dyin' too young."

"I can handle it, Mom," Will stated firmly.

"I know. But *I* can't."

And Will knew that to his mother's mind she'd never said a truer thing.

Chapter Three

Cassie looked up from her study of the vegetable garden to see Will Taylor striding across the open yard from the house to the outbuildings, his long legs covering ground at a rapid pace. He didn't stop until he reached the corral where, once inside, he fitted a brown horse with a bridle then walked it over to where a blanket and saddle straddled the top rail, ready for use. With practiced ease he saddled up and, with the agility born from years of repetition, swung into place. Nudging the horse forward, he arrived at the gate. From that height, he leaned down to let himself through. He did the same thing a short distance away at another gate—putting into practice what he'd preached earlier in the day.

Only when he'd disappeared from view did Cassie realize that she'd been staring after him as if mesmerized. She instantly turned her back, highly irritated with herself. She'd left the house to enjoy the outdoors—the fresh air, the sunshine. Now she was tense again. She should just ignore him. She'd soon be on her way back to Houston with the signed contracts in her briefcase and Love fading into the background. She could forget again that the town even existed, and Will Taylor along with it.

As proof that she was once again in command of her psy-

che, Cassie continued to explore the area. She examined the
windmill up close. In town they'd had town water or electric
pumps for their own individual wells. Windmills had been
used by the surrounding ranches and farms, and she'd only
seen them from a distance. She found the henhouse, a potting
shed where Sylvia had some seedlings waiting to be
planted…but she stayed away from the cluster of outbuildings
which, she could see now, were mostly three-sided with metal
roofs.

She was starting to enjoy herself again—the warm spring
sun, the delicate scent of flowers in the air—until she spotted Robbie Taylor in the backyard sitting under the shade tree.
His head was lowered, his chin on his chest; he might have
been asleep. But the last thing she wanted at this delicate stage
was to stumble upon the old man unawares and give him the
impression that she was applying pressure to his decision-
making process. She needed to give the Taylors wide berth
until they made their final decision—other than at meals, of
course. She had to show up for those or they'd wonder why
she hadn't, and possibly take affront. Another aspect of staying on the ranch she hadn't foreseen. She had to tread carefully…and the best way she could see to do that was to isolate
herself in her room. If necessary, for the majority of time that
she had to spend here.

Thinking to put her plan into action, she started indoors, but
her intent lasted no longer than the time it took to get to the front
porch. The big gray cat, still curled in the rocking chair, awakened at her approach. Blinking sleepily, the animal stretched,
then gave every indication that it wanted to be petted.

Cassie hesitated. The cats she'd had as a youngster had
been on the wild side. She still had a couple of scars on her
hands as evidence. But she'd always loved cats and had
longed for one that would enjoy being petted.

"I hope you mean this," she said as she sank into the accompanying rocker and tentatively touched the feline's head.

The cat stood up, stretched again, then flowed smoothly from one rocking chair to the other, ending up in her lap.

Smiling, Cassie stroked the plush coat from neck to tail.

"The Duchess likes to have her ears rubbed," Sylvia Taylor said from behind her, making Cassie start. She hadn't known the woman was anywhere near.

Sylvia stepped outside, joining her on the porch.

"Is that her name?" Cassie asked for something to say.

"We call her the Duchess because she thinks she is one." Sylvia tilted her head, considering the pair. "She doesn't usually take to folks so fast."

As Cassie moved to rub the cat's ears, the animal began to purr. It had been a long time since she'd had any connection with a pet. In Houston, she stuck to houseplants.

Sylvia crossed to the porch railing, made a leisurely survey of the road out front, then turned to ask, "What have you been doin' with yourself all these years, Cassie?"

Cassie kept her reply short. "Working."

"For the same man you work for now?"

"Most of it."

"You look like you're doing just fine."

"I am."

A moment passed, uncomfortable for Cassie in its silence. She braced herself for more questions.

But instead of continuing to pry, Sylvia abandoned her place at the railing and came back to open the screen door. "Have to see to supper," she explained. "Don't worry about hurtin' the Duchess' feelin's when you want to stop. She's what a friend of mine calls a love sponge if she decides she likes you. You call a halt whenever you're ready."

"I will," Cassie murmured.

Once the woman was safely inside, Cassie sighed. Yet another reason to stay in her room. She was prepared to answer a few general inquiries about her life in Houston, but she was determined not to go into any depth. And the Duchess aside, Sylvia's miffed feelings would definitely complicate things.

She gave the cat another ear rub, placed her back in the companion rocker, then went inside.

AT SIX O'CLOCK Cassie presented herself in the kitchen, drawn by voices along with wonderful aromas of cooking foods. Each of the ranch Taylors was there, but none was seated. Sylvia was busy dishing up, while Will, his hair damp and freshly combed, leaned against the counter. Robbie stood off to one side staring out the window.

Cassie smiled briefly at no one in particular before taking her seat.

"Right on time." Sylvia approved.

The two men exchanged a look before they, too, took their places. By the time Sylvia joined them, the table was filled with fried chicken, green beans, mashed potatoes and home-made biscuits

As good at it looked and smelled, though, Cassie wasn't the least bit hungry, and neither, did it seem, were the others. Yet everyone went through the motions. Will, having done the hardest physical labor, ate the most. Sylvia ate the least—even less than Cassie, who emptied most of her plate because she felt she needed to. They went through the motions of conversation, as well, keeping the topics far away from the one that dominated everyone's minds.

After refusing cake and coffee for dessert, Cassie said, "The meal was delicious, Sylvia. Thank you." Then excused herself and immediately left the room.

During the afternoon she'd made some inroads into the book she'd attempted to start earlier. It was by her favorite author and she returned to it after dinner. She hadn't been reading for long, though, when someone knocked on her door. She found Will standing stone-faced in the hall.

"We'd like you to come down now, please," he said. His pale eyes gave nothing away.

Cassie accompanied him to the kitchen, where the table had been cleared of all but used cups. The cake sat untouched on the counter.

Sylvia offered a tight smile, but Robbie turned his head away, refusing to look at her.

Once Cassie had slipped into her chair, Sylvia came directly to the point. "Dad says he'll sign, but on one condition."

"Two!" Robbie interjected, seemingly having decided to take an active part. "I wanna know what that boss 'a yours plans to do with it!"

Cassie experienced a burst of victory, but kept her expression schooled. "And the other condition?" she asked.

"It's not enough money," Sylvia replied. "Not for somethin' that's so important to us."

Cassie answered Robbie first. "Mr. Michaels buys land as an investment for the future. He's been buying and selling land for years all over Texas. He considers your strip of land as just such an investment." Her gaze moved to Sylvia. "How much more did you have in mind?" she asked.

Sylvia countered, "How much are you willin' to offer?"

Cassie pretended to reluctantly consider the matter, but in the end she moved up one preapproved level.

The amount made Sylvia clear her throat and glance at the two men. "Would you mind if we took a little more time to talk?" she asked.

"Of course not," Cassie agreed. *Don't press your advan-*

tage too soon, Jimmy had taught her. *Let people have enough time to get past the finish line.*

Cassie returned to her room and again picked up where she'd left off in her book. Although she didn't expect to read more than a few pages, she read many more than that. And, as time wore on, she gave several disquieted checks to her wristwatch before, finally, there was another knock on her door.

Cassie had prepared herself to find Will in the hall again, but instead, this time it was Sylvia. Traces of moisture glistened in the woman's eyes and her cheeks bore two spots of color.

"We're ready now," Sylvia said simply. And as they started downstairs, she added inexplicably, "Dad's makin' a call."

Cassie frowned, but made no comment.

The two men continued to sit at the table, their expressions grim but resolute.

Once again Cassie seated herself and waited for one of the family to speak.

Robbie twitched several times before he said gruffly, "Okay, I'll sign." The words seemed to be pulled from him. "I've called Ray. Told him he has'ta get hisself out here, so he's on his way. Might as well get this over and done with."

Now Cassie understood what Sylvia had been referring to on the stairs, and it was exactly what she *didn't* want. As Jimmy's agent, she'd wanted to arrange her first meeting with Ray Taylor herself. On her schedule, when she was ready. Jimmy had told her, and she'd found through experience, that it was more productive to negotiate with one party at a time when dealing with multiple owners. And preferably out of each other's hearing. But what could she do?

She swallowed her consternation and agreed, "All right."

"He'll sign, too—" Robbie continued bitterly "—lickety-split like, 'cause he's never cared about the Old Home Place."

"Dad!" Sylvia seemed shocked that he'd say such a thing in front of an outsider.

"Just tellin' the truth," Robbie retorted. "I had'ta practically beg him to keep that bit 'a land in both our names when he sold me his share in the ranch just days after our daddy died. Couldn't get away from here fast enough."

"Granddad." Will spoke wearily, cupping a hand over the back of his neck to rub the muscles there. It was as if he'd heard that complaint at least a thousand times before.

"Well, he did." Robbie remained unrepentant. He rattled his empty coffee cup on the table. "How about another shot 'a this stuff, Sylvie? I think I'm gonna be needin' it."

Without asking, Sylvia collected a cup for Cassie before filling all four cups with steaming brew. "I'd better make some more," she said.

While the woman busied herself with the automatic coffeemaker, Cassie made some quick mental alterations to her plan for presenting the offer to Ray Taylor. But who knew, this could possibly work out for the best. If both brothers signed their contracts tonight, she could be back in Houston by midday tomorrow, impressing Jimmy with the swiftness of her success.

Then she became aware of the others in the room with her. Of the way Will sat staring bleakly out the window over his grandfather's shoulder, his expression grim. Of the old man hunched over in his chair. Of Sylvia—did the men even know that she'd cried? Or had she given in to emotion only when she was out of their sight? The land they'd agreed to sell was a part of their heritage and it was hitting them hard.

Awareness such as that made Cassie uncomfortable. Early on, Jimmy had taught her never to get close to the people she was negotiating with. *Keep a distance between you and them,* he had said. *You're not involved in their lives. You're just*

working a deal they want or they wouldn't be talking to you.
In the three years she'd been negotiating for him, she had
never before been this uncomfortable with what she was
doing. Was it because she'd grown up in Love and knew these
people—if only nominally—from that time?

She rejected her feelings of discomfort. Her goal remained
the same—to secure this sale and bring it back to Houston.
And the sooner she could do it, the better. She could even
leave tonight, right after Ray Taylor did. Which meant she
wouldn't need to see her mother. She wouldn't be in town
long enough.

"Your coffee's gettin' cold," Sylvia murmured, settling
back into the chair across from her.

Robbie snorted and stalked outside. Will quickly followed him.

Sylvia glanced at their retreating backs. "Don't worry," she
said. "When Dad gives his word he never goes back on it."

"I'm not worried," Cassie replied.

Sylvia shook her head sadly as she spooned sugar into her
cup. "Doin' this is hard for those two. But sometimes a person has to do hard things." Her eyes lifted. "I guess you
comin' back here was a hard thing, too. I've often wondered
what happened to you, Cassie. I'm glad to see you're doin'
so well."

Cassie's nerves were beginning to wear a little thin, and
Sylvia's probe, gentle as it was, caused a flicker of panic to
race through her body. Sylvia would never guess it from looking at her, but she longed to be on her own again. A decision
had been made, though, an acceptance given. She had to stay
where she was. And she had to find a way of answering Sylvia's questions without giving insult. She checked her watch.
The ranch wasn't that far out of town; it shouldn't take Ray
Taylor long to get here.

To her relief she heard the approach of a car, then doors open and close. Footsteps soon sounded on the front porch.

Sylvia hailed, "Come on in," to the newcomers, which also served notice to the two men in the backyard, if they hadn't heard the arrival on their own.

Will and his grandfather entered the kitchen at the same time as the two men who had come down the hall.

Physically, the twins were nothing alike. Where Robbie was rangy and deeply tanned with a thick head of cottony hair, Ray was shorter, with much paler skin, a rounder body and clipped gray hair that fringed a shiny dome. Ray Jr., in his early fifties, was a younger version of his father, except his hair had only started to lose color and recede. Both men were dressed in suits and ties.

There were no hugs or fond greetings exchanged between the brothers.

"I hope this is important," Ray said irritably, snapping out each word. "Junior and I were busy. We were going over our books."

"Good," Robbie snapped back. "'Cause when you get home, you'll have more money to add in."

Ray scowled. His gaze moved past Sylvia and Will to settle on Cassie. "Who's this?" he demanded.

"The person who's gonna give you the money," Robbie replied.

Cassie was quick to offer her hand. It was past time for her to step in. "C. A. Edwards," she said, giving Ray Taylor's hand a firm shake before doing the same with Ray Jr. "I represent Michaels Enterprises of Houston, and Mr. Michaels, my employer, has a proposition he feels might be of interest to you."

"I don't like initials on a woman. What's your first name?" Ray asked.

"Cassie."

It was obvious her name meant nothing to Ray, but his son's eyebrows shot up.

"All right, Cassie," the older man said. "What's this deal that's so important Robbie told me to drop everything to get myself out here for?"

"At least it got ya out here," Robbie inserted.

Ray's scowl darkened. "Don't start that with me, Robbie."

"All I'm sayin' is—"

Sylvia edged closer to Will, who, at her urging, intervened.

"Why don't you let Cassie do the talkin', Granddad?" he suggested.

Cassie continued before Robbie could do more damage. "My employer is making an offer on the strip of land you and your brother own between the highway and the railroad track. I have the contract in—"

Robbie interrupted. "She wants to give us a bunch of money for it, Ray. I'm willin', and I told her you would be, too. Bein' how much you like money and all."

Cassie wanted to shut her eyes and moan, but instead she repeated, "I have the contract for your consideration, Mr. Taylor. You can take it with you, if you like. Or I can return with you to your home to answer any questions you might have."

"A *bunch* 'a money, Ray," Robbie said.

Sylvia quickly supplied Ray with the contract Cassie had given them earlier.

Ray glanced at it, read the amended amount on offer and handed it back. Then, simply and unequivocally, he said, "No."

Cassie had never been in a situation described in some books as being so quiet a pin could be heard to drop, but this was one. Ray Taylor's refusal had sucked away everyone's breath, including her own.

Robbie stared at his brother. "I don't think I heard ya right, Ray," he said. "Say it again."

"I said...*no.*"

Robbie sputtered, Sylvia reached for Will's sleeve, and Will's lips tightened into a flat line.

"Now, if that's all there is to this," Ray said, obviously pleased with himself, "Junior and I will go back to our account books." He motioned for his son to precede him to the front door.

"But...you can't!" Robbie protested as his brother was about to step into the hall.

Ray stopped, turned and squinted back at him. "Watch me," he said. Yet before starting off again, he paused to offer a previously forgotten courtesy to the women. "Nice to meet you, Miss Edwards, and Sylvia, always nice to see you." He nodded to his great-nephew. "Will."

At about the same time as the car's engine started outside, Robbie groped for his chair and fell into it.

"Well," Will said grimly, "I guess that takes care of that."

Cassie couldn't believe that everything had gone so wrong so fast. If she didn't know for a fact that the ranch Taylors needed the money, she'd almost believe that Robbie had sabotaged the deal on purpose. He couldn't have been more provocative.

"How could you do that, Dad?" Sylvia whispered shakily, dabbing openly at her eyes. "How *could* you?"

Robbie still seemed stunned. "Ray's never turned down money in his life," he said. Then anger took over. "He's never cared about this ranch—not any part of it! He'd rather be a city man than get his hands dirty! Never wanted anythin' but to be a bigwig in town. Throwin' his weight around. Lordin' it over folks."

Cassie gathered her thoughts. As much to reassure herself

as to reassure them, she said, "I'll talk with him tomorrow. Possibly I can persuade him to change his mind."

"He's doin' it to spite me!" Robbie swore.

Will cradled his neck. "Granddad, I think we've all had enough for this evenin'. I know I have. Listen to what Cassie's sayin'. She's the one who knows what she's doin'."

For a brief moment Will's blue eyes met Cassie's before switching back to his grandfather. Cassie wasn't sure what surprised her most—the apology she'd read in his gaze, or the compliment he'd paid her.

Will continued, "I've got to see to some things outside, but Mom probably just wants to call it a night. You should, too, Granddad."

"I'm doin' the dishes," Sylvia declared, a waver in her voice.

"I'll be glad to help," Cassie heard herself offer. It was hard to remain aloof from the family's distress.

Sylvia smiled sadly and started to shake her head, but before she could state her refusal, Will cut in. "No! That's not necessary. I'll take care of things when I come in later."

"I'm doin' 'em, Will," Sylvia insisted.

Will slipped his arm around his mother's shoulders and said firmly, "We'll be fine." Then he gave her a bracing hug.

After gazing up at him for several seconds, Sylvia patted his cheek.

While the others busied themselves with their separate chores, Robbie sat with his white head hanging, his gaze fixed on his loosely clasped hands.

He'd been so sure about his brother, Cassie thought. Sure enough to bait him. He hadn't wanted to sell the land in the first place, but after he'd agreed, he hadn't expected this. He looked crushed.

Feeling the need to offer some hope, Cassie pledged quietly, "I will go into town and talk to your brother tomorrow."

"I'd sure appreciate that," Robbie answered, his voice a husky whisper, his eyes never lifting.

Once in the privacy of her room, Cassie fell back across the bed and allowed herself the privilege of moaning out loud.

She *wouldn't* be going back to Houston tonight. Or possibly tomorrow, either. This deal wasn't going to close early…if it closed at all.

A sudden thought occurred: What Will had said about her to his grandfather…did he truly mean it?

She sat up sharply. *No!* Now, of all times, she had to stay focused on what lay ahead.

She had to come up with a way to persuade Ray Taylor to change his mind. She had to think, to plan—

Go get 'em, girl, Jimmy would say.

And she would.

Chapter Four

Cassie awoke the next morning filled with confidence that she could save this sale. Repairing the damage that had been done yesterday wouldn't be easy, but a direct appeal to Ray Taylor's business sense would likely produce the desired result.

She called his home first thing and after a brief conversation with his wife she discovered that he'd already left for Handy's and that he would be there all morning. Cassie showered and dressed and made her way downstairs.

The house was quiet. It was already past nine o'clock, long after the ranch Taylors had started their day. Even the kitchen, which seemed to serve as the family's nerve center, was empty. Cassie jotted a note and was looking for a good place to leave it, when Sylvia Taylor came in from outdoors.

"Good mornin'," the older woman greeted her. "My, don't you look nice. That bright red color certainly suits you."

"Thank you," Cassie murmured, glancing down at the businesslike but still feminine suit she'd purchased for the trip. Maybe, psychologically, she'd felt she'd need the boost the color would give her, or maybe she'd just liked the way the jacket fitted. Either way, it was the battle armament she'd chosen for the day.

"Would you like some eggs for breakfast?" Sylvia asked,

and tipped the ceramic bowl she carried forward slightly for Cassie to see. "They're fresh. I just gathered 'em."

"I rarely eat breakfast," Cassie said.

"How about coffee, then? Or tea. We have all different kinds. Even some of that herbal stuff some folks prefer."

Cassie shook her head. "No…actually, I'm on my way out."

Sylvia's expression sobered, revealing the worry lines that had been camouflaged by her smile. "You're goin' into town to talk to Ray." It was a statement, not a question.

"Yes."

Sylvia slid the bowl onto the counter. "Think it'll do any good?" she asked.

"I hope so. I'll certainly do my best."

"I'll keep my fingers crossed for you," Sylvia said, and lifting one hand, showed Cassie her crossed fingers.

Cassie answered by crossing hers for a second as well, and then she walked outside to her car.

WILL COULD HAVE AVOIDED meeting her. He saw her car coming down the drive in plenty of time to just keep going down the road as if he had business elsewhere. But he didn't do that. Instead, he turned the pickup into the drive at the same instant as she rolled to a stop on the other side of the gate so that they blocked each other's path.

He hopped out of the truck. "Mornin'," he called as he unhooked the catch and swung the gate open. Then he walked to her car.

He wasn't sure what he was doing or why he was doing it…or even what he'd say next. Last night he'd been so tired he could have slept standing up against the wall, but his last waking thought had been of her. Instinct took over as he tipped his hat back and squinted down at her.

"You off somewhere?" he asked.

She was all dressed up again in clothes that could have come out of a magazine. Only this time instead of being conservative black, her suit was scarlet red. And instead of the crisp blouse he couldn't remember the color of, her blouse today was soft and white, with a fine gold chain clasped around her neck. Not a hair was out of place, her makeup was skillfully applied. She smelled nice, too, like some kind of exotic flower. Though not overwhelming, the scent was potent enough to come upon a man unawares and dance around his senses, making him want to go to places and do things he hadn't planned before.

She answered his question. "I'm going into Love to see your uncle."

He couldn't take his eyes off her. There was something about the way she— Something that made him—

He stepped back, breaking the spell. He had to leave this alone. He didn't have time in his life for a dalliance right now. And that was assuming she'd be interested. Which she wasn't—not from the cool way she reacted each time she saw him.

"Well, don't let me keep you, then," he said gruffly and, climbing back into his truck, reversed onto the side of the road and watched as she accelerated past. She did wave thanks, though. Which was something.

On his way up the drive he wondered if she'd have any luck getting his uncle Ray to change his mind. The two brothers had been at odds from the moment they'd first left the womb. One was a born rancher; the other was a born businessman. Will had spent many an hour during his growing years listening to his grandfather's tales about the pair as youngsters. How Ray had done everything he could to avoid his chores around the ranch. How he'd hated riding horses and working cattle. How even something as basic as looking after the tack had totally appalled him. In his turn, Robbie had hated school and "book learnin'," and had looked upon being cooped up all those hours as punishment. Ray, of course, had loved every minute.

He, himself, was a blend of both men. He loved the ranch and everything that went with it, but he also enjoyed the "book learnin'" part—which had given his grandfather more than a few nervous moments over the years.

Will grinned as he drove the truck around back to the feed barn, hopped out again then, after letting down the tailgate, shouldered the first of several sacks he'd picked up in Love that morning.

His grandfather hadn't had anything to fear along those lines, though, because in the end his good grades in school had earned him a scholarship to A&M—something that his grandfather had approved of, as had his dad. And he wouldn't trade his life on the ranch for any other, even with all the problems still thrown in.

CASSIE PARKED AMONG the small group of cars already taking up slots in Handy's parking lot. It wasn't so much the volume of people who shopped at the grocery store at any one time as it was the constancy of the in-and-out traffic. From the time the store opened in the morning, till the time the store locked up at night, customers were passing through its doors. And it had been that way since Cassie was a little girl. Everyone in town and the surrounding rural community shopped at Handy's.

Cassie took a breath, smoothed her hair, adjusted the collar of her blouse and stepped out. She doubted if anyone inside would recognize her. But if, by chance, someone did, or if one of the Taylors had mentioned it to someone, who'd mentioned it to someone else, who'd…she was prepared.

With her head high, she stepped into the familiar store. Just as little about the outside had changed, little on the inside had either. There were newer registers at the four checkout stands, and newer-styled carts to push around, but she had a feeling that if she wanted a certain type of cereal, or bread, or milk…it would be in exactly the same spot as it had been ten years before.

Two checkers were on duty, both ringing up customers. Cassie recognized the middle-aged women as long-term employees, but they didn't notice her as she walked along behind them, crossing the front area of the store to the narrow set of stairs that led to Ray Taylor's office. She could see him standing behind the windows, hands clasped behind his back as he viewed the goings-on in the aisles and at the checkouts. He might have been some kind of monarch surveying his domain.

Cassie hadn't called for an appointment because she was fairly certain that he would refuse. If she came in person, he would find it more difficult to reject her without listening to what she had to say.

At the top landing she rapped smartly on the door.

"Yes?" Ray Taylor called out, bidding entrance.

He frowned as she stepped into the room. "You again."

"Mr. Taylor, if you have a few minutes I'd like to speak with you. Last night—"

"I said all I needed to," he broke in impatiently.

"Please, Mr. Taylor. I won't take much of your time."

"I'm a busy man, Cassie."

He spoke as if he knew her, which meant Ray Jr. had told him the significance of who she was. Cassie met his gaze levelly, holding it, refusing to back down.

The seconds drew out until, finally, he agreed. "All right, then. Five minutes. But that's it. It's all I have time for."

He pulled one of several nondescript chairs away from the

wall, stationed it before his desk and motioned her into it. Then he went around and took his own seat. Just as he had last night, Ray Taylor wore a business suit and tie and looked every inch the busy executive. Even if technically a few years earlier he'd gone through the motions of handing over the day-to-day operation of his empire to his son, reality showed that Ray Jr. was relegated to a far smaller desk at the rear of the room and that his desk had far less business-related materials cluttering its surface than his father's. The real power continued to rest in the older man's hands.

Cassie reached into her briefcase. "You drive a hard bargain, Mr. Taylor," she said, withdrawing the contract. "Possibly *this* will be of more interest to you." She flipped to the right page, marked through the dollar amount, increasing it to Jimmy's second agreed-upon level, then passed it over to him.

He glanced at the new number and without blinking an eye, passed it back. "No," he said.

Cassie leaned forward. "I'm sure you appreciate that my employer considers this a fair price for the property."

"I do. I'm just not accepting it," Ray Taylor said.

"You're a very astute businessman, Mr. Taylor. Surely you can see the potential a sale of this kind could bring. An infusion of money in this amount is a shot in the arm to any enterprise. You have a piece of property that's not working for you. If you sell it to us, you could—"

He rose to his feet, declaring, "Your five minutes are up." He didn't say it unkindly, just firmly.

The time elapsed had been at most three minutes, but Cassie was in no position to protest as she scrambled for an argument that might sway him. "I can increase the amount," she said, although she didn't think additional money was the answer.

"I'm not interested."

"I still feel there has to be a way we can come to an agreement. Questions that I haven't answered. If I could just have a little more—"

He came around the desk, gathered her arm, pulled her gently to her feet and accompanied her to the door. "I know all I need to know," he said as he delivered her to the landing. "Now, if I can't help you with anything else…you have a nice day, Cassie." And with a gentlemanly smile that was decisively dismissive, he closed the door.

Cassie was still blinking as she stood clutching her briefcase and the contract when Ray Jr. came upstairs.

"Oh…hello," she said, stuffing the contract back into the case as she tried to regain her aplomb.

He didn't seem surprised to see her there or to find her in her flustered state. "He means what he says, you know," he said quietly.

"But why? Why won't he even consider, when—" She broke off. Was it any use to ask Ray Jr.? He was his father's puppet. He wouldn't tell her anything.

"He just won't," Ray Jr. said. His eyes narrowed. "You know, I wouldn't have recognized you last night. You look so different. Does your momma know you're in town?"

Cassie dove for cover by checking her watch and saying, "I—I have to go. It's past time that I—" She stopped herself from making excuses, straightened her shoulders and reminded herself, yet again, that she wasn't the young girl she used to be. The girl whose first instinct was to run and hide. "Thank your father again for me," she said calmly. "Tell him I appreciate his courtesy." Then she walked down the narrow set of stairs, out past the checkers and baggers and customers who, thankfully, continued to look upon her as if she were a stranger.

CASSIE SAT IN HER CAR, the key in the ignition unturned. Was there something else she could have done? Some other tack she could have used? Would asking the ranch Taylors be of any help? An entire mountain of ill feeling seemed to exist between the two brothers. Would knowing the cause make a difference? Ray Taylor was intractable. He was determined not to budge. It seemed that nothing she said, nothing she did, was going to sway him.

Shutting her eyes, she dropped her head onto her folded hands resting on the steering wheel. Was this going to be the first time she would fail Jimmy? She'd had difficult moments in negotiations before, but never anything like this.

She sat back, dug out her cell phone and placed the call to Houston.

Diane, who'd taken over her old job as Jimmy's executive assistant, quickly connected her with their employer.

"Howdy, Cassie, how's it goin'?" His positive, assertive, friendly voice boomed across the miles. "You about ready to head home?"

She could almost see him—stretched back in his chair; his shiny black boots crossed on top of his desk. He was an East-Texas-farm-boy-made-good and liked to play the part of showy entrepreneur to the hilt. Custom western suits, bolo ties, a snowy white Stetson set atop perfectly styled silver-gray hair, his hands impeccably manicured, his shave barber-fresh. He'd intimidated the life out of her when she'd first gone to work for him, until she'd gotten to know him better and let herself relax.

"Well…yes. Only, I have some bad news, Jimmy. It's not looking good out here. In fact, it's not going to happen." She heard a thump as his boots hit the floor, followed instantly by the squeak of his chair as he rocked forward to listen intently. "One of the parties—" she continued "—Ray Taylor, refuses to sign. He's dug in his heels and won't do it."

"Why not?"

"It something between the two brothers. Robbie Taylor says he's doing it to spite him. Robbie has agreed to the sale, by the way."

"Good."

"Ray and I talked to a degree last night, then I met with him this morning…and he won't do it."

"You need to find out what the problem is."

"I'm not sure that will help," Cassie replied.

"Is not knowin' helping?" As usual, Jimmy came directly to the point.

"No."

"Then have at it, girl! You're gonna have to dig deeper for this one." She knew that a wide smile had spread across his features. Having never met a challenge he didn't relish, he didn't think other people should let anything stand in their way either.

Cassie drew a silent breath and said, "I doubt that anything will change by Wednesday." Wednesday was her third day at the ranch, her allotted day to be finished.

"Then stay longer." Jimmy's solution was simple.

"But—"

"Stay as long as it takes. I got one of my feelin's about this one, Cassie. And you know what that means!"

"But—" she protested again, knowing it would do no good.

"You can do it. I know you can, you know you can. So, do it! Lemme know how you're gettin' on." And with that vote of ultimate confidence, he hung up.

Cassie clicked off her phone and stared sightlessly ahead of her. *Stay longer. Stay as long as it takes.* Words she didn't want to hear. Words that if Jimmy only knew what they would cost her... She hadn't told him anything about her connection to Love. He knew that she'd been raised in a small Central Texas town, but not the name of it, because she hadn't wanted anything from her early life to in any way taint her new one.

Someone approached the driver's side window, bent down, looked inside and said, "Cassie? Is that you?"

Cassie would recognize the voice anywhere. *Her mother!* Could this day get any worse?

"Hi, Bonnie," she croaked, using her mother's first name as her mother had always insisted.

Bonnie Edwards beamed at her.

Cassie made herself get out of the car and accept the hug that had to be accepted, then she pulled stiffly back.

Bonnie's overabundance of hair was as dark red as ever, compliments of the same henna tint she'd used since Cassie was little. It spilled over her shoulders in a wild array of natural curls that reached the middle of her back. Rings from the Near or Far East decorated each multi-pierced ear and even one of her nostrils. Her long fingers and several of the toes that showed out of her sandals were decorated with rings as well. A large crystal pendant hung from her neck to nestle among the multicolored, crinkly voile drapery of her blouse, which matched her multicolored, crinkly voile skirt. And, thanks to her strict adherence to her daily dietary regimen, she remained on the verge of being too thin.

"I never expected to see you here, Cassie." Her mother's eyes, several shades lighter than Cassie's dark brown, moved over her, examining her keenly.

Cassie clasped her arms reflexively across her chest. "I'm in town on business."

During their ten years of separation, mother and daughter had occasionally had strained conversations on the phone, but the only time they'd met in person had been four years earlier when Bonnie had gotten over her aversion to cars enough to come to Houston to take part in some kind of out-there seminar. Afterward, she and Cassie had had dinner. The meeting had not gone well, though, and later Cassie had castigated herself for even trying.

"I can see that your heart isn't in harmony," Bonnie said, reaching out as if to cup Cassie's cheek. "If you'd just let me clean your aura and set your body and mind in balance—"

"I don't have time for this," Cassie broke in, avoiding the touch.

"Cassie—"

She escaped into the car. "I promise I'll stop by before I leave. But right now I have to—I have to go." She turned the key and reversed out of the space. Her mother hadn't changed. She'd *never* change. Cassie flicked a glance to where Bonnie stood, gave her a tight smile and pulled out of the parking lot.

She was trembling as she accelerated away. It had been like this between the two of them since she'd grown old enough to rebel. She'd refused to be a part of her mother's world, to be dragged from one place to another as she accompanied Bonnie on yet another of her ridiculous missions to better the lives of the people of Love, yet seeing those same people watch them, talk about them, laugh at her mother's strange ways and beliefs.

At school she'd hear girls talking among themselves, complaining about how their mothers wouldn't let them do this or that, or how they'd taken them to church on Sundays, or to social events. And sometimes they'd claim they were so *embarrassed* by something their mothers had done or said. She'd have given anything to have had one of their mothers as her own. Or for her mother to be normal!

Cassie loved her. It was just…the way her mother lived. In her own universe, doing things her own weird way, without a thought as to how she was being perceived. And she couldn't understand why Cassie wasn't exactly like her.

CASSIE HAD STOPPED SHAKING by the time she reached the turnoff to the ranch, and she pretty well had herself in control again…at least on the surface. She parked the car where she had before, beside what she now knew to be Will's pickup, and went into the house.

All she wanted was the isolation of her room, but once again that solace was denied her. Sylvia and Robbie were sitting in the living room, tense, as if waiting for her return.

"What'd he say?" Robbie asked before she could start up the stairs.

"He refused."

"Dagnabbit!" Robbie swore.

Sylvia looked down, her disappointment evident as she said, "It's over then."

"I told ya he was doin' it on purpose!" Robbie burst out. "If I say the sky's blue, he's gonna say it's gray! If I say it's rained an inch, he's gonna say an inch and a quarter! No matter what, he's gonna—"

Sylvia interrupted the tirade. "So that means you'll be leaving soon. I guess there's no reason for you to stay tonight even."

"Well, actually, I need to talk to you about that. Would it be possible for me to keep the room a little longer? I know you have other guests scheduled to arrive, and if it's a problem, I can find somewhere else."

Sylvia watched her closely. "I'm not sure I understand. You mean…you want to stay longer for a vacation?"

"No," Cassie answered quickly. "It's not that. It's just— I'm not through trying to convince Ray to sign."

Robbie's head snapped up. "You're not?"

"No."

Hope dawned in Sylvia's eyes. "The only guests we have comin' for the next couple of weeks are that family that's arrivin' today. And like I said before, they're stayin' in the bunkhouse. And it's only for a few days. You can have the room you're in for as long as you like."

By the time Sylvia finished speaking, she was smiling broadly. Suddenly, the situation had started to brighten! Her smile was infectious and Cassie managed a smile as well.

The back screen door clapped shut and boots thumped through the house until Will joined Cassie in the doorway.

"What's up?" he asked, noting the women's smiles and his grandfather's renewed friskiness. "Did Uncle Ray change his mind?"

"Not yet!" Robbie replied. "But he's gonna. This little gal's gonna keep after 'im till he does!"

Will's eyes settled on Cassie and she felt her blood course faster through her veins.

Why was she continuing to react this way? If pressed, she could understand it happening the first day of her return to Love. She was bound to be sensitive at first to everything and to everyone who had played a part in her past life. But not this morning at the front gate, and not now when she had more weighty matters to deal with. Well, *now* was a bad gauge for comparison. It was too soon after she'd seen her mother. Her entire mind and body were, to use Bonnie's term, out of balance. But rather than having her aura cleaned, she needed some time alone to regroup.

"I'm going to try," Cassie clarified Robbie's optimistic statement.

"So you'll be stayin' longer, then," Will said.

Sylvia spoke up. "I've told her she can stay as long as she likes. In fact…Cassie, you don't have to pay for your room. You'll be our guest. Our real guest."

Cassie immediately shook her head. "Oh, no. Jimmy…Mr. Michaels…wouldn't hear of it, and neither would I."

Sylvia waved away her objection. "We'll talk about that later," she said. Then, standing up, she proclaimed, "You know, I'm startin' to feel better about things." Something caught her eye out the front window and she hurried over to look. "Seems the Warrens are here," she announced.

A car horn tooted several times as the family's van rolled up the driveway, making Will wince.

His mother gave his cheek a playful tap as she passed by him on her way to the front door. "Be nice now. You know this is repeat business. We want 'em to have a good time."

Robbie struggled out of his recliner and, copying his daughter-in-law's actions, mock-cuffed Will's chin as he, too, headed for the door. "Be nice now," he teased, his voice falsetto.

"I'm not the only one she was talkin' to!" Will called after him.

"I'm nice. I'm always nice," his grandfather boasted and, chuckling, stepped out onto the front porch with Sylvia.

Cassie had taken a step or two toward the stairs under the guise of clearing a pathway for Sylvia and Robbie. She took a couple more. The truth was she didn't want to be so close to Will. And she wasn't in the mood to meet the newly arriving family.

With her hand on the banister, she said, "I think I'll go to my room."

But she'd only mounted the first step when Will said again, "So you'll be stayin' longer, then."

His repetition made Cassie pause. "Do you have a problem with that?"

He smiled wryly. "I could."

Her body tightened. Something about the way he'd said that… She looked at him, trying to read his intent. "What did you say?" she challenged.

He shifted his long frame. "I'm sayin', it could get inter-estin'." Then after a pause, he said, "You…tryin' to untangle Uncle Ray and Granddad."

The way he looked, the way he moved, was having a strange effect on Cassie's knees. "Untangle?" she murmured.

"This has all been goin' on for a long time. You're gonna need somebody to give you a history lesson."

"I come from Love, remember?"

"It's family history I'm talkin' about, not town."

She should just leave, finish going upstairs, but she couldn't make herself move. Something was happening here, something that went well beyond the words he was actually saying.

"Are you volunteering?" she asked.

"Who? Me?"

After that, all she could do was stare at him.

The newly arrived family's excited voices heralded their approach to the porch. Will glanced their way and then back at her. "You better get goin' if you're still plannin' to."

Cassie was still having trouble trying to figure out which way was up, much less what she was planning. But a child-ish squeal broke her inaction and she quickly hurried to her room. And once there, for the first time since her arrival, she locked the door—unsure whether she was doing it to keep everyone else out, or to keep herself inside.

THE WARRENS TURNED OUT to be a sturdy middle-aged cou-ple with a ten-year-old daughter and a nine-year-old son who were all cheerfully out to have a good time. David was a den-tist in San Antonio and Cindy, his wife, was a stay-at-home mom who home-schooled the children. The parents had been weekend guests at the ranch a month earlier and had enjoyed it so much they'd promised their children the same treat.

Cassie learned all this within the first few minutes of meeting the couple after venturing down to the kitchen at lunch time.

"I'm sure you've already found this out for yourself," David said to her, "but the Taylors are wonderful people and excellent hosts. And Sylvia—" he winked at their hostess "—is such a great cook I've had dreams about her fried chicken…and her barbecued brisket…and her chicken-fried steak—"

"And her biscuits!" Cindy supplied.

"Ah! Can't forget her biscuits!" He brought the fingertips of his left hand up to his mouth and made a kissing sound as he brought them away. "I mean, the lady can cook!"

"Are we gonna have biscuits for lunch?" nine-year-old Seth asked hopefully.

"Don't be silly," his older sister, Melissa, disapproved. "We've already had lunch."

"We just love the bunkhouse!" Cindy enthused. "It's so quaint! What we thought we'd do first is take the kids down to the creek. Would that be a problem?"

Sylvia smiled. "Not at all. Just stay in the pasture behind the house. There aren't any cows there. They're in other pastures with their calves—which is somethin' you'll need to see, but you have to be careful because those mommas are real protective of their babies. Will'll take you out tomorrow sometime to see 'em."

"Baby calves, kids," Cindy could be heard saying as they left the house by way of the back screen door. "See, I told you you were going to have fun!"

Sylvia glanced at Cassie after they were out of earshot and shook her head, grinning. "This is goin' to be interestin'. Our first kids to visit the ranch. Hope they aren't our last." She motioned Cassie into a chair. "Would you like somethin' to eat? We have some cold fried chicken, or I can make you a nice sandwich."

"Cold chicken sounds wonderful."

Cassie watched as Sylvia bustled about, preparing a small salad for three and cutting and buttering thick slices of home-made bread.

"Dad likes his dinner in his room, then he takes his after-noon nap," she explained, making up a tray. "Will's packed his meal today. So, when I get back, it'll just be the two of us. Help yourself to some iced tea, or I made some lemonade this mornin'. Be right back."

Cassie did help herself to lemonade and was sipping it when Sylvia returned. "Why might these kids be your last?" she asked, curious.

Sylvia delivered their food to the table and slipped into her chair. "Because Dad and Will were dead set against me doin' this in the beginning. They didn't want *any* visitors comin' to stay at the ranch. Will complained he didn't have time to "wrangle dudes." And Dad—he thought it went against ev-erything the Taylor ranch stood for. Of course, neither one of 'em had any trouble leasin' a part of the ranch out to deer hunters in the fall. We've been doin' that for about four years now. Until—" She stopped, sighed, then continued, "But my idea's worked out pretty good. Up to now, anyway. I just hope these kids won't cause any trouble."

"They look nice enough." Cassie bit into a cold piece of chicken that could have made a certain colonel green with envy.

Sylvia shrugged. "Well, with kids, it's what you don't see that worries you." The woman grew silent again as she picked at her salad with her fork. "I kinda wish they weren't here for another week or two, though. You know, not until after every-thing's settled with the sale." She looked up, concerned. "You don't think it'll take longer than that, do you, to get a solid answer? I mean, I know Ray's already said no and all, but…"

Her words went on, but Cassie was no longer listening. The idea of having to be in Love for even that long appalled Cassie. And she knew she would have to be *in* Love. She was going to have to find a way to get through to Ray Taylor and that meant being around him and his family…*in town.* She'd decided to keep her home base at the ranch, first, because she knew it was what Jimmy would prefer, as she did herself. And, second, because if she were to stay at the only motel in Love, she'd never know when her mother might come to call and turn everything upside down.

"I should hope not," she replied earnestly. Then was unsure whether she'd spoken over something Sylvia was saying.

But Sylvia seemed pleased by her answer. "Was Ray still as determined as last night?" she asked.

"Yes, but he did listen to me." Cassie didn't say for how long.

"Those two," Sylvia said, shaking her head, "both just as stubborn as a pair of ol' billy goats."

Cassie seized on the opportunity. "Mrs. Taylor…Sylvia. The way Robbie keeps talking about Ray—can you tell me what's caused the hard feelings between them? If I know, I might be able to work around it. Or I might be able to use it to get through to Ray."

Sylvia sat back, shaking her head as she laughed softly. "Ahh, that's a big job you want answerin'. And I'm not laughin' because it's funny. It's more…sad, really, but it's been goin' on for so long, we're all just used to it. There's some things you come to believe you can't change, so you—"

The telephone in the hall rang and Sylvia went to answer it. She spoke for a short time then came back.

"That was the leader of one of my church committees and

she's goin' to be stopping by in a little while for some hand-iwork I've been doin' for the group, so I'll have to get it to-gether for her. You just make yourself at home here, Cassie. Whatever you want, you get it. Don't stand on ceremony." She started to turn away, but stopped. "Oh! What we were talkin' about—you should talk to Will when he comes in this eve-nin'. Him and his granddad are close and he can probably give you a better perspective than I can. He can *sure* give you the male point of view, and bein' it's two males that are causin' all the trouble..." She didn't finish the sentence, but she didn't need to. It finished itself.

Cassie smiled faintly and nodded, what remained of her appetite failing. Talk to Will, the woman had advised. She didn't *want* to talk to Will. But she couldn't say that to Sylvia.

Chapter Five

Cassie stayed in her room throughout the afternoon, telling herself that if she tried hard, she could pretend that she was someplace else. Somewhere where no one knew her, where one pressure didn't pile onto another until it all seemed too much. But because her bedroom faced the front road, she heard when the church committee leader paid her call to collect Sylvia's handiwork—whatever it was—and then drove off after a friendly exchange on the porch. And later, she heard the children, returned from their time at the creek, laughing and playing energetically in the yard around the house. At times Robbie Taylor's voice mixed with theirs—telling more of his tall tales? Then Sylvia, David and Cindy joined the others on the porch.

A small part of Cassie yearned to go downstairs and be included in the fellowship—a yearning that she quickly extinguished. She wasn't the "real guest" that Sylvia now deemed her. She was here for only one reason—to complete her job. And because of that, she had to retain a businesslike detachment.

As time wore on, though, she became increasingly restless, moving from spot to spot in the small space and pausing occasionally to look out the window. In Houston, she was a creature of the present. She stayed busy, not letting herself think about anything that wasn't in the here and the now. She never considered the future beyond the fact that she would keep doing what she was doing—working as Jimmy's agent—until…well, until she couldn't do it anymore. *And then what?* a tiny voice within her asked. She'd retreat to a place where she'd sit lost and alone and wait for the end? That wouldn't happen to her! She wouldn't be alone. She had friends. She even had a couple of ex-boyfriends who—*Who, what?* the tiny voice asked again. Even though she still counted both men among her friends, as soon as either relationship had started to deepen, something had made her pull back. And now both men were busy with their lives, forming other commitments, as were her other friends, two of whom had recently gotten married, and another who'd had a child. She was seeing less and less of them….even now.

Cassie turned sharply away from the window. It was this infernal waiting that allowed for so much introspection. Normally, she avoided self-examination. There was nothing wrong with living in the moment, with not thinking about the future or dwelling in the past. The past. She tossed her head. What past did she have, other than growing up in Love? Which was something she did well not to think about. And which was damned difficult not to do when she was in it!

She crossed the room, retrieved her suitcase from beneath the bed and set it on the quilt. Coming here had been a mistake. She should've told Jimmy the truth…asked him to find someone else to handle this negotiation. Even Diane, the twenty-two-year-old assistant, could've done better than she had so far. She certainly couldn't have done worse. And if Jimmy had conducted the transaction himself, he would have Ray Taylor eating out of his hand by now.

She would tell him the truth. And after that she'd tell him she was leaving—

Her body stilled. What was *wrong* with her? Even after learning the reality of what she was facing, she knew how Jimmy would react. He would consider what she was doing running away. And the phrase *run away* wasn't in Jimmy's vocabulary. Neither was *give up*.

Cassie pushed the suitcase back into place, and as she straightened she saw that it was almost six o'clock. The long hours of waiting were over. From this moment, she was back on the clock. After dinner she would talk to Will. And after that she'd decide what she would do next. And it wouldn't be run away.

TWO LEAVES HAD BEEN ADDED to the kitchen table to accommodate both family and guests around its laden surface. Uncomfortably, Cassie found herself seated off Will's right hand and side-by-side with Sylvia. David and Cindy Warren sat across from them, and the children were at the table's far end by Robbie. As bowls and platters were passed around, the naturally curious dentist and his wife took turns questioning her.

"Cassie, is it?" David asked as he helped himself to a hearty portion of mashed potatoes. At her confirming nod, he continued, "Where are you from, Cassie? I don't believe we heard earlier."

"Houston," Cassie said and she felt Will's quick glance at the omission of her hometown roots.

"What part?" Cindy queried.

"Northwest."

"Oh," the woman returned immediately. "We have friends who live in Spring. Are you near Spring?"

"It's not far away."

"And what do you do there?" David asked, but before she could answer, he peered down the table and reprimanded his young son who was using the salt and pepper shakers like dancing feet, making them clatter against the tabletop. "Seth! Behave yourself," he said sternly, and Seth instantly stopped.

"I'm in real estate investment," Cassie said casually. "Actually, the man I work for is in real estate investment."

"Ah." David nodded. Then stabbing his fork through the thick, crunchy crust of a perfectly done chicken-fried steak, he gave an even more satisfied, "Ahh," as he delivered it to his plate.

"Are you here for a few days like us or for longer?" Cindy asked, passing her husband the cream gravy.

"Possibly longer."

"Well, you couldn't have picked a better spot," David chimed in. "Sylvia, if this tastes as good as it looks—" He patted his thick waistline and compared it with Will and Robbie's more rangy frames. "I don't know how you two don't each weigh a ton, eating this good food every day. I certainly would."

Cindy laughed. "It's because they work hard, honey. They work it off."

"It's the country air," Will quipped.

"And a clear conscience," Robbie added with a wink at the two children.

"And the blarney," Sylvia said, grinning.

Friendly exchanges continued throughout the meal, with Will contributing his fair share. For someone who had resisted taking in lodgers on the ranch, he certainly seemed to be doing his best to be hospitable.

Cassie tried hard not to notice the strength and pleasing shape of his long-fingered hands or the way his shirt, open at the neck, allowed a few fine golden chest hairs, only a little darker than his hair, to peep free of constraint. Or the way he seemed so relaxed—the exact opposite of her!

Cassie knew she was going to have to talk to him, to request the help that he himself had proposed that morning.

She'd been waiting since lunch to ask. But her stomach, which had been tight throughout the meal, constricted even more as the meal drew to a close.

As everyone rose from the table, Robbie asked the children if they'd like to learn to throw a lasso. The children, of course, were thrilled. David and Cindy said that they were going to sit on the front porch and relax, and Will, after saying he had some work left to do, was at the back screen door before Cassie could make herself move.

"Uh…Will, could I have a word with you, please?" she asked.

He stopped short. "Sure," he said. His pale eyes moved over her as he waited for her to begin.

No one had actually left the room yet, and since Cassie didn't want to make her request in front of an audience—especially Robbie—she hedged, "Could I…walk with you, please?"

"Ho-ho!" David Warren teased, resting both hands on his wife's shoulders as he stood behind her. "That sounds like a country pickup line if I ever heard one!"

"David, stop it," Cindy chastised, smiling.

"Well, I don't see any rings on either of their fingers!"

"Come on," she said, tugging his arm, "let's get you out of here before Sylvia kicks us off the ranch."

"I was just playing," David defended as his wife pulled him into the hall.

Cassie managed to maintain her cool exterior, but on the inside she was burning with embarrassment and annoyance.

Sylvia wordlessly shook her head and Robbie rolled his eyes, both prevented from saying anything by the children's presence. Then Robbie scooted the pint-sized pair past Will out the door, and started them along the worn path to the working heart of the ranch.

"Sure, come on along." Will answered her earlier question as if nothing had occurred in between.

After a bracing breath, Cassie passed through the screen door that he continued to hold open for her.

WILL COULDN'T HELP but notice the way the beige slacks and pale blue shirt she now wore fitted her body, showing off a tiny waist and curving hips that swayed ever so slightly as she walked.

She'd hardly said a word during supper, responding only when directly addressed. But that was the way she seemed determined to operate. *A woman of few words,* he thought with some amusement. But in this instance *she* was the one who'd asked to talk to *him.* He decided to let her be the one to call the shots.

She glanced over her shoulder after a few steps, her dark eyes checking his position before she swung around to face him. "Earlier today you said that I need a family history lesson. Your mother tells me you're the best person to give it to me. Would you?"

The request had a rehearsed sound to Will's ears. He decided to toss in a monkey wrench and see what happened. "Why didn't you tell the Warrens you're from Love?"

She took a moment to answer. "Because it's none of their business."

"It's not because you're ashamed or anythin', is it?"

"No," she answered quickly. Too quickly.

He shifted position and lazily crossed his arms. "Then why not admit it? Everyone's from somewhere. You're from here. Or is it that you'd like to forget that you're from here?"

Her cool demeanor began to crack. "I don't see—"

"Houston's a big place. Never seen a place quite so spread out. You can drive for miles and still be inside the city limits. Do you like it better than here?"

"What I like doesn't matter," she retorted with a tight little edge. "I'm here to do a job, not—"

"I'd just like to know," he said easily.

Her brown eyes flashed. "In Houston, people leave you alone. They don't keep asking questions when you've made it perfectly clear that you—"

"So you do like it better. *Because people leave you alone.*"

"Yes!" she snapped, then took a visible breath before reclaiming her cool facade.

But Will knew better now. She wasn't as coolly calculating as she pretended. What good it would do him and why he should care were two things he would have to look into later. Right now, though, he just couldn't seem to stop himself from being curious about her.

He squinted into the distance—he was fast losing light. And he still had to see to the horses, and do a little work in the shop, and then, once in for the night, do a whole lot of catching up on the computer. "Okay," he said. "I'll help. But not now. How about later?"

"How much later?" she prompted.

He gave a slow smile. "Will an hour, hour and a half do?"

"That's fine with me."

"Then it's a date." He smiled wryly. "This'll sure make David Warren happy."

She frowned, momentarily confused, before she snapped back, "David Warren can—"

"Go someplace hotter'n a Texas summer?" Will supplied.

She looked at him, and for the briefest second he thought she was going to smile, too. Instead she said levelly, "I'll see you then." And headed back for the house.

Will, setting off in the opposite direction, started to whistle.

As CASSIE OPENED the back screen door, she knew she could *not* return to her room. She'd had enough of the place. Instead, she went over to where Sylvia was putting away the meal's leftovers and stationed herself at the sink. She needed to stay busy. The busier, the better.

Sylvia glanced up. "You don't have to do that."

"I want to," Cassie replied and ran a plastic tub full of hot soapy water into which she started plunging glasses and cups.

"Well, I won't fight you on it," Sylvia said. "I'm kinda tired tonight."

The two women worked in companionable silence until Cassie said, "You should have a dishwasher."

Sylvia turned from putting away the last of the leftovers in the refrigerator. Dipping her fingers into the soapy water, she rinsed them, then reached for a dish towel. "That's what Will says. He tried like crazy to get me to agree to one when we started refurbishin' the bunkhouse, but there's just somethin' satisfyin' about doin' the dishes by hand. You can think about things while you work, and when you're done, you feel this nice sense of accomplishment to have the kitchen all clean again."

"But with guests…"

"I know. With one or two people it wasn't so bad. But with more…maybe I should've done it."

"You still can," Cassie suggested.

Sylvia shook her head. "Dishwashers cost money."

Cassie didn't know what to say. She couldn't tell Sylvia that she already knew about the family's tight financial situation, and neither could she make promises about an eventual agreement that she might not be able to fulfill. She let the subject drop.

Silence stretched between them again, until, this time, Sylvia broke it. "You can tell me to mind my own business if you want to, Cassie, but I can't help but wonder about you and your mom. She's gonna be hurt if she hears that you're stayin' out here with us."

Cassie bobbled a plate, but managed to keep it from harm.

"I saw Bonnie this morning," she said, answering because she could hear the sincerity in Sylvia Taylor's tone. The woman was truly concerned.

"You did?"

"Outside Handy's."

"Ah," Sylvia murmured. Then added strongly, "You know, Cassie, things aren't quite the same as they used to be around here. Your mother—"

"Do you mind if we don't talk about my mother?" Cassie asked tightly.

She could feel the older woman's eyes fix on her, trying to delve deep inside to see things that Cassie didn't want anyone seeing.

Cassie continued to wash and rinse plates and place them in the rack on the counter. One by one, Sylvia continued to dry and put them away.

Finally, Sylvia said, "Love's grown some since you've been away. Young folks movin' out and some of 'em movin' back again, startin' their families. Other folks movin' in with theirs. You, ah, have you started a family yet, Cassie?"

Cassie shook her head.

"Are you married? David Warren mentioned that you're not wearin' a ring, but women sometimes take their rings off or don't wear them for any number of reasons."

"No, I'm not married," Cassie answered. Questions, always questions…but always filled with Sylvia's good-hearted interest.

Sylvia sighed, "Will's not married either. Sometimes I don't think he'll ever marry. I've almost given up hope. I always wanted a grandbaby or two." She looked out the window toward where Robbie had the children tossing ropes near one of the outbuildings and chuckled. "Although, honestly, at times tryin' to keep Dad in line is a lot like tryin' to deal with a nine-year-old. Maybe that's why he gets on with 'em so well. Which is somethin' that's sure surprisin' the heck out of me. I thought he was gonna fuss about havin' to deal with the kids, and there he is out there havin' a grand ol' time!"

As Cassie plunged the last stainless-steel pot into the soapy water, Sylvia said, "I'll take it from here. You go outside and enjoy yourself. Weather's been so nice this spring. Not near as hot as last spring or the one before."

Then she surprised Cassie by giving her a quick hug. "Thanks, Cassie. I truly appreciate the help."

Flustered, Cassie could only murmur, "I'm…used to staying busy." She tried to make light of it by shrugging, but Sylvia's motherly affection unsettled her. Bonnie wasn't much of a hugger and most of the household chores that Cassie had performed regularly while growing up had gone largely unnoticed.

CASSIE HAD NO DESTINATION in mind when she set off from the house, until childish laughter drew her to Robbie and the children.

"'At's it! Ya did it that time!" Robbie loudly proclaimed his approval. "See, I told ya. Ya just give your wrist a little flick."

Seth was beaming as he danced over to where his loop of rope had closed around an old tree stump.

Melissa sat cross-legged on the ground a short distance away, absorbed in herding a beetle with a long piece of straw, her length of rope forgotten at her side.

Robbie winked at Cassie as she joined them.

"I wanna do it again!" Seth cried as he ran back.

"Well, ya know what to do, you just hafta do it!"

The boy painstakingly recoiled his rope and awkwardly tried to circle the loop as he'd been shown. He failed in his next attempt and stomped miserably around in reaction.

"Keep tryin'!" Robbie urged. "Over 'n' over till you get the hang of it. Somethin' worth doin' is worth practicin' to get right."

The boy firmed his lips and started over. Once again he missed, but instead of complaining as he had before, he did as he'd been told and kept at it.

"Straighten your arm out a little," Robbie called before moving closer to Cassie's side. "Boy could be a good roper," he told her, "given the opportunity."

They applauded and cried out when the boy caught the stump again.

"He's got the determination," Robbie said as he watched his charge move back into position.

"You may have started something," Cassie said.

"Better 'n a lot of stuff kids get into these days."

But instead of continuing to lasso the stump, Seth decided to rope his sister. His first attempt settled right into place, making her screech at the same time as she threw the rope off and took off after her laughing brother.

When they disappeared around the nearest outbuilding— which Cassie now saw was the refurbished bunkhouse—Robbie grinned and said, "Guess I better go after 'em, 'fore they get into trouble and get me into it, too. Hey, kids!" he called. The only response was another girlish screech and more devilish brotherly laughter. *"Kids!"* he called again, and disappeared, walking stiffly, to find them. Moments later the children erupted into view, the chase still on as they ran back to the house, with Robbie continuing to trail behind.

Cassie had a short debate about what to do next. The idea of going back to her room still didn't appeal; neither did sitting on the front porch with David and Cindy. She decided to strike off on her own.

She could go for a walk and see the creek that the Warrens had visited earlier. She even knew the creek's name—

Love Creek. It was the creek that had given the town its name. Spring-fed, its source somewhere in these hills, it meandered past the outskirts of town until, eventually, a number of miles later, it emptied into a lake on the other side of the county seat. Her mother had "sensed" that the creek held special powers, and she and Cassie had spent long hours at the spot where its course passed nearest to their home. Bonnie in meditation, and Cassie enjoying the freedom to wade among the rocks with the clear cold water gurgling around her ankles and lower legs. She turned away from the sweetness of that memory. None of the past was good here.

She cocked an ear. She could hear no sounds of anyone about, so Will must have ridden off or gone somewhere. It was safe for her to explore the area a little.

As she'd noted the day before, the outbuildings were predominately three-sided, with metal roofs and concrete slabs, and each seemed to be used for a different purpose. In one, a not unpleasant grassy scent permeated the air, tickling her nose, and reminding her of the feed store in town. There were bags and boxes of various sorts, and all kinds of supplies. Another building was an open shop-type area, with a workbench and vise and assorted hand tools, along with boxes of nails and coils of barbed wire. A section of it looked like a garage, with the tools and equipment to keep the ranch vehicles running. Another building housed a tractor, and parked next to it, outdoors, was a red pickup truck, older and more battered than the one Will drove on the road. In all likelihood it never left the ranch, if it ran at all. Also outside, scattered about, were other types of implements that Cassie guessed could be fitted on the tractor and dragged. And not far from them was a fuel tank set on stilts.

The last building was easy to identify from the corral abutting one side. It looked far older than the other structures, more weathered, but it had been built very sturdily and was fully enclosed.

Two horses were free in a nearby pasture. The pair stopped nibbling grass blades long enough to inspect her before, one by one, they lowered their heads back to the grass. Cassie gazed at them. She'd always loved horses, but from afar. She'd touched one once, smoothed her fingers along its hairy cheek, but she'd never ridden one.

Will suddenly emerged from the stable, leading a large red-brown horse by a halter. He seemed just as surprised to see her as she did to see him. He and the horse crossed over to where she stood outside the corral gate, and once they were through, he was the first to speak. "Are you in that much of a hurry to get outta here?"

Cassie, stung by her stupidity in thinking him gone, and also by his uncanny ability to read her thoughts, answered tightly, "You could say that, yes."

"You didn't look all that unhappy about ten minutes ago when I saw you with Granddad and the kids."

Cassie retreated behind her previous shield. "I have a job to do—"

"Don't you ever get tired of sayin' that? Don't you ever relax?"

"Do you?" she retorted before she could stop herself.

For once he didn't have a quick comeback. He was just as driven in his need to make the ranch prosper as she was in her need to settle this contract. Then she began to think better of her aggressive stance. She did, after all, need his help.

As a peace offering, she motioned to the horse. "What's his name?" she asked.

"Jimmy."

Her head snapped up. "Is that really his name or are you being—"

"His name's Jimmy. Been that way since he was born eight years ago." He motioned toward the horses in the pasture. "That chestnut sorrel out there—she's his mom—her name's Polly. And the other one, the dun…he's Jake. Polly is Mom's horse and Jake is Granddad's. They both have a few years on 'em."

"And Jimmy is yours."

"That's right."

She moved uneasily, unable to think of anything else to say. Mostly, she was aware of *him*. At this moment, both Will and the horse seemed larger than life to her. They could have been supernatural beings from one of Bonnie's "other realms." Handsome and valiant and vital…

The horse stamped and tossed his head, breaking Cassie's line of thought, which made her want to kiss the diamond-shaped blaze on his long hairy nose. He was a large horse, but he wasn't larger than life. And neither was Will.

She flicked her hand toward the house. "I should be getting back. I didn't mean to disturb you. I was just…looking around."

She started to turn, but Will stopped her by making an offer.

"You know, if you want, we can do our talkin' now. There's no use makin' you wait until later."

She looked at him. He'd hooked his arm under the horse's neck and was casually patting and rubbing the animal's cheek, keeping him pacified.

"You aren't too busy?" she asked.

Will laughed dryly. "I'll be busy on this place all my life. You want to wait that long?"

The twinkle in his blue eyes told Cassie that he was teasing.

"Well…sure," she said. Thinking that she was agreeing to his prior offer.

He playfully mistook her answer. "Be careful," he warned, "I might hold you to that one day." Then laughing again, he stepped away from the horse. "Hang on a minute and I'll be back. I'm just gonna turn Jimmy loose with the others."

Though there was plenty of room as he walked the horse past her, Cassie instinctively backed away. And as she did, she realized that she'd do very well to remember to keep just such a distance later, too…when it was only Will and herself.

Chapter Six

"You mind if I see to a few things while we talk?" Will asked upon his return.

Cassie said quickly, "No. Not at all."

"Come on into the stable, then," he invited, and showed her in by a side door.

Occasional rays of light were visible through the cracks in the walls, giving added natural lighting to the interior. The area was divided into two sections, set apart by a flat-board fence. In the section where they stood on a hard rock floor, years, possibly generations, of old tack and equipment were strewed about or hanging from nails, alongside more up-to-date versions. The next section over was a shelter for the corralled horses, with a soft dirt floor and a wide doorway that allowed them to enter and leave the stable as they liked. The scents of feed and hay and leather were heavy in the air.

Will cleared a few things from the top of an upturned wooden barrel and offered it to her as a seat. "Best I can do in here. Okay?"

Cassie settled onto it. "It's fine," she murmured and Will nodded.

She watched as he moved behind the fence to where, through the spaces between the boards, she saw an almost identical upturned wooden barrel to the one she sat on. It held an array of grooming-type implements—a metal comb, a brush, a bottle of some kind of liquid—possibly liniment? Along with several other articles she couldn't identify.

"So what is it you want to know exactly?" he asked as he collected the gear.

For a second, Cassie couldn't remember! Then she reclaimed her thoughts and said, "Tell me about your grandfather and his brother. Why are they so at odds?"

He crossed back into the storage area to put the items away. "They've always been that way. They're twins but they're complete opposites. They don't look like each other and they don't think like each other. As a result, they rub each other the wrong way. Granddad's always loved the ranch, Uncle Ray… Well, I guess he might have some sort of feeling for the place, but his main interest is in Love and the businesses he has there."

Cassie considered what he'd told her. "But there has to be more to it than that. They're both so…angry."

When Will finished his task, he leaned casually against a wooden support post and crossed his arms. "The one thing they have in common is that they're both about as stubborn as they come. They could teach mules how to dig in and not budge."

Cassie smiled faintly and waited for him to continue.

"Granddad's big beef is that Uncle Ray isn't loyal enough to the family name or the family heritage. He still resents that Uncle Ray isn't here workin' the ranch with us. Uncle Ray made his decision a long time ago. And Granddad holds it against him."

"If that's so, then why wouldn't your uncle be happy to sell the strip of land?"

"Probably because Granddad wants him to."

"You mean he's only refusing to be opposite?"

Will shrugged.

"But it feels…more than that," Cassie said.

"Could be because he's still mad at Granddad for winnin' the girl. Uncle Ray was interested in my grandma before my granddad got around to proposin'. But then Granddad was interested in her first. So that makes things kinda confused."

"But that has to be forty or fifty years ago."

"Yep. Then Uncle Ray got married a few years later and didn't ask Granddad to be his best man. Then when my daddy was born, Uncle Ray didn't come out to see him until he was three months old. So to get back at him, when Ray Jr. was born, Granddad waited six months to go see him. On and on, one thing after another. It's just the way it is between those two."

Cassie's spirit was ebbing. All she was learning was how impossible her goal would be to achieve. "So what you're telling me is that I'm wasting my time. That I should just go back to Houston and forget about it."

He shook his head. "No. My daddy and Ray Jr. were good friends growin' up. They liked to fish and hunt together, and because of that granddad and Uncle Ray buried some of their differences for a while. The boys brought 'em together and that lasted for a time even after they grew up. Then things happened and pretty soon they were the way they used to be."

"So? I don't understand what you're saying."

"I'm sayin' that Uncle Ray thinks the world of Ray Jr., even if it doesn't always look like it. And that if anyone can get through to him, Ray Jr. can."

Cassie shifted position, unconvinced, and the barrel beneath her wobbled, then began to topple over. She gave a soft cry as she struggled not to fall. Will was at her side before the barrel stopped rolling, steadying her, even though she no longer was in danger of falling.

"I'm all right. I didn't expect— I didn't mean—" The words caught in her throat.

Will was so close to her that she could hear the rapid thumping of his heart, or maybe it was her heart. She didn't know. Her hand had somehow reached out for his chest—to hold him away? To hold herself away? His strong, capable hands on her arms made her feel weaker, not braced. That golden hair, those sky-blue eyes, the rugged lines of his face…

He smiled slowly and when he spoke, his words were husky. "Didn't expect you to want to get started so quick. You don't let any grass grow under your feet, do you?"

Cassie had no idea what he was going on about. Or why, every time she got near him, her mind seemed to hit some sort of erase button, leaving her to founder. "I don't—"

He dipped his head and his lips touched hers in a soft butterfly kiss that was soon followed by another and another. Drawing away, he smiled again—that slow pull of his lips that, if only she'd let herself admit it, she had started to wait for. Then he righted the barrel, saw her back to her seat and stepped away, for all the world as if the moment hadn't happened.

"Ray Jr. is the person to talk to," he said, turning to search for something among the boxes on a shelf.

If her heart weren't beating so fast and her lips weren't tingling from those kisses, Cassie might have thought the whole thing a dream. She took a couple of steadying breaths, striving to seem just as unaffected about what had happened as he was. It had been a spur of the moment thing; it meant nothing. Nothing at all.

She cleared her throat. "I had the impression that all the strings were in your uncle's hands."

Will must have found whatever it was he wanted, because as he turned back toward her, he slipped it into his jeans pocket. "Ray Jr. may take the path of least resistance, but that doesn't mean he's not his own man. He's got a lot goin' for him. He's just up against a hard rock. He's been up against it all his life, though. So he knows some ways to get around."

"This morning he didn't seem interested in helping."

"You saw him?"

"Yes. At the store after I saw your uncle."

"Did you ask him to help?"

"No, but—"

"I'll be headin' into town tomorrow mornin'. If you want, why don't you come along and we'll both talk to him."

"I can talk to him on my own."

"That's true. You can. But it might carry more weight if I'm with you. Ray Jr.'s a little more into family connections than his daddy is."

Cassie couldn't refuse. "All right," she said, "I'll come with you."

"Good. You ready to head back?" He retrieved his hat from a nail just inside the door, set it on his head and waited for her reply.

"Yes…yes, I'm ready," she said and this time, careful to keep a distance between them, strove hard not to so much as glance at him as she accompanied him to the house.

WELL, HE SHOULDN'T HAVE DONE that, Will thought as he sat staring at the computer screen. He could hear the children outside playing and the other adults in the backyard under the shade tree as they waited for the right moment to open the hand-crank ice-cream maker his mother used for her special blue-ribbon recipe. Cassie had fled to her room right away, but he'd had a harder time getting free. Only the press of the work that his mother knew well he was behind in had kept him from getting roped into the social occasion outdoors.

Except…a half hour had gone by since he'd closed himself into the small second kitchen pantry that he shared with rows of last year's vegetables and fruits his mother had judiciously preserved in glass quart and pint bottles, and he still hadn't completed one entry. He couldn't put his mind to it. His eyes kept traveling to the horseshoe nails that he'd searched for like an idiot, stuffed into his pocket and then set out on the short bookshelf by the monitor after entering the "office." By quirk of fate, because he hadn't counted them, there were three nails…one for each of the kisses that he'd given her. She had barely reacted; her lips parted slightly, her body unmoving. But an earthquake had been taking place in his body, with maybe an erupting volcano thrown in. He hadn't expected to be affected like that. He'd quickly run for cover, and she seemed to have been okay with that, but she'd gone very quiet on the way back to the house and then disappeared from sight.

This wasn't something he needed right now. He had enough to think about and to do. Tonight he'd planned to work on the tractor, make sure it was ready for the hay ride his mother wanted him to provide for the guests tomorrow afternoon. And he'd needed to try to catch up here. In the days that his granddad had been out with the cattle full-time, he'd known each and every cow in their herd by sight. Knowing their history, the lineage, how heavy a cow's calves were, if she had breech births, if she'd started to go barren. He'd kept it all in his head. Will had a lot of that same information in his head, too, but keying those records onto a computer spreadsheet made it easier for him to keep a run of everything and brought the ranch into modern times.

Although here he sat, the tractor ignored and the computer just stared at.

All because he'd kissed a girl.

CASSIE GROANED when she awakened the next morning to a rooster's crow. She pulled the pillow over her head, but he wouldn't stop crowing and the sound, though muffled, got through.

She'd had a horrible night. Waking up for long periods and then sleeping only in snatches. As a fanciful preteen, she would have almost fainted at Will Taylor kissing her. As an older teen, she probably would have, too. Yet the reality of it actually happening was more disturbing. And that she should feel that way was even more disturbing than everything else, when obviously it had meant nothing to him. He'd gone on to talk about Ray and Ray Jr.—

She sat up with a jerk and looked at her watch. It was well past seven o'clock! He'd told her to be ready to leave at seven forty-five. She threw off the bedcovers, slipped into her robe and, after peeking to see that the hall was clear, hurried into the bathroom.

Just as she was about to close the door, Will stepped out of his bedroom. He was fully dressed, thank heaven. He'd probably been working for the past couple of hours and had only come upstairs to get something.

Her first instinct was to finish shutting the door without saying a word. But he was looking at her and he was starting to smile.

"Mornin'," he said quietly.

Cassie hadn't looked in a mirror yet. Her hair was probably standing straight up and the makeup she'd been too un-nerved to remove last night probably made her look like a raccoon or worse. She ran a smoothing hand over her hair and peeped out at him through the remaining door crack.

"Good morning," she murmured.

"Late start?" he asked.

Her chin lifted. "I'll be ready on time."

"Good, 'cause Ray Jr. likes to eat breakfast at Reva's at eight. That's where I thought we'd corner him."

And Reva's would be filled with other Love regulars, too. Cassie groaned again in her mind. She'd been far more prepared to meet townspeople yesterday than she expected she would be today, unless her upcoming shower could work miracles.

His gaze moved over the little he could see of her. "Are you always such a bright and cheery person this early?" he teased.

"On my good days," she returned and shut herself safely inside the narrow room.

She could hear Will's chuckle through the door.

THE WARRENS, IT SEEMED, were early risers and the family was in the kitchen at the table when Cassie entered the room. A huge stack of hotcakes, a tub of butter, a bottle of syrup, crispy strips of bacon—the visitors were about to dig in.

"Cassie…good morning," Sylvia greeted her, smiling warmly, and the salutation was taken up by the Warrens. "Can I get you anything before you leave? Some coffee? Some orange juice?"

"You're leaving?" Cindy questioned, surprised.

"Only for an hour or two," Will said, moving away from his position at the counter to snatch a strip of bacon. "She's comin' into town with me."

"Ah-ha!" David exulted. "What'd I tell you?"

Cindy dug her elbow into his ribs. "Shhh," she said.

The children giggled as they reached for the syrup at the same time and began a tug of war to see who'd win. Both parents' attention turned to stop the tussle before something broke or spilled.

"I'll come to the door with you," Sylvia said to Will and Cassie, and then followed them out onto the porch.

"Phew," she said, fanning herself. "I've forgotten how energetic kids that age can be." She grinned at Will. "It's been a long time since you were that little."

Robbie spoke up from his chair at the jigsaw puzzle. "'Bout time we start growin' our own again. Can't wait forever." He thumped a puzzle piece into place with a balled up fist and peered up at Will from beneath bushy eyebrows, mischief in his grin.

"You're gonna live forever, ol' man," Will bantered back. "You're too ornery for the devil to want you anytime soon."

"It's wings I'm after, son. An' I can feel 'em sproutin' already!" He wiggled his shoulders.

The gray cat leaped onto her favorite rocker and, bracing her front paws on the arm nearest Cassie, looked up at her, expecting to be petted.

"The Duchess has really taken a shine to you, Cassie," Sylvia said. "You can count that as an honor."

"I like her, too," Cassie murmured, smoothing her fingers over the cat's soft fur, being sure to rub both ears.

"We'd better be goin'," Will said after a moment spent putting on his hat.

"Where you off to?" Robbie asked, unkinking himself from the chair.

"We're goin' to talk to Ray Jr., Granddad."

Robbie snorted. "And you think *that's* gonna work?"

"Do you have any other suggestions?" Will returned.

"Leave it alone, Dad," Sylvia urged. "Let 'em do what they can. And breakfast's on the table, so you need to get a move on before those kids eat it all."

The old man shambled off, shaking his head and grumbling under his breath about his brother.

Sylvia turned from watching him. "Well, good luck's all I can say. I hope it'll do some good."

CASSIE SENSED Will's quick look several times during their drive into Love. They were in his pickup truck rather than her car because he said he needed to haul something back to the ranch.

She was practically hugging the passenger door, the wide space between them pointed, but it was the only way she could get through this morning. The shower had not worked a miracle of any kind and her shell of professionalism was fragile. She looked no different on a cursory surface examination—she wore another suit, this one a more sober light gray, and her makeup was back in place, as was every hair—but inside she was squishy.

Will turned into the parking lot at Reva's, found an open slot and cut the engine.

"You've been pretty quiet," he said, propping an arm on the back of the bench seat as he turned to look at her. His hand didn't quite reach her, but it was close.

"I've been thinking about what to say," she lied.

She looked straight ahead, avoiding looking at him.

"And what did you come up with?" he asked.

"I've decided to let you take the lead. As you said…family and all. You probably know the best way to approach him."

"He's my cousin. I'll just talk to him."

"Of course."

He frowned. "What's happened to you, Cassie? I understand that you might not want to have much to do with this town. You probably don't have a lot of good memories of it. But it's not a bad place."

"We're not here to talk about me," she said tightly.

"Well, maybe we should."

She checked her watch. "It's ten minutes after eight," she pointed out and reached for the door handle.

"Is it because of what happened yesterday?" he asked.

Her fingers froze on the metal bar. "I'd just as soon forget that, if you don't mind."

"What if I do mind?" he countered.

She could hear his smile in his voice. That slow pull of his lips that made her—

"Hey, Will, what are you doin' here?" The voice came from outside the truck, making Cassie jump. Ray Jr. leaned down to look in the open driver's side window, his fleshy face transformed by a smile.

"Come to see you, Junior, that's what." Will opened his door. "Brought some company with me, too." He motioned toward Cassie, who had exited the truck as well and come around to join them.

"Cassie," Ray Jr. said, his smile fading. He glanced at Will uncertainly.

"Ray Jr.," Cassie said.

"Thought we'd join you for breakfast," Will said. "That is, if it's okay with you."

"Well, sure," Ray Jr. agreed, recovering his smile.

The men stood back to let Cassie enter the café ahead of them. She would just as soon have followed them because on first glance the room seemed filled with people. In the initial few seconds she reverted to her younger self and had to fight a spurt of panic. But she quickly saw that the roomful was maybe ten or fifteen people, spread out in groups at several tables along with a couple of singles sitting on counter stools. Only one or two seemed to have noticed their arrival. Until—

"Mornin', Ray Jr., you're late," a man at the most crowded table called, causing his companions—and everyone else—to twist around. One chair remained empty at their table, undoubtedly reserved for Ray Jr.

"Will!" a man at another table called out. "Long time no see!"

Cassie could feel everyone's eyes inspecting her curiously, but no one seemed to make a connection as to who she really was.

More greetings were exchanged and Will moved to shake various hands. Most were middle-aged or older farmers and stockmen, come to town in their work clothes. Others were local businessmen like Ray Jr. Caps and cowboy hats ruled the day, and the only women present, besides Cassie, were Reva and her helper.

"It's been too long since you've paid us a visit," Reva complained to Will as she hurried over with a steaming carafe of coffee to fill their cups after he and Cassie had settled at a table near one of the front windows. Ray Jr. had stopped off to speak to his friends, but she didn't hesitate to fill his cup as well. "The usual, Ray Jr.?" she called out to him. And receiving his "You betcha," she looked at Will. "What'll you have?" Then at Cassie. "And you, Miss?" Their order in hand, she sailed away in an aura of complete competence that only long years in the business bestowed. A thin woman of indeterminate age with sandy-colored hair and freckles, she ruled her café with an iron hand inside the proverbial velvet glove.

Cassie was hard-pressed to find anything that had changed inside the place. The tables were topped with the same beige-speckled Formica, the chairs were the same low curved-back wood, and as always the menu was posted above the back counter on either side of a bright red advertisement for Coca-Cola. Napkin holders, salt and pepper shakers and ashtrays decorated each table, along with plastic holders for packets of sugar and small white bowls for tubs of liquid creamer.

After Ray Jr. joined them, he quickly downed several large swallows of coffee.

"Dad's on a tear this morning," he said in explanation. "I'm needin' this. The hotter, the better!"

"What's he on a tear about?" Will asked.

Ray Jr. sent Cassie a quick look. "This 'n' that. You know. Business."

"Does it have anythin' to do with the Old Home Place?"

Another quick look at Cassie. "It could."

"It's your dad we came here to talk about, Junior. Just how set is he in turnin' this deal down?"

Ray Jr. fiddled with his cup. "Pretty set. Like I said to her—to Cassie—yesterday morning, he really means it. I haven't seen him this dug in since, well, since I wanted us to start sellin' the knickknack things the church ladies make to the tourists passing through. You'da thought I was suggesting we sell skin magazines, or something. He hit the roof!"

Reva arrived with their orders and without a wasted movement, she set down a plate of fried eggs, grits and sausage in front of Ray Jr., a similar plate in front of Will, and then moved around to Cassie, where she slid an order of wheat toast and jelly onto the table in front of her. "Sorry, Miss," she apologized, quickly supplying Cassie's missing flatware and napkin from those already set out on another table.

Ray Jr. looked up from peppering his eggs. "Don't you know who this is, Reva?" he asked. "This is Cassie. Our Cassie. Cassie Edwards!"

Reva paused, hands on hips. "No," she said in disbelief. "Our Cassie? I don't believe it."

"Well, it's true," Ray Jr. said and reached for the salt shaker.

If the other regulars in the café hadn't overheard the information for themselves, Reva was going to be sure to tell them about it. And everyone else she saw in the future, until everyone in the area knew.

Cassie made herself give a small smile. "Hello, Reva," she said and strove to look as poised as she possibly could.

"Well, bless your heart! I never woulda guessed in a thousand years! What brings you back to town? You come to see your momma?"

Cassie's smile faltered and she quickly shored it up. "I've seen her, yes," she said.

She could feel Will's steady gaze. This was one of the moments she had dreaded…and to have him here to witness it—

"Hey, Reva," he said, shifting his attention to the café owner, "did I forget to order some toast? 'Cause I sure meant to."

"Comin' right up, Will," Reva said, and hustled back behind the counter.

Had he done that on purpose? Cassie wondered. Rescuing her by diverting Reva's attention? He seemed to have an uncanny ability to know when she needed help. But if he could sense that, what else could he sense? She darted a glance at him and was relieved to see that he was eating. His toast soon appeared and Reva quickly headed to the cash register to accept a customer's payment.

Neither man spoke much as they ate, while Cassie spread a little strawberry jam on her toast and nibbled at it. Her stomach didn't want food, but she had to do something.

Finally, as the men finished with coffee, Will returned to his earlier subject. "You think maybe you could get your dad to see reason, Junior? I'm only askin' because it's important."

Ray Jr. leaned forward, his gaze probing. "Things are gettin' tight, huh?" he asked.

"Pretty tight."

Ray Jr. nodded.

Will continued, "We lost the huntin' lease a couple of weeks ago. Man we were workin' with has decided that his company needs to cut back on expenses. He's not gonna be entertaining his customers in the fall…at least, not on the Circle Bar-T."

"Uh," Ray Jr. breathed, as if taking a sympathy stomach punch. "You trying to line up someone else?"

"In my spare time," Will answered dryly. "You know how

it is, though. It's hard to make a good connection. We never had any trouble with those ol' boys from Waco. They never broke any of the rules. Always cleaned up after themselves. With someone new—" Will shrugged "—who knows?"

"I can keep an ear out for you," Ray Jr. offered. "See if somebody knows somebody who might be interested."

"I'd appreciate that. But what you can do best is to work on Uncle Ray. Maybe get him around to where he'll meet with Cassie again."

Ray Jr. nodded doubtfully. "I'll try."

Cassie leaned forward herself. "Do you know of any specific reason why your father's so adamant?"

"Not really. Nothing that's not—" he shrugged "—you know…the usual."

Cassie sat back. This didn't look good. They seemed to hit one dead end after another. Maybe she could convince Jimmy to forget about the prospective sale. It wasn't as if there weren't other places. But he'd said himself that he had a "feeling" about this property, and he always listened to his feelings because they rarely proved incorrect.

Will tipped his head toward the almost whole order of toast that remained on her plate. "Do you want to finish that?"

"I'm finished," Cassie said.

They all stood up. "Good talkin' to you, Junior," Will said as he clapped his cousin on his shoulder. "How's the new shop doin'?"

For the first time since Ray Jr. had greeted Will in the parking lot, a wide smile covered his face. "Doin' good, actually. Lots of people seem to want cards and party supplies. Didn't surprise me, but it did Dad."

"Mom's birthday's comin' up next month. I'll stop by and see what you got the next time I'm in town."

"That's great!" Ray Jr. said, then after a quick check to his watch, curbed his enthusiasm to say worriedly, "Gotta get going. Dad'll be wondering where I am." He raised his voice. "Put it all on my tab, Reva, includin' your tip."

Reva, readying a new pot of coffee, waved a hand in agreement.

"You don't need to do that, Junior," Will said, frowning as he reached for his wallet in his back pocket.

Cassie dug in her purse as well.

"Least I can do, don'tcha think? Everything considered? Not to mention all the meals I used to eat out at your place when your daddy and I were either going out or coming back from one of our huntin' or fishin' trips. I still think on those times as some of the best in my life." He noticed Cassie's extended hand and folded bills. "And you. You didn't eat enough to keep a bird alive. So put that away."

Reluctantly, Cassie followed his direction. Further protest wouldn't do any good anyway because he was already on his way out the door.

In the parking lot, one of the men who'd been at Ray Jr.'s regular table called to Will from his pickup truck. Cassie waited on the sidewalk as Will went to talk to the man. When he joined her again, he looked somewhat abashed.

"Tim Hassat—you remember Tim?—he's asked if I can help him out for a half hour or so over at Swanson's. You can come along, if you want, or—"

"I can find something to do," she cut in.

His pale eyes narrowed. "Could end up bein' closer to an hour. I'm sorry about this, but—"

"Don't worry about it. It's not a problem." Staying with him could be the problem. Not that she wanted to be in Love itself any more than she had to. Especially now that word would be quickly spreading about her identity. "I need to find some clothes. I only packed enough for three days."

He gave his slow smile that could tingle her toes. "That's right. You travel light." He tapped the hood of his truck. "Hop in and I'll give you a lift."

Cassie looked up Main Street. She could walk to the store she had in mind, but it was a distance. Mainly, though, she didn't want to make a spectacle of herself. She'd trudged those same streets too many times as a child with her mother, who even then refused to have anything to do with the ownership or operation of a car.

She made an effort at refusal. "But Swanson's is just across the street."

Will was already getting in the truck. "Where to?" He grinned.

The truck started rolling the instant Cassie followed suit and said the store's name. This time Cassie forgot all about hugging the passenger door until they were halfway there, and then she could see no reason to.

"Ray Jr. has a new business?" she asked for conversation.

Will nodded. "He and Uncle Ray opened it a couple of months ago. This one's supposedly Ray Jr.'s to run on his own, though. His 'opportunity to prove himself.'"

"I thought your uncle had turned the businesses over to him some time ago."

Will glanced at her. "Oh, he did, but it's a little hard to tell, especially since he won't let Ray Jr. make any of the real decisions. How'd you know that?"

"I just…heard."

The truck reduced speed from slow to very slow as they neared the shops in the center of town, then they pulled into one of the fronting diagonal slots.

With the engine still running, Will issued a quiet challenge. "You know a little more about everythin' happenin' around here than you let on, don't you?"

Cassie knew she'd slipped up and decided to own up to it. Nothing was going according to her original plan anyway. "It's always best to know all you can about a situation before you enter into a negotiation. It gives you a stronger hand."

His eyes narrowed. "So you know about our little problem on the ranch, too."

"I didn't know about you losing the lease."

"Not many people do, up to now."

"Is it—" She stopped. She'd be putting herself too close to the situation if she asked. But what the heck? Again, nothing was going according to plan. "I take it, losing the lease presents a major difficulty."

"On top of everything else? Yes."

Bleakness seemed to settle over him as she watched. The lines time, trouble and responsibility had etched on his face deepened. He drew a long breath and released it. Then, as she continued to watch, he pushed the worry away and was actually smiling when he looked at her again.

"But that's what we're workin' to fix, isn't it?" he said.

Chapter Seven

Cassie emerged from the shop a half hour later, a bag with enough clothes to see her through a week clasped in her hand. It hadn't taken her a lot of time because there wasn't much to the array of choice. Jeans, shorts and T-shirts, skirts and blouses, casual dresses along with a small number of more stylish selections…the store's inventory might seem limited now, but Cassie remembered a time when she had pressed her nose against the front window and dreamed of wearing the more normal clothes on display rather than her mother's hand-sewn and mail-order oddities.

Shoes were next, and since there was only one shoe store that she knew of in town, she crossed the street, all the while keeping an eye out for Will's truck. He'd told her he didn't mind waiting if he was to arrive before she finished, but that was something she didn't want to make him do.

The occasional person she passed was starting to look at her closely, as if trying to fit the young person they remembered with the adult woman they were now seeing. Word had spread. As yet, no one had spoken with her other than the clerk at the clothing shop. And Cassie didn't remember her. She must be one of the town newcomers Sylvia had mentioned.

Cassie didn't make the situation easy for any of them. She

kept her head up, her chin high and her eyes straight ahead. If they came away with nothing else after seeing her, it would be that she wasn't about to hide as she used to. Her insides might feel like jiggling Jell-O, she might be having to battle panic…but she wasn't going to cower away.

A blond woman about her age was inside the shoe store with two small children. Cassie knew instantly who she was—Lynette Simpson. Her first instinct was to pass on by, but she made herself go in. Mr. Riggins, who'd owned the store forever, barely glanced up from trying to fit the youngest child, a boy of about four, with a pair of boots. The little boy was twisting and kicking and doing everything he could not to stay in the chair. His brother, about a year older, was running around and knocking over displays while screeching at the top of his lungs. Lynette threatened one with no boots, which seemed to be what he wanted anyway, and the other with a spanking when they got home, which he seemed not to think much of a threat. Mr. Riggins, looking harried, was patient.

Cassie perused the displays that were still standing and waited, her back slightly turned to the mayhem. After five minutes of ear-splitting screeches, thumps and threats, Cassie heard Lynette say, "Okay, we'll take 'em," having finally reached the breaking point.

The youngest boy wiggled free and, giggling, joined his brother in a chase about the store. They ran wide circles around the chairs until the youngest, zigging when he should have zagged, collided with Cassie's legs.

"Oh, my goodness!" Lynette exclaimed. "Now look what you've done!" She hurried over to where Cassie was rubbing the side of her knee and began an apology. "I'm *so* sorry. I hope you weren't hurt. My boys, they're just—" She stooped to pick up the shoe Cassie had dropped, and when she straightened she looked at her properly for the first time. Recognition dawned. "Cassie? Is that you?" she breathed. "I'd heard—when my mother called to tell me you were in town, I just didn't believe her. But here you are! Right in front of me!"

Wide blue eyes moved avidly over Cassie—her children, who were still misbehaving, temporarily forgotten. Lynette looked essentially the same as Cassie remembered her, except for a certain unkemptness as well as a little more weight.

Lynette smoothed a hand over her flyaway blond curls and attempted to wipe a chocolate ice-cream stain from the front of her blouse.

"You look—you look so different," she said as if marveling that it could be true. "So—" She seemed at a loss for the proper descriptive word.

"Lynette," Cassie murmured. She'd wanted to be friends with Lynette all those years ago when they were children, and they had been for a few short weeks one summer, then school had started and Lynette had pulled away.

"Um—" Lynette looked around for her boys who had been corralled by Mr. Riggins "—what have you been doin' with yourself?" She laughed uncomfortably. "I guess you can see what I've been doin'—havin' babies. I'm married to Donnie Parks. You remember Donnie?… He was a couple of years ahead of us? Do you have any ba—" She laughed uncomfortably again. "My goodness, my mother isn't gonna believe that I've seen you. How long will you be in town?"

"I'm not sure," Cassie replied.

"Well, well, isn't that somethin'." Lynette seemed to be trying to think of ways to carry on the conversation, but was too rattled, either by her children's bad behavior or the unexpectedness of the meeting, to find a subject. Finally, she said, "I suppose your mom's happy to have you visit. You know, maybe tomorrow evenin' I could stop by and we could go over to Reva's. I can't do it tonight, because Donnie—

"I'm not sure what I'll be doing tomorrow," Cassie interrupted her, "or if I'll even be here."

"Oh." Lynette paused, nonplussed. "Then maybe I can get Donnie to change his plans for tonight and we can—"

"I'm not staying in town. I'm at the Taylor's ranch on business."

"Oh," Lynette said again.

Mr. Riggins *oofed* loudly as one of the children kicked him in the shin, and Lynette hurried back to her motherly duties. Gathering her children and the boot box, she headed for the door. But not before sending Cassie an uncertain smile and a little wave.

Mr. Riggins, who had to be nearing eighty by now, looked ready to collapse. But he wouldn't rest until he'd assisted his waiting customer. Cassie quickly made her request—a good pair of athletic shoes—and gave him her size. He trotted out of the back room a few minutes later, box in hand. Cassie tried on the shoes, then, after paying for them and wishing the old man a good rest of the day, stepped back out onto the sidewalk.

A quick check showed her that Will's truck still was not in any of the parking slots. Though it had seemed longer, she'd probably spent only about fifteen minutes in the shoe store. If Will's possible hour held true, she had more time to spend.

With bags in hand, she strolled up the sidewalk, looking in all the store windows. Remembering the barber shop with its red-and-white striped pole attached high up to one side of the front doorway, and the ice cream parlor where she'd sneaked an occasional treat outside of her mother's strict food program. And farther down, standing off on its own, she came upon the post office where Will had… She swung around and checked again for the truck's arrival. It still wasn't there.

But another person she recognized was walking toward her. One of the neighbors on the street where she'd grown up. The woman glanced at her, looked away, and then her head snapped back again. She'd obviously heard the news, too. But Cassie walked on, and the woman didn't stop her.

The sun was warmer today, a promise of what was to come in full summer. The air was so much drier here than in Houston, though. To her, it made the heat more bearable. She'd almost forgotten.

"Cassie?" A familiar voice called her name.

Cassie shut her eyes for several seconds before turning. "Hello, Bonnie," she murmured.

Her mother looked her typical self, but her smile wasn't as bright as it had been the day before; the expression in her eyes was more question. "I didn't expect to see you again."

"I told you I'd stop by before I left."

Now some of the people in cars were slowing to look at them. Bonnie, as always, didn't notice. Cassie did.

"What a person says and what a person does can make an interesting puzzle," Bonnie stated.

Cassie drew a silent breath. More of her mother's gobbledygook. She shot another look down the lines of parked cars, desperate to see Will. And she did! He was just pulling into a slot about half a block away.

"I'm sorry, Bonnie, but my ride is here. I have to—"

Her mother caught her arm as Cassie was about to draw away; her fingers cool on Cassie's skin. When Cassie looked at them, her mother let go.

"I want to see you, Cassie. It's not a good thing for a mother and a daughter to be apart for so long. Come home.

Let me make some of my special tea. Let me give you some of your favorite honey cakes—remember how you used to love them when you were young? I baked them last night."

"I can't. Will is here and—"

"Will?"

"Will Taylor."

"Hello, Mrs. Edwards," Will said, coming up behind her, his long legs having covered the distance in no time.

Cassie hadn't been aware that he was so close. If she had, she certainly would have done everything in her power to prevent this moment from happening.

Bonnie looked him up and down. "So that's the meaning of the force I was told to expect. It's you!"

Cassie intervened quickly. "We have to go. Will doesn't have time for—"

Her mother tilted her head and smiled up at him. "Would you like a honey cake, Will? And some of my special tea?"

Cassie wanted to curl up and die. Right there on the spot. Her mother had a way of making everything so much worse. A way of causing her—even in her grown up and confident shell—to lose sight of all but the horror of the moment.

"No, Bonnie," she said briskly, "he wouldn't."

Will seemed to contemplate her mother's invitation. Cassie was about to start pushing him toward the truck when he said, "I'm not sure I've ever had a honey cake."

"Then you're in for a treat," Bonnie promised.

There was an awkward moment when Cassie should have said something, but she couldn't. She was afraid that if she opened her mouth she'd scream *No!* so loudly that people would come running to see why.

They headed down the sidewalk toward the truck, Cassie

on legs that worked of their own accord. But at the truck, Bonnie shook her head, turning down Will's offer of a ride.

"I'll meet you," she said, and with a beatific smile continued to walk.

CASSIE SAT IN COMPLETE SILENCE. Will made no move to start the engine.

Finally, he asked, "Have I done somethin' wrong?"

A pained expression passed over Cassie's nicely drawn features. "Oh, no," she said, "everything is just…wonderful."

"You don't want to go to your mom's house?"

"I thought you were so busy!"

"I am. But what's another half hour?"

Cassie ran a hand through her hair and looked away.

Will gazed out over the steering wheel. Suddenly he didn't want a honey cake either. *Hell.*

He looked back at her. She didn't know it, but some of the fine hairs were out of place from the earlier sweep of her hand. It reminded him of the way she'd looked that morning, when she'd peeked out at him through the crack in the bathroom door, with her hair all over the place from sleep and her makeup mostly disappeared. He felt a stirring in his body, just as he had then. She'd looked good from the moment he'd first seen her. All buttoned down and collected. But if he had to give a preference, he liked the slightly mussed version and the face that went beyond pretty without artificial assistance.

"I heard your mom ask, but you turned her down. You said it was because of me. But it's not me, is it? It's you. You don't want to go."

Her head whipped around. "Do you blame me?" she demanded. "My mother is a lunatic, okay? You know she is.

Everyone in town knows she is. I'm surprised everyone in the state doesn't know it!"

Will frowned, surprised by her ferocity. "No," he disagreed. "She's just…Mrs. Edwards."

"Uhh!" She expelled a disbelieving breath.

Will didn't know what to do. Inadvertently he seemed to have stomped on a raw nerve. He knew Cassie had left town as soon as she was able, but he'd had no idea that she and her mother were so alienated. But then, Bonnie Edwards was a little…unusual. It could stand to reason.

"She's expectin' us," he said quietly.

"She'll forget all about us if she sees what she thinks is a white crow, or hears something in the breeze," she answered, her voice brittle.

"I don't think she will."

Cassie was silent. Then she said, "All right. But don't blame me if this gets weird!"

"I'd never blame you, Cassie," he said. "A person can't be blamed for the kind of parent they have. Junior can't make Uncle Ray different. And you can't change your mom."

She folded her arms and looked pointedly out the side window. "If we're going to do this, can we just…go?"

CASSIE FELT AS IF she were in a waking nightmare. Short of pretending that she was suddenly, violently ill, she couldn't see a way of getting out of it. And even if she did, Will would see through her ploy in a second and she would be even more humiliated than she was at this moment.

He didn't understand. How could he understand? He had Sylvia for a mother, not Bonnie.

They slowed to a stop in front of a small wood-frame house where amulets hung from the eaves, and crystals, sparkling like raindrops in the sun, dangled from numerous tree branches. Like Sylvia, her mother had a garden, only Bonnie's took up the entire front yard and was filled with anything and everything that her mother might consider held some kind of magical power. To the neighbors, it must have been an eyesore, with the various large and small objects that Bonnie had found in her wanderings painted in bright colors and with mysterious decorative designs to guide a path to the front door. The high thin notes of a flute floated on the air. *Home,* Cassie thought. And she cringed inwardly.

She chanced a quick look at Will. The chaos he saw didn't seem to bother him in the least. He just sat there as she did, waiting for her mother to show up.

"I don't think she's going to come," Cassie said, her hands pressed tightly together in her lap.

"It takes a little while to walk."

"She knows all the shortcuts."

Another minute passed, increasing Cassie's tension.

"Let's go," she directed. She'd lost all semblance of her newfound inner confidence and she was sure that it showed. But she didn't care.

He looked at her steadily for a moment, then started to turn the key—but her mother stepped into view from between two houses and the opportunity for escape passed.

Like a wraith, Bonnie walked beside them without acknowledgment and went up the path to the house. She paused only long enough to drop what looked to be a small rock into a collection of others in a glass bowl on the narrow porch. She didn't even turn to see if they were following as she went into the house.

Cassie took a bracing breath, opened the truck's door, and feeling something like a wraith herself—or maybe it was a leaf being blown along in a furious wind storm—she traced her mother's steps, with Will right behind her.

The interior of the house was just as oddly eclectic and strangely put together as the exterior. Fringed scarves and candles and symbols from various eastern religions mixed with Bonnie's own interpretations of ancient beliefs and lore. Incense sweetened the air as the flute continued its haunting notes. The room was filled with furniture—old, overstuffed and ranging from pieces that might be prized to those that belonged on a trash heap. Flowers filled various vessels. And, Cassie noted, there were still no time pieces of any kind. Her mother hated clocks.

Cassie kept herself from looking at Will. She didn't want to see what he might be thinking now. Even when she'd found a friend to play with for a time, she'd never invited the friend here. She was too ashamed.

Her cheeks were flushed as she watched her mother come from the kitchen carrying a plate of cookie-sized honey cakes in one hand and an oddly shaped teapot in the other, all of which she set on the low table in front of the couch. Bonnie then gathered three cups from the tall cabinet by the front door and, smiling tranquilly, sank onto her knees on the floor and motioned for Cassie and Will to seat themselves on the couch across from her.

She lifted the plate of honey cakes to Will. "I gather the honey in late spring. It's the best time, I think. The bees tell me it is."

Will sampled the cake. "It's delicious," he pronounced.

"Cassie?" her mother prompted, offering the plate to her.

Cassie took a cake and nibbled it. It was good; she remembered they had been her favorite throughout her childhood. "It's good, Bonnie," she murmured.

Her mother seemed to sense when the water for the tea was about to boil because she disappeared with the teapot, only to reappear a moment later, the teapot full. Why she hadn't left the teapot in the kitchen earlier was a question only Bonnie could answer.

A minute later she poured a cup of weak tea and tasted it herself before pouring for her guests. "I think you'll like this, too. I found it just the other day."

Cassie was unsure what the word "found" could mean. It could be anything. She thought to warn Will, but he'd already taken a sip and was smiling. Cassie cautiously tried it herself and identified it as a version of Earl Grey.

"Your uncle had it in his store," Bonnie said to Will.

"That's a nice lamp you have over there." Will nodded toward a large clump of rock or mineral sitting on a console that was glowing salmon pink and orange from the inside out. "What is it?"

"A salt lamp from the Himalayas. It brings calm to the evil winds. Don't you feel it?"

"Mmm…sure," Will hesitantly agreed.

Cassie felt no such calm. Evil winds abounded.

Bonnie leaned forward, looking at Will with luminous eyes. "I *knew* you'd feel it." She switched the look to Cassie. "I told you he'd come, remember? Before you left. You were so unhappy and you wouldn't let me help. But I told you he'd come! And he has!"

Cassie had had all that she could take. She looked at Will, beseeching him to put an end to this, uncaring that he would know the depth of her desperation.

He stood, pulling Cassie up with him. "We have to go, Mrs. Edwards. Thanks for the cake and tea."

Bonnie sank back on her heels, momentarily disappointed, then she jumped to her feet as well. "Here," she said, "take some of these with you."

She wrapped two cakes in tissue paper and held them out

as an offering. "Eat them when the moon is starting to rise and you'll be together for the rest of your lives."

Tears of anger, humiliation and frustration sprang into Cassie's eyes and she almost ran from the house. Will, after mumbling his thanks, followed her.

After all the embarrassments over all the years, she hadn't thought it could get any worse. And it had! How could she face Will again? How could she get into the truck with him and ride back to the ranch? The tears that she'd kept from shedding in the house now rolled over her cheeks. This was all too much. Jimmy would have to understand. She couldn't stay here. She *had* to leave.

She fumbled with the truck's door handle. She had no other option but to ride back to the ranch with Will. Love had no taxi service. Then she'd get in her car and drive back to Houston. She wouldn't tell Jimmy what she was doing until after she'd done it. If he wanted to fire her, he could. She just had to get away…

She was still fumbling with the handle when Will came up behind her and covered her hands with one of his.

"Cassie!" he said tautly. "Stop it!"

"I want to go, Will," she moaned. "Just…let me go!"

His voice softened, mellowed. "Cassie…I'm not tryin' to stop you. I'm tryin' to help. Move your hands away and I'll open it."

The calm assurance of his tone got through to her, settled her down. She instantly withdrew her hands and stepped back. As he swung the door open she tried to wipe her tears away, but fresh ones kept taking their place.

He leaned inside, deposited the wrapped honey cakes on the dashboard and straightened. Then, carefully and gently, he settled an arm around her. When she allowed that, he did the same with his other arm, until he was holding her.

The strain of the day, of the entire trip, was exacting its harsh toll. Cassie's breaths were broken and her tears increased as she relaxed into the warm strength of his body. Until, finally, the tears lessened and stopped, and she was able to push away. Almost reluctantly, his arms released her.

He leaned into the truck again and produced a handful of tissues. She took them gratefully, wiped her cheeks and blew her nose, then did her best to smooth down her hair.

"Hop in," he directed quietly, "before your mom looks out and starts to worry."

"She won't worry," Cassie said bleakly and climbed into the truck.

Will looked at her before closing her door, but didn't argue. Then he, too, climbed in and got the truck rolling.

Cassie closed her eyes. She should be ashamed of the way she'd broken down, especially with Will there to see. But she was too emotionally spent to find the energy to be ashamed.

Although she wasn't looking, she knew when they left the town behind and made the turnoff to the ranch and bumped over the railroad tracks. But they didn't make the turn into the Circle Bar-T's drive. Instead, they continued to go straight.

Cassie sat up and opened her eyes. "Where are we going?" she demanded, raking up a little of her old, hard-won inner confidence.

Will glanced at her. "I didn't think you'd want to meet the crowd at the ranch just yet. So we're takin' a little detour."

He was right; she didn't want to meet the "crowd," but her car was there and she still planned to get into it and go back to Houston.

As if he could see into her mind, he added, "I also didn't think you'd want to be makin' any rash decisions. At least not until you've had a chance to think 'em through."

Just before a narrow bridge, he slowed the truck and pulled

it off the blacktopped road onto a graded trail that led down a sloping embankment on one side of the bridge. They came to a stop a few feet from the slowly moving creek.

Without a word, he set the hand brake, pushed his door open and walked to the front of the truck, where he stood gazing out at the water for a few minutes, before leaning back against the truck's grille.

He was giving her time to pull herself together, Cassie realized. And the realization made her conscience sting. The least she could do was let him know that she appreciated it.

She joined him at the front of the truck, and because it would be easier to talk without having to face him, she leaned back against the warm grille as he did, to gaze out at the narrow stream.

Without knowing it was imminent, she heaved a long sigh. It felt good, though, and it helped her to begin. "Will—I'm sorry for what—I'm sorry for what happened earlier. My mother—"

"Is a nice lady. She's different. But she's nice."

Cassie shook her head. "She's a lunatic," she said softly, her chin dropping. "You can't pay attention to anything she says. She's off in another world most of the time. She doesn't care or even think about…anything else."

"She loves you," he contradicted.

Cassie shook her head again, her throat tight.

"You're thinkin' about leavin', aren't you?" he asked.

Cassie made no reply.

"All the fight's been knocked out of you."

Although that was exactly how she felt at the moment, she couldn't let that pass. "I wouldn't say that."

"If you leave, that's exactly what you're sayin'."

"If I leave, it's because I want to, not—"

"Want to?" he broke in. "I thought you wanted to see this deal through."

"I do. But—"

"Then why not do it?"

He pushed away from the truck to lean into the driver's window. A moment later he was back and he had the tissue of honey cakes in his hand. He looked at her, winked, and opening the tissue said, "I think we're safe to eat these in broad daylight, don't you?"

Cassie found a smile from somewhere deep inside and chose one of the honey cakes. That he was accepting her mother's daft prophecy in good humor eased a little of her mortification.

"I should think so," she said, and bit into the sweet goodness at the same time as he bit into his.

"Mmm," he approved after they'd finished. "Your mother sure makes a mean honey cake! But don't tell that to my mom. She thinks she has the corner on bein' the best cook in the county."

"I won't," Cassie promised. She kept to herself her certain knowledge that he wouldn't think as much of some of her mother's other concoctions.

He glanced up to check the sun's height in the sky. "Guess we'd better get goin', huh? I've got a lot to get done before this evenin'. You comin' on the hayride?"

"Do I have to?"

He grinned. "No, but it could be fun. We're takin' the kids out to see the calves. That's always good for a laugh."

"I'll think about it," Cassie murmured.

She was smiling more easily as she got back into the truck, until she glanced a short distance above the horizon…and there saw the ghostly pale visage of the newly rising moon.

Chapter Eight

Cassie couldn't believe it was only a little past noon when they arrived back at the ranch. So much had happened in the space of four hours.

Yet even with the short break Will had provided, she still wasn't ready to be "on show." So it was with relief that she learned the Warrens were at the creek again, that they'd packed a picnic lunch, and that they didn't expect to return until the middle of the afternoon.

"Those kids are wearin' me out!" Robbie complained as he dropped into his usual seat at the table.

"You're enjoyin' 'em and you know it, Dad," Sylvia teased as she measured brown sugar, ketchup, Worcestershire sauce and various other ingredients that Cassie knew to be the makings for barbecue sauce into a pot on the stove.

Robbie eyed Will. "How'd it go with Ray Jr.?" he asked.

"It went," Will replied.

"Took you a while," Robbie observed.

"Tim Hassat asked me to help him out over at Swanson's. He and Ned needed another pair of hands to get his tractor back in shape."

"Yeah," Robbie agreed. "Since Terry's joined up with the army, Ned's sure missin' him, I bet."

Ned, Cassie knew, was Ned Swanson, the owner of the garage. And Terry was his youngest son. The last time she'd seen Terry he hadn't been much older than Seth Warren was now.

Will settled his hat in place in preparation for going outside. "You mind missin' a little of your siesta, Granddad?"

"Not a bit."

"How about comin' out back with me? I could use a hand myself."

Robbie was out of his chair before Will finished speaking. "You bet!" he responded enthusiastically, and, stuffing his hat on his head, hurried to be the first one out the door.

Will and Sylvia shared a smile before Will turned to Cassie.

"You gonna be okay?" he asked.

Cassie nodded wordlessly, her gaze held by his.

Time passed. A few seconds, a minute…she had no idea.

Then Will gave a short nod and followed his grandfather outside.

Sylvia, at the stove, continued to stir the contents of the pot, but she must have seen the look shared by Cassie and her son because her expression became thoughtful.

Cassie couldn't seem to propel herself into action. Upon entering the house, she'd thought to go directly to her room, but the prospect of being so alone there prevented her from doing it.

"Would you like a cup of coffee?" Sylvia invited.

Nodding distractedly, Cassie took a seat at the table. If Will hadn't intervened, she'd be on her way back to Houston right now, and she felt a pang of unease because she wasn't. Her life at the moment seemed to be spiraling out of her control. Nothing was as she would have chosen it.

Sylvia slid a steaming aromatic cup, filled almost to the brim, in front of her, then, pouring one for herself, settled into a chair as well. "Mindy Parks called to tell me you were in town," she said conversationally. "She didn't know I already knew."

Mindy Parks was Reva Henderson's best friend. "Word's spreading," Cassie murmured.

"How do you feel about that?" Sylvia asked.

"I expected it."

Sylvia spooned sugar into her cup. "Darla Simpson called to tell me Lynette met you in the shoe store. She said Lynette said that you looked amazing. Like some kind of TV reporter, or something. Your hair, your makeup, your clothes—"

Cassie laughed disbelievingly and fiddled with her cup handle.

"She did." Sylvia smiled. Her tone altered. "She also said Lynette saw you with your mother, and that she'd *heard* you and Will went to visit Bonnie."

"Oh, the joys of small-town life," Cassie quipped unsteadily.

"Most people don't care, you know."

"And some people care too much—"

"It's not every day that one of our own comes back, Cassie, and is so obviously doing well."

Cassie was beginning to feel as if the new Cassie she'd created in Houston was slipping away from her. The people…her mother…they were trying to suck her back into the life she'd worked so hard to escape.

"People should mind their own business," she snapped.

"Does that include me?" Sylvia asked.

Cassie lifted her eyes, saw the woman's gentle expression, and looked back down again. "No."

"Then let me tell you somethin', Cassie. Things truly aren't the way you seem to remember them. You were a child, you were hurting…your mother—"

Cassie cut in. "Do you know that I don't have a picture of my father?" she demanded tightly. "Not one! My mother threw them all away after he died. She even took the one I had by my bed." *She hadn't meant to say that!* She hadn't even known she'd been thinking it…but there it was.

Sylvia leaned around to turn off the burner under the barbecue sauce. Then she reached to cover Cassie's hand.

Cassie wanted to break the contact. She didn't want Sylvia's sympathy. But her hand stayed where it was.

"I remember your father," Sylvia said quietly. "He was slender, with hair about the same color as yours that he wore down to his shoulders. And he always had a smile for everyone." She smiled in remembrance. "Your parents created quite a stir when they came to town. You were just a tiny baby."

"I can't remember what he looked like," Cassie confessed.

Sylvia's smile ebbed. "He died when you were three or four, didn't he? I think he fell doin' some kind of work at the county courthouse."

"I was three. I don't remember."

"Carpentry work. Handyman work. That's what he did. And he was good. People liked him despite—" She paused. "Well, they *were* very different."

Cassie swallowed tightly, her eyes fixed on the table.

Sylvia squeezed her hand. "People are more acceptin' of things now, Cassie. So much has happened over the years— your mother's ideas… well, some of 'em aren't so strange anymore. Organic gardening, yoga exercises, meditation— those were some of the things she was always goin' on about. Maybe the town just needed some time to catch up."

Cassie withdrew her hand. "I'm not going to believe you if you try to tell me that suddenly everyone thinks she's a visionary."

"No, I wouldn't say that. It's more…she belongs here. She may have a funny way of sayin' things and a funny way of actin'…but she's ours."

"To be laughed at!"

"No one ever laughed, Cassie."

"Yes, they did," Cassie countered, lifting her gaze from the table.

Sylvia gave her another of those long, seeking looks. "Kids maybe," she conceded. "Did some of them laugh at you?"

Cassie lifted her chin and Sylvia read the answer on her face. Then she said, "What would you say if I told you that a few of those same kids are goin' to your mother now for tarot card readings, and are takin' what she tells 'em seriously?"

Cassie blinked.

"And one of their mothers as well," Sylvia continued. "I don't believe any of that stuff myself, but they seem to."

"No," Cassie maintained stubbornly, "I don't believe it."

Sylvia shrugged.

Everything that Sylvia had just told her played again in Cassie's mind, and she still resisted. There might be differences on the surface, but underneath the town was exactly the same. It mattered to her, though, that Sylvia not think she was impugning her word.

"I know you're only trying to help, but…"

"Give the town a chance, Cassie," Sylvia advised. "And you may see some things you didn't see before."

Cassie stood, wishing she'd done this earlier. "I, ah, I…" She stumbled over the words that would let her escape.

Sylvia smiled up at her. "Would you like a tray up in your room for lunch? I'll fix you one the same time I do Dad's. And don't forget—we're takin' everyone on a hayride later, then we're eatin' barbecue."

All Cassie could do was nod.

SHE TRIED TO STAY in her room the entire afternoon. Heaven knew she'd already been through enough for one day. But after a couple of hours and a pleasant lunch that she'd done only minimal justice to, she came downstairs with the excuse of returning the tray.

Sylvia was hard at work preparing the side dishes for the barbecue when Cassie entered the kitchen. With a flagging smile, Sylvia told her to set the tray on the counter, then went back to shredding a cabbage.

"Is there anything I can do to help?" Cassie asked. Earlier, she'd changed out of her business suit and into a new pair of jeans and a pastel pink cotton T-shirt, as well as exchanged her heels for the new athletic shoes.

Sylvia brushed some loose hairs away from her eyes, then said, "I could use a few tomatoes from the garden. Would you go pick 'em for me? Oh, and a couple of cucumbers, too. I brought in the beans earlier when I cut the cabbages. The garden has just been wonderful this year. Everything's comin' in early. I took a chance with my tomatoes, puttin' 'em in before what could've been a last freeze, but the last freeze didn't happen and we started eatin' tomatoes before anybody else," she bragged. "This is gonna be a grand season for cannin' and freezin'."

Cassie made her way out to the garden and, carefully picking her way between rows, completed the task assigned to her. She was on her way back into the house, her bounty in the basket Sylvia had provided, when she came upon Robbie hobbling up from the outbuildings. She fell into step beside him.

"You gotta watch Sylvia," he teased, glancing into the basket. "Stand still for a minute and she's got you doin' somethin'. She's even found a way to put you to work!"

Cassie couldn't help but smile. "I volunteered," she informed him.

They reached the chairs under the shade tree and Robbie tapped her arm, motioning to them. "Let's sit out here for a few minutes and cool off. If we go inside, Sylvia'll just find somethin' else for us to do."

Cassie glanced at the kitchen screen door. She could still hear Sylvia shredding cabbage, so a few extra minutes shouldn't hurt.

Robbie slumped into a chair as she settled on another. He crossed his legs, hung his hat over one knee, and then looked around. His weathered features reflected pride in what he saw.

"Ray'll never understand the simple joy of doin' what we're doin' right now. Sittin' in the shade, lettin' the breeze go by, appreciatin' the rewards of a lot of hard work—the kinda hard back-breakin' work that puts grit between your teeth and sweat on your brow. Where you hafta be smarter than some dumb animal that thinks it's smarter than you and is determined to prove it. Where you hafta keep the water flowin' into the tanks for the herd, and the fence up and mended, and the horses looked after." He shook his woolly white head and snorted in disgust. "He actually thinks workin' for eight hours in that store 'a his and then goin' home is hard work!"

"It's beautiful here," Cassie murmured judiciously.

"Darned right it's beautiful!" Robbie agreed. "Lots of Taylors have thought so. Me, my son, my daddy, my daddy's daddy. It was hard on the women early on. S'pose it still is," he conceded. "But they loved it, too. So does Will—" His throat closed at the mention of his grandson's name, emotion seeming to overtake him. He leaned toward her, his eyes intent. "That's why I agreed to sell the Old Home Place, ya

know. 'Cause 'a Will. That boy don't deserve what's happenin' to him. He don't deserve all the worry he's had heaped
on him. He's worked hard all his life on this place. Had ta
leave school 'fore he was done to come back and fill his daddy's boots. Doesn't have time for a wife or kids. He's makin'
too many sacrifices…and all I hafta make is one!"

The old man grew silent. Cassie waited, but when he continued to be lost in deep thoughts of his own, she murmured
a leave-taking—which went unacknowledged—and let herself back into the house.

SHE ENDED UP HELPING Sylvia for the next hour and was in
the kitchen when Will put in an appearance.

"Well, I think we're all ready outside," he said. "Got the
flatbed hitched to the tractor and spread some hay around on
it. When is it you're wantin' to take everybody for a ride?"

"I was thinkin' about four. The Warrens should be back and
rested by then. Cassie, is that good for you?"

In the face of everything, Cassie couldn't refuse atten-
dance. "Sure," she said.

Will gave her a quick smile before turning. "I'll keep an
eye on the time," he promised his mother before the screen
door thumped shut after him.

Sylvia sighed. "I wish that boy could slow down a little.
Sometimes I feel bad pushin' the idea of havin' people stay
with us when it causes Will even more work. If we could *just*
get Ray to agree to—" She stopped, looked at Cassie and finished somewhat awkwardly. "Sign the contract, we could afford to take on some help. Then Will wouldn't have to work
so hard. Or worry so much. Sorry, Cassie, I'm not sayin' that
to add any pressure. I know you're doin' all you can."

Sylvia didn't know how close she had come to leaving,
Cassie thought. Then she experienced a tug of guilt that she

had allowed her mother's behavior to make her lose sight of her original goal. "I understand," she said.

Sylvia took stock of all their preparations. "I think we're ready in here, too. Thanks for your help, Cassie. I'd still be workin' if you hadn't pitched in."

"I enjoyed it," Cassie said and meant it. She had enjoyed working side by side with the other woman, who laughed easily and often.

Boisterous voices closed in on the house, announcing the return of the Warrens. David Warren was the only one to come inside, though, and that was to return the picnic basket.

"The kids are having the time of their lives!" he proclaimed, his face pinkened from the sun. "And so are Cindy and I. We'll keep coming back as long as you let us, Sylvia. And we'll tell all our friends. That lunch you packed us was great, too. As usual!"

"Well, thank you," Sylvia said, and quickly added, "I hope y'all are gonna have some room left for barbecue later."

David lifted his eyes to heaven. "Ah, your brisket! You bet, as Robbie always says. This country air!" Then he hurried outside to his wife and brood and they headed off for the bunkhouse.

Sylvia smiled with satisfaction as she turned to Cassie. "A happy man," she said.

CASSIE HAD NEVER BEEN on a hayride before and enjoyed the long, leisurely tow around the empty pasture. Then Will towed them into another pasture where they could see the cows and their calves close up. Will dumped some extra hay for the mothers, who got busy eating while their youngsters started to play, giving little kicks and running this way and that. One of the calves ran straight toward Will, then sensing that he was coming too fast, put on the brakes so hard that he lost his balance and toppled over, performing a somersault as Will stepped easily out of the way. The calf then got up, shook himself and came over to sniff Will's hand. Will caught hold of the calf and called to Melissa and Seth, asking them if they wanted to come see him. At David's nod of permission, the kids slid to the ground and cautiously approached the animal—which, from their awestruck remarks, was a lot bigger than they'd thought.

"Now you always have to be careful, just like you are right now," Will said. "This baby's momma is *very* protective. She'll charge you if she thinks you're about to hurt him."

"Oh, we'd never do that," Melissa said as she touched the calf's hairy black neck.

"But the momma doesn't know that," Will said.

Melissa nodded and Seth joined her, a little more tentatively, in touching the calf.

After a few minutes passed, Will lifted the children onto the flatbed and, with a nod at the parents and a wink for Cassie, he started up the tractor and towed them around the pasture a little longer, looking at other cows and calves before heading back to the ranch house.

Sylvia met them outside the bunkhouse where she and Robbie had set up a couple of collapsible tables that were now filled with food. The guests piled off and, plates in hand, helped themselves to the abundance. They sat as they found places, on the bunkhouse steps and narrow porch, and on the stump that Seth had learned to lasso. Will, following cowboy tradition, hunkered down with his plate. From all the *ums* and *awws* that followed, the Taylors had made another hit.

Following the meal, everyone helped to clear the tables, including the children. And this time, David and Cindy insisted upon doing the washing up. Will hurried off to do more chores, Melissa and Seth started playing around the side of the house and Sylvia sat in the kitchen with a cup of coffee, talking with David and Cindy. Only Cassie and Robbie remained with nothing to do. And together they drifted toward the chairs under the shade tree.

They said little as the sounds of the others' activities drifted over them. Then Robbie became so still that Cassie suspected he'd fallen asleep. She even became sleepy herself. The succession of restless nights—both before and after her arrival at the ranch—and this morning's early start as well as the various stresses of the day and the aftereffects of a pleasant meal, all combined to make her drowsy.

She was just drifting off when Robbie shattered the tranquillity by saying, "I think I'm gonna have myself a little talk with Ray tomorrow mornin'."

Surprise jerked Cassie to full awareness. "You are?"

Robbie seemed very pleased with himself. "Yep. Think you could help me get into town? I don't want Will and Sylvia knowin' about it."

Cassie frowned, troubled. "Well, yes, but—"

"Good. I'm thinkin' about nine-thirty. That all right with you?"

"Certainly, but I'm still—"

"What they don't know, ain't gonna hurt 'em."

"But how are we going to do it? Will probably will be working, but Sylvia would notice."

He gave her a devilish wink. "I'll deal with Sylvia, don't you worry."

Cassie still wasn't assured. "Considering what happened last time, do you think it's wise for you to—" She stopped. She didn't want to insult him.

Robbie lifted an eyebrow. "This time it'll be different," he said.

And there was something in his voice that caused her to believe him.

SYLVIA MADE ICE CREAM AGAIN that evening at the behest of the children. Though the light was fading, Will still hadn't come in from the pastures by the time it was being served. Robbie took his bowl with him to his room, and Cassie slipped upstairs without anyone noticing.

She stretched out on the bed fully clothed and instantly fell asleep, so tired that even her worries couldn't prevent it. When she awakened some time later, full darkness had fallen and all was quiet inside the house and out. Her muscles felt as if she hadn't done as much as twitch in the time she'd spent asleep. It was an effort to move. But she couldn't remain dressed and she wanted to brush her teeth.

After checking that Sylvia's and Will's doors were firmly closed, she made her way as quietly as she could to the bathroom. Back in her room, though, she was wide-awake and restlessness overtook her. She tried pacing across the limited floor space, but it wasn't enough.

Glad that she'd yet to change into her night clothes, she once again stepped into the hall and made her way downstairs onto the front porch. She had no idea what time it was and had left her watch on the writing desk beside the bed. She should have looked before she left, but then, did it matter?

She stepped to the railing and gazed out into the night. It was so quiet here. No speeding cars, no sirens…just the occasional cricket calling to its mate. The air was cool and she folded her arms across her chest, hugging herself for warmth, as she looked into the star-filled sky and breathed the nighttime scents of the cooling land. It was hard to believe, being this close to nature, that anything outside of nature was important.

But certain things were important. The ranch Taylors were a part of this land and in order to keep it, they needed to make the sale. *She* needed to make the sale as well, but had nothing to show for her three days spent trying. What did Robbie have up his sleeve that he wanted to talk to Ray about? And why keep the meeting a secret from Will and Sylvia?

Will worked with the elements of nature all the time—the cattle, the horses, the grasses, the weather. In the city, how to dress for the day and whether or not to carry an umbrella was all-important. And animals were mostly either treated as pets or observed in the zoo.

Cassie inhaled another breath of nighttime air and felt a release from the restlessness that had seized her. For now…just for now…she would ignore tomorrow and everything that might come with it.

She closed her eyes and drew another relaxing breath, lifting her face to the starlight.

She wasn't aware of another presence until the tiny hairs on the back of her neck lifted in warning. Her body stiffened and she whirled around, only to find Will standing bare inches behind her.

To WILL'S MIND, he'd never seen anything as appealing as Cassie with her face lifted to the stars. In the pale light, she might have been an elfin princess or a statue carved by a master. Far out of his reach…and yet, so close that he could touch her. For those seconds when she was unaware, he'd had to fight himself not to reach out. Now all he wanted was to touch her. Only she was looking at him as if he were an intruder. Which he was. He held back.

"You couldn't sleep either?" were the words that came

from his mouth. They were low, husky. He hadn't planned them. If he had, they might have been better put.

"How did you—? I didn't hear—"

He looked down and wiggled his sock-covered feet. "Boots make a lot of noise at night."

"What are you doing up?" she demanded, either not having heard or not having absorbed his earlier question.

"I couldn't sleep. So I put my clothes back on and came down."

"Well," she said, still irritable, "you shouldn't walk up behind a person like that!"

"Sorry," he said.

She shrugged and turned away from him, pretending to look at the stars again. But it wasn't the same. Her body was tight, tense.

As a polite host to a guest in his home, he should have apologized again and gone away. But he had no intention of doing the latter. He stayed where he was, right behind her. Only he softened it by resting his hand on a porch support and kind of leaned into it.

"I like to come out here at night when the house is quiet and Mom and Granddad are sleepin'." He laughed softly. "It doesn't happen all that often these days. Most nights I'm asleep before my head hits the pillow."

She said nothing.

He continued, "There's just somethin' so peaceful about it. In the daytime, too many things are happenin'. They just get in the way. At night, it's you and the crickets…if they don't have somethin' better to do."

"Except tonight," she answered tartly.

"Am I botherin' you?" he asked.

There was a pause, then she shook her head in the negative. But though she might deny it, her body was still as tautly drawn as a good line of barbed wire.

She eased away from him, one step to the side and back…then another.

"How'd you like the hayride?" he asked.

"It was nice," she answered.

She hadn't looked at him since she'd turned away.

He leaned his shoulder against the post. "I think the kids had fun."

"I—I think I'll go in now. It's cooler out here than I thought."

"Hold it. I'll give you my jacket." He had his worn denim jacket off and around her shoulders before she could blink. "There. That better?"

He was facing her now…and she was looking up. And Will couldn't hold off any longer. He had to taste her lips again and feel the softness of her body up against his.

CASSIE KNEW SHE NEEDED to rush away, not to place herself in jeopardy. But his husky voice was her undoing, that and his slow, slow smile. When he dipped his head down to hers, she caught her breath—as if that would help—and then all resistance melted as the warmth and vitality of his mouth covered hers in a kiss that was so exquisite she lost all care as to who she was or who he was, and why this might be something they would both regret later. Her hands moved over his chest, then onto his shoulders and neck, where they pulled him even closer. He caressed her back, one hand gliding over her hips while the other ventured on its own to her breasts…when she, at last, broke free.

His jacket had fallen onto the floor at her feet and she almost stumbled over it as she backed away. Will bent down to pick it up. She watched his golden head lower and raise and wondered if she'd ever forget the springy softness of the hairs at the nape of his neck and the way her fingers had played through them.

She took another step. She had to put more distance between them. If he so much as reached out to steady her, she didn't know what would happen. Her heart was tapping madly against her rib cage, her breaths were quick and unsteady, her body felt on fire.

"That shouldn't have happened," she breathed.

Will watched her steadily. "But it did."

"I didn't mean for it to."

"I did."

She shook her head, denying what he'd said.

He gave another slow smile.

Cassie took yet another step back and continued to shake her head. She was almost at the door.

"I meant every second of it," Will elaborated.

"Will…I'm not here to— I'm going back to Houston just as soon as I can. I'm not here to *start* anything."

"Sometimes things just happen, Cassie."

"Not between us!"

"Why not between us?"

"I'm Cassie. Cassie Edwards. You know who I am!"

"You're female, I'm male…and we're both unattached."

"It's not just that!"

"No, I'm thinkin' it's a little more than that."

Cassie looked at him, confused. "Will, I can't—I don't—"

He closed the distance between them. But instead of catching hold of her and again sweeping her up against him—as a part of her wanted him to do—he settled the jacket back in place over her shoulders.

"I'm the one who's goin' in, Cassie," he said softly. "You stay and enjoy the stars. You were out here first."

Then, pausing only long enough to brush a fingertip lightly along the curve of her cheek, he walked silently back into the house.

Of its own accord, Cassie's hand lifted to cover her cheek. But there was nothing automatic about the haze of tears that blurred her vision as she stumbled to the railing and, there, held on for everything she was worth.

Chapter Nine

The rooster awakened Cassie again the next morning and she greeted it with about as much enthusiasm as she had the day before. And as the flood of memory from last night engulfed her, her dismay only increased.

What had happened between her and Will—the way he had talked after—the way she had felt…before, during and after… A moan escaped her tightly held lips. She didn't need more complications! Why was this happening now? She was here to do a job. She wasn't here to…what? To play out an attraction that, she now had to admit, had carried over from the pubescent years of her childhood through the present day. She moaned again and tried to escape by hiding under the bedcovers. She'd stay here all day if she could.

But memory of her commitment to Robbie to drive him into town to see Ray made her check her watch for the time. It was now even more imperative that she get the contract signed so she could leave this place as quickly as possible. Before she did anything to wholly embarrass herself. Will could have his pick of women. Any involvement with her would just be light amusement for him. For her, on the other hand—no, she wouldn't let herself go there, not even in her mind. She had to concentrate on what she was here for. Robbie seemed to think that he had a way to get through to his brother, so she would give him every bit of assistance that she possibly could.

The rooster seemed to have his internal alarm set at around seven-twenty and since Robbie didn't want to leave until half-past nine, Cassie took her time showering and dressing. She'd rather not go downstairs much before that, on the off chance that she could run into Will. Their next meeting was going to be awkward enough; she didn't want to start the day off with it.

THE KITCHEN WAS ABUZZ with activity when Cassie finally put in an appearance. The Warrens were at the table finishing with a lazy breakfast, Robbie sat with his coffee cup cradled in his hands, Sylvia was at the counter packing a lunch for the Warrens to take with them on their trip back to San Antonio, and Will's chair was empty…just as she had hoped.

Her eyes met Robbie's after she'd greeted all the others and he motioned her into her chair with a little tip of his head. As soon as she'd settled into it, Sylvia passed her a filled cup.

"It's our last morning here, Cassie," David said regretfully. "I sure envy you getting to stay on longer. If I didn't have patients already lined up for tomorrow, I'd say we'd stay on, too."

"Melissa's missed all the piano practice she should, David," Cindy said quickly. "And Seth has karate." She hurried not to give the wrong impression. "Not that I wouldn't like to stay longer. It's been so much fun!"

Only Cassie was aware that Robbie discreetly tapped Melissa's elbow.

"We didn't get to ride a horse!" the young girl cried, as if hit by a sudden thought. "I told all my friends I was going to ride one, and Seth did, too! Oh, please—" She darted around the table to station herself between her parents. "Please, please, please!" she begged first one, then the other. "Let us ride a horse. *Please!*"

Seth looked momentarily confused, but quickly added his voice to his sister's. "A horse….we want to ride a horse!"

Sylvia turned from the meal she'd just finished putting together and said, "Well, I don't see why you can't. That is, if it's all right with your mom and dad. I have a fat old horse out in the pasture who could do with a little exercise."

David frowned. "Why didn't you say anything about this before, Missy?"

"I forgot. But I really want to. I really, really do!"

"Me, too. I do, too!" Seth agreed.

David sighed, glanced at his wife, then apologized to his hostess. "If you don't mind, I guess—"

"Eeeee!" both children exclaimed and started pulling on their parents' arms, prompting them to get up.

"You have to watch us, Daddy. Mom, you too," Melissa decreed.

Sylvia laughed. "Then let's do it." She wiped her hands on the kitchen towel she had over her shoulder and dropped it on the counter.

"Dad, Cassie…you two want to come along?" she asked before leading the group outside.

Robbie shook his head and Cassie did the same before taking a sip of her coffee.

The children gravitated to Sylvia, one on each side, as they started for the door.

"My horse's name is Polly and she's older than you are, Melissa. I've had her for a long, long time…."

As they moved farther away, her words faded.

Cassie lifted an arched eyebrow at Robbie, who grinned widely in return. "Is this where we're supposed to make a quick getaway?" she asked.

"You bet it is," Robbie said, and unkinking himself from

his chair, he took a note from his breast pocket to leave on the counter. "Cost me enough. That little gal drives a hard bargain."

"You paid her?" Cassie said.

"It was the only thing I could think to do."

Cassie motioned to the note as she stood up. "What's that say?"

"You remembered somethin' you forgot in town and asked me to come along."

Cassie tilted her head and narrowed her eyes. "You're a wily old man when you want to be, aren't you?"

"C'mon," he urged her into the hall and toward the front door. "Let's get movin' 'fore Will comes in and wants to know what we're up to."

He couldn't have found anything that would have gotten Cassie moving faster.

ROBBIE WAS TUNED exclusively into his own thoughts as they drove into Love. With each passing mile he grew more and more somber. Cassie itched to know his plans. What was he going to say to Ray? What could it be that would make him think that, after hearing him out, Ray would suddenly change his mind and be ready to sign? Cassie had the contracts with her, just in case. But Robbie kept his own council and she had to content herself with the knowledge that the situation couldn't get any worse than it already was.

She pulled her car into a slot outside Handy's and turned to look at the old man.

He stirred and said, "Might be best if you wait out here."

"I'd rather come with you."

He shrugged without protest and opened his door.

By the time they reached the narrow staircase leading to Ray's office, everyone at store-level was aware of their presence. Both cashiers, the bag boy, what customers there were in line or in the aisles…everyone stopped what they were doing to watch them. Word must have also been out that the two brothers had clashed and that somehow Cassie was involved.

Robbie ignored them, intent on his objective. Climbing the stairs was difficult for him—Cassie could see by the way he moved that it hurt—but he kept on climbing until he reached the top. And there, instead of knocking, he called out his brother's name.

"Ray! It's me. Open the door."

The door swung open half a minute later, a surprised and irritated Ray on the other side.

"Goldernnit, Robbie!" Ray protested. "Can't you at least try to be civilized?"

"I thought I was," Robbie retorted. "I didn't just open it up and let myself in."

Ray's gaze shifted to Cassie. "Why's she here?" he demanded. "I've already made it clear that—"

"I got somethin' to say to you." Robbie pushed past him into the room.

Ray's lips tightened, but he let Cassie through as well, then shut the door with a decisive thump.

The brothers stared at each other for a tense moment after they were all seated. Then Ray bit out, "If you've got something to say, say it because I'm supposed to be at a chamber of commerce meeting in—" he pulled back his sleeve "—twenty-five minutes."

"You still headin' up that thing or did you finally let somebody else have a turn?"

Ray's eyes widened. "If you're just here to insult me—"

"An' what about the mayor's job…I hear you're groomin' Ray Jr. for it. How many times were you elected?"

The color heightened in Ray's cheeks. "Are you coming to a point?" he demanded.

Cassie's heart sank. Robbie was doing it again. Didn't the man understand that angering the person he wanted to bring over to his side was exactly the wrong way to go about it?

Robbie leaned forward. "What I'm 'comin' to' is that you've done real well for yourself, Ray. People think highly of you. They respect you."

Ray waited. So did Cassie.

Robbie continued, "An' maybe…maybe I should start respectin' you, too."

Cassie didn't know she'd been holding her breath until she heard the soft hiss escape through her lips.

Ray seemed just as taken by surprise as she was. Then surprise turned to anger. "If this is your way of trying to soften me up—"

"It's my way of tryin' to make amends! I made some mistakes over the years. When you came to me all those years ago and asked me to buy out your share of the Home Place…I shoulda done it. No matter what."

"But you didn't!"

"No, I didn't."

"And I came this close—" Ray measured a sliver of air with his fingers "—this close…to losing this place. And did you care? No, you didn't care!"

"I *said* I was wrong," Robbie asserted.

Ray's anger grew as the old hurt freshened. "I was extended as far as I could take it. Bills were piling up, invoices needed paying…the bank note was past due. My babies needed food and shots. And *you* couldn't be bothered!"

Robbie winced. "You never told me all that."

"What was I supposed to do? Beg? I told you I needed it real bad. I told you the business needed it. That if I wasn't able to get hold of some money quick—" He stopped and took a breath, attempting to calm himself.

As silence descended over the room, Cassie sat without moving. She felt a voyeur into parts of the brothers' lives that she knew neither would want open to the view of others.

Finally, Robbie said gruffly, "But you worked it out. You saved the store. And now you have others."

"No thanks to you," Ray returned sharply. "I did it by myself, by the hard sweat of my brow. Ask Ray Jr. how often he saw me at home when he was a young boy. How do you think it made me feel to see him off fishing and hunting with your Johnny all the time? *I* wanted to take him fishing!"

"You don't fish!"

"I could've learned!" Ray snapped.

Another stretch of silence. The brothers cut at each other in waves that built then crashed onto shore, only to form again.

"Well, I'm here to say I'm sorry." Robbie's apology was aggressive.

Ray rolled a shoulder, stretched his neck, then rubbed the side of his face. Finally, just as aggressively, he accepted. "Well, all right!"

Silence again. Cassie moved slightly, the muscles in her back complaining. Neither brother noticed.

"So," Robbie began, his voice once again gruff, but now with no hint of aggression, "if this is what's been gummin' up the works, I'm hopin' we can put it behind us. If not for me…for Will. He's not a part of any 'a this stuff that's between us. An' it's the *ranch* we're about to lose, Ray. Haven't lost it yet, but it's close. One more hard hit an'… He shook his head, the worry hard on him.

"Will's a fine young man."

"That he is."

"But I still won't do it."

Robbie's head snapped up and for the space of a few seconds he seemed to be wondering if he'd heard correctly. He got his answer from the stubborn set to his brother's jaw.

"I can't believe you can be this mean, Ray," he said softly.

A muscle ticked in Ray's cheek, but he made no denial.

Robbie stood up to blindly make his way to the door. None of the cockiness of his entry remained in him. He looked a beaten man.

Cassie followed closely behind him. But before leaving the room, she turned to check on Ray.

Ray remained seated at his desk, the impending meeting seemingly forgotten. His expression wasn't that of a victor.

ROBBIE SAID NOTHING as they left the store, got into the car and started back to the ranch. Cassie was concerned for him. She didn't like the bleakness that had settled over his features or the hollowness in his eyes. From what she'd seen over the past few days, his spirit, if not his body, was indomitable.

"You, ah, you tried," she said in an attempt to draw him out.

He humphed.

She went back to steering. He wasn't ready to talk yet. And he might never be ready to talk to her. She was in the unenviable position of knowing things she shouldn't. What Ray had said put Robbie in a bad light. And even though, at the time, Ray might not have told him the extent of his financial woes, it still didn't fully excuse Robbie's refusal to help his twin.

"I guess by now you wish you'd stayed with the car," he said tiredly.

Cassie glanced at him. "I'm all right."

"It wasn't easy, ya know, goin' to see him and apologizin'. But it was all I could think to do." He paused. "Well…I was wrong. Now I've probably messed everythin' up worse."

"There wasn't a lot to mess up. It was pretty bad before."

He looked out the window. After a moment he said, "I couldn't give Ray the money. Ranch was stretched as far it could go after five straight years 'a drought. We were sellin' off cattle just to keep from havin' to feed 'em. And gettin' next to nothin' for 'em in the bargin. Screwworm was bad then, too. Had to spend all your time doctorin' or you lost 'em that way. I didn't have two nickels to rub together."

"Did you tell Ray that?" Cassie asked.

"Hell, no."

"Why not?"

"I had some pride left. It was hangin' on by a thread, but— I s'pose pride was all I had. I know he's held it against me, but I didn't think he'd hold it against Will. I thought once he had me grovelin' at his feet—"

He stopped talking to again stare out the window.

AT THE RANCH, Robbie went directly to his room. He pleaded tiredness, but Sylvia sent Cassie a questioning look.

There was no time for the two women to talk, though, because the Warrens were about to leave. Though the horse ride had been a put-up job, both children had enjoyed it thoroughly and wanted to say a last goodbye to Polly before getting in their van. Hospitable as ever, Sylvia walked the family to the pasture and then saw them off, waving as they drove away.

Afterward, she flopped down in the rocker next to Cassie and the Duchess and breathed a huge sigh of relief.

"Whew! They're nice people—nice kids—and I hope they want to come back…but not anytime soon. I need a week or two to rest up! And to tend to things I kinda let slide. My poor flowers—" she looked at the beds hugging the porch "—and my garden! About all I managed to do was keep it all watered." She rocked for a few minutes before she asked, "What was that about with Dad earlier? Did you really forget somethin' in town or was he the one wantin' to go?"

Cassie felt as though she were walking on eggshells. She felt a need to protect what she could of Robbie's dignity. "He asked me to take him in to talk to Ray."

"Hmm. And did it do any good?"

"No."

Sylvia sighed, and the Duchess, sensing her distress, abandoned Cassie's lap for her owner's. By force of habit, Sylvia began rubbing her ears and the cat started to purr.

Cassie moved restively. She needed to think. There *had* to be something she could do. Something…

She used the excuse of wanting a glass of iced tea to get off on her own. She offered to bring one to Sylvia as well and the offer was quickly accepted. She had ice in the glasses and was about to pour in the refrigerated tea when Will came inside through the back door.

Cassie didn't know how to react, how he would react. Like her, did part of him wish that last night had never happened…and the other part wish that even more had?

He gave her one of those slow smiles.

"I'll take one of those, too," he said, flicking a finger toward the tea.

Cassie reached for another glass and felt his eyes move over her.

"You're all dressed up this mornin'," he said. "You been into town?"

Cassie nodded, rooting in the freezer section for ice.

"Did Ray Jr. call?"

"No." When Will had coached her on the familial history between the two brothers he hadn't mentioned Ray's visit to Robbie to ask for help. Was he aware of it? Or was that something Robbie had kept to himself, once again out of pride? She locked onto the question as a way of moving away from her unsettled feelings. "Will, do you know about your uncle having had some pretty bad financial problems a number of years ago?"

She poured the tea and handed him a glass. Their fingers brushed in the exchange and Cassie's heart gave a little flip.

Will was slow to answer. When he did, he surprised her by saying, "I've heard somethin' to that effect. Uncle Ray wanted to sell Granddad his part in the Old Home Place and Granddad couldn't do it. My daddy told me about it. He was just a boy—around eight or nine, I think—when he overheard Granddad and Uncle Ray talkin', but Granddad never said a word to him about it. Not then and not later."

"Your Uncle Ray believes he could have helped."

Will frowned. "But Daddy said Granddad *couldn't*. He didn't have the money."

"That's what Robbie told me, too. And I believe him."

Will gave her a long look. "Do you think this might make a difference?"

Cassie shrugged. She didn't know. Pride and stubbornness could build an impenetrable wall.

"I'll go talk to Granddad," Will offered and started to swing away.

Without thinking, Cassie caught hold of his arm. She immediately let go, but not before every nerve in her body zinged into acute awareness. "No," she said tautly. "Let me handle this. Let me—" She lost track of what she was about to say.

Will's rugged attractiveness, the growing warmth in his blue eyes… The situation was fast getting out of hand. What was happening to her? Because this was more than physical appeal. But she couldn't let herself think of Will in that way. She couldn't. She wouldn't.

The front screen door bounced shut and footsteps sounded in the hall.

"What's happened to the tea?" Sylvia asked cheerily as she entered the room.

Cassie and Will had quickly moved away from each other, but it wouldn't take a detective to figure out that something had been going on. Sylvia paused, looking from one to the other. But she let the moment slide away uncommented upon.

"The Duchess abandoned me for a grasshopper," she said, "so I thought I'd come in and check."

"I was just...on my way," Cassie murmured, and two glasses in hand, led the way back to the porch.

Sylvia stayed behind with Will for a minute, which gave Cassie a few precious seconds to pull herself together. She could *not* be falling in love with Will Taylor. All right, yes, she'd had a crush on him growing up and there was, to this day, a residual attraction. She'd already admitted that. But *love?*

Sylvia took her glass from Cassie's unresisting fingers and settled again in the rocker. Cassie slowly sank into the rocker's twin.

Thankfully, Sylvia didn't seem in the mood for chatter. She contented herself with sipping her iced tea and looking sagely off into the distance...while Cassie merely tried to keep up with her reeling emotions.

"Jimmy?" Cassie spoke into the tiny cell phone. Her connection was spotty. It kept cutting in and out.

"I'm here," he all but shouted, forcing her to jerk the phone from her ear.

She walked from one end of the porch to the other. Sylvia had left her on her own a few minutes earlier and she'd decided to make the call that, before today, she'd dreaded to make. "Let's see if this is better," she said.

"You sound fine to me."

"You, too. I must be in the right spot."

He brought his voice back to normal modulation. "You have that deal wrapped up yet?"

"Not yet, but I think I may be on to a possibility. A misunderstanding that happened years and years ago."

"Good girl! I told you you could do it!"

Cassie laughed uneasily. "I haven't done anything yet."

"But you will. How's the country air out there? I sure as heck envy you. Makes me want to pack up and see some sights."

"It's…very nice," Cassie said.

"They got you up on a horse yet?" he teased.

"I went on a hayride," she admitted.

He laughed. There was a murmur of a feminine voice— Cassie recognized it as Diane's—and when Jimmy came back he was all business. "Gotta go, Cassie. Let me know when you get this deal signed and sealed." Then he was gone in a click and Cassie, too, disconnected.

For a long time she didn't move. Had she been overconfident? Would simply telling Ray that Robbie had been equally stretched financially make that much of a difference? He'd accepted Robbie's apology, even if he'd accepted it in hostility. Yet he still hadn't budged.

She needed to see him. And the sooner, the better.

The sooner, the better in every way.

Chapter Ten

Cassie drove into town without the slightest idea of whether Ray Taylor would be in his office or not. He'd said he had a chamber of commerce meeting. It might be over; it might not. A quick check at the store informed her that she would have to wait.

Back in the parking lot, she looked around. Reva's was the only logical place for waiting. It was close to Handy's, and she could keep an eye out through the windows that overlooked Main just in case she might see Ray entering the store.

She pulled across the street and walked inside.

A different set of people sat scattered at the tables and counter, not as many as at early breakfast the day before, but enough to keep Reva and her assistant busy. A few of the people looked to be visitors passing through; the rest, familiar faces, were from Love and its environs. Reva glanced up from filling coffee cups, waved, and promptly made her way over.

"Hi, Cassie!" she said warmly. "Good to see you again. Would you like a menu?"

"I'll take a burger, no onions, and an orange soda."

"No fries?"

Cassie shook her head. "No."

"Comin' right up," Reva said and hurried off to post the order for the cook.

Cassie was aware of people looking at her—some surreptitiously as they talked with their companions, others far more openly. Finally, one of the latter group, an older woman in her sixties with silver hair, a small face and a dimpled smile, broke ranks to walk over to her table.

"You may not remember me, Cassie" she began. "I'm Mrs. Lynn, I taught you in fifth grade."

Cassie remembered her. "Mrs. Lynn."

"Everyone's buzzing about you being back. And about how nice—how successful—you look. Where do you live now, Cassie? Are you thinking of moving back to Love?"

"I live in Houston, and, no, I'm not moving back."

"Oh," the woman lost some of her smile. "Why, that's a shame. We don't like losin' our own."

Another person, a younger woman about Cassie's own age with long red-brown hair that she pulled back into a clip, came shyly to join them. "Remember me, too? Lottie Stewart? It's so nice to see you again. What have you been doin' with yourself?"

Cassie remembered her, too. Another classmate. "Hi, Lottie. Mostly working."

"Oh, who for? Are you on TV? Somebody said somethin' about maybe you were."

"No." Cassie shook her head. "Nothing so glamorous."

A short silence followed. Cassie still didn't like answering questions, but it wasn't as onerous as she'd once expected. If this had happened the first day or two that she'd been back, she wouldn't have been able to stand it. Did she have Sylvia to thank for immunizing her with her gently probing questions? She glanced around. Most of the watchers had gone back to their meals. And the several who still met her gaze didn't seem to be disapproving. One, she was taken aback to see, was Wes Eastbrook. He'd been part of the group of boys who'd teased her at every given opportunity. He sent her a small smile.

Mrs. Lynn continued, "Well, it's good to see you again, Cassie. Don't make it so long before you come back."

"Yeah," Lottie agreed. "Don't make it so long."

The two women returned to their tables, where soft whispering with their tablemates ensued.

A short time later Reva delivered her hamburger and cold drink and Cassie made quick work of them. She was hungrier than she'd thought. She was just debating whether to pay for her meal and leave, or wait a little longer—she'd yet to see Ray return, although she hadn't been watching all that steadily—when Wes Eastbrook stopped off at her table on his way out.

Cassie's stomach tightened as she looked up at him. Several years her senior, he'd always been big for his age. Now he was a big man. Massive shoulders, thick trunklike body, powerful thighs.

"Nice to see you again, Cassie," he said awkwardly.

She couldn't make herself say anything. She just stared up at him, tongue-tied. He and his friends had been responsible for so many of her nightmares, and her "daymares" as well, if there was such a thing. For a period during her adolescent years, they'd waited for her in the halls at school, in the school yard…outside the post office.

"Mind if I sit down a minute?" he asked and took Cassie's blink as permission. He seemed to fill the other side of the table. He also seemed to be having trouble finding what it was he wanted to say. His eyes slid to her and then away and then came back. Finally, after a deep breath he admitted quietly, "I owe you a big apology. What me and my buddies did…it was wrong. We shouldn'ta done it. I got kids now myself, and I wouldn't want one 'a them runnin' into someone like me.

We prob'ly made your life a misery." He stared down at the table. "I've thought about you off 'n' on for years, about what we did—what *I* did—an'…I just wanna say I'm sorry. And that I hope things are all good for you now."

Dumbfounded, Cassie strove to find her voice. Never in a thousand years would she have expected Wes, or any of the others, to express any form of regret.

"I—"

He lifted his large body from the chair. "You don't hafta say anythin'. I just wanted to set things straight with you. You can believe me or not—an' I wouldn't blame you if you don't—but if I ever catch one 'a my kids doin' somethin' like what I did…" He left the punishment hanging in the air. Then he started to walk away.

"Wes," she called after him, her throat tight. "I—thank you. I accept…what you said."

He paused, nodded, then went out the door.

Cassie sat very still, her emotions turbulent as his words echoed in her mind. Her world seemed to be shifting. What she'd experienced, what she'd believed…

As Mrs. Lynn and her companions left the café, they took a moment to call goodbye. So did Lottie, who left on her own.

In a kind of dreamlike state, Cassie answered their well wishes with well wishes of her own, then she paid her tab and fled. She couldn't handle any more of this "niceness" at the moment. She needed time to think, to absorb, to adjust to what had happened.

And she needed to speak to Ray.

"YOU AGAIN," Ray Taylor complained as she intercepted him in the parking lot of his store. "Don't you ever give up?"

"Not when I think there's been a misunderstanding."

"There's no misunderstanding."

"But there is! There's something Robbie didn't tell you today or all those years ago. He didn't have the money. He *couldn't* help you. It wasn't that he didn't want to, as you seem to think. He couldn't do it! The ranch was in as bad a shape financially as your store was. Think back. There'd been a drought for five years. Other people must have been going through the same thing, too. It was probably one of the reasons why your store was having problems. People were having to pull in, to put off buying things. Everyone was hurting."

"Did he tell you to tell me this?" Ray demanded.

"No. He doesn't know I'm here."

He narrowed his eyes. "You sure do want to get hold of that property, don't you?"

Cassie lifted her chin. "Yes. It's what I was sent here to do."

"And you'll do anything, say anything, to get it!"

"No! I'm telling you the truth, Mr. Taylor. As I said, think back."

He continued to look at her, his eyes tiny slits. Then he said, "It's still not going to make any difference."

Cassie frowned. "Do you hate your brother and his family that much?"

She startled him by being so direct. "No!" he cried, shocked.

"Then why are you doing this?"

Ray Jr. came up on them at that moment. "Dad? Cassie? What's going on?" He looked from one to the other, his round face concerned. He could see that his father was upset.

Cassie knew she'd pushed too hard. Jimmy wouldn't like the way she'd handled herself. She should stay calm, no matter what. She took a breath, released it. "Please, Mr. Taylor, think about what I said. I'm telling you the truth."

Ray Taylor ignored her. He turned his back and walked away, straight into the store.

Ray Jr. stared after him. Then, shaking his head, he said,

"Whatever it was, you sure got through to him. I've never seen my dad be so rude to a woman before."

"I hope I did," Cassie murmured, then she got into her car and headed back to the ranch.

WILL FINISHED UP on the fence, stowed his gear and swung back up onto the gelding's back. Jimmy danced around, protesting being made to work. They were in a pretty spot by the creek where the grass was lush and the sun dappled the ground through the tree leaves.

"I know...I know," Will said in sympathy to the horse, "I'm not much happier about it than you are. Been a rough day all around. And I'd like to stay here, just like you would, but we can't do it. Not today."

The horse settled down and Will urged him forward. They moved along the line of fence, checking for spots that needed work, and also keeping an eye on the cows and calves in this far pasture. It didn't take a lot of thought, just attention, and his mind wandered where it seemed to wander a lot these days—to Cassie. His mom hadn't said anything, but he knew she had a good idea of what she'd've interrupted if she'd been a few minutes later coming into the kitchen during his midday break. He hadn't meant for it to happen—hell, he hadn't meant for any of it to happen, and yet it had...and it kept on happening! There was something about Cassie that he just couldn't resist. He was drawn to her like a bee to clover. All she had to do was look at him.

It didn't seem to matter that this wasn't the right time. That he wasn't ready. That, from the look of it, she wasn't ready either. Something was going on between them.

He'd waited all his adult life, hoping that one day he'd meet the right woman—a woman he could love as his father had loved his mother. A woman who would love him back in the same way. Anything less just wouldn't be enough. Was Cassie the woman?

He found some wire pulled loose from a post and slipped out of the saddle to tighten it, then he hopped back up and moved on.

He wanted to get to know her better, but he wasn't sure she was going to let him. She held herself so tightly contained. For self-protection? Coming back to Love couldn't have been a picnic for her. He hadn't realized quite how hard until she'd almost lost it after they'd visited her mother.

He'd held her then, offering what comfort he could, and she'd let him. Then last night, on the front porch. He whistled under his breath. That had been good for an almost sleepless night. It didn't help, either, that she was just down the hall.

He didn't care who her mother was. Bonnie Edwards was…Bonnie Edwards. The strange lady around town. How she acted, how she talked was her business. Her behavior didn't hurt anyone…except, it seemed, Cassie to this day.

He veered the horse to the left and checked a drinking tub, making sure there weren't any leaks and that the water was flowing smoothly from the windmill at its side. A couple of cows lumbered up to drink, their calves trailing behind them.

Will spoke to them softly as he and Jimmy headed off, back to ride the fence.

He had a quandary about the future, though. Even though it was the Home Place, it would do them all kinds of good to make the sale. But when the sale was accomplished—if it was accomplished—Cassie would go back to Houston. And even if it wasn't accomplished, again, Cassie would go back to Houston.

To a boyfriend? To a "significant other"? And when that happened—even if there wasn't a boyfriend or an "other"—how was he going to be able to press his case? He couldn't take that much time away from the ranch.

"You know, Jimmy," he said dejectedly to the horse, "sometimes I envy you. High point to your day is a good brushin', some fresh water and a nice bunch of oats."

Then he started to laugh, because he didn't think he'd enjoy being a gelding.

WHEN CASSIE ARRIVED BACK at the ranch, Sylvia was sitting in the kitchen going through a box of photographs. Numerous prints were spread out on the table. She held one in her hand as she sat back, smiling.

"Oh, I haven't done this in years. Look. This is Will. He's nine months old and see where he is?" She showed Cassie the photo of a cowboy mounted on a horse with a baby tucked in front of him on the saddle. "That's my Johnny, Will's dad. By the time I took this, he'd already had Will up and ridin' around the horse pasture with him for a couple of months." She showed her another photo. "And this is Will at four." A very young towheaded boy sat alone in the saddle atop a full-sized horse. "He was goin' out in the pastures with his daddy and granddad by this time. Boy teethed on a saddle. I come from a farm family, not a ranch one. We didn't have any horses. So I was always a little worried, but I didn't need to be. Johnny and Dad looked after him."

Cassie was drawn to the snapshots and slipped into a chair. "This is Robbie," she said, pointing to one near at hand. The man she was looking at was much younger and stood much straighter, with a shock of brown hair instead of white, but it was unmistakably him.

"And here's Ray," Sylvia said. "These must've been taken before their daddy died. So they'd be in their—" she calculated "—mid to late twenties. They were thirty when he died." Ray was markedly slimmer than he was now and had a full head of brown hair worn slicked down close to his head. And though he was dressed in jeans and a long-sleeved western shirt, he didn't look nearly as comfortable in them as Robbie did.

Sylvia passed her another photo. "And this is Johnny when he was little. And this was him about the time we met." She held on to the photo for a moment, touched a finger to his suspended-in-time face then sighed and passed it on. "I miss him to this day. He was the love of my life."

Cassie vaguely remembered Will's father…at a greater age, of course. He could barely be twenty here, if that. She could see some of his father in Will, but more of his mother.

"He was only forty-two when he died," Sylvia murmured.

"How did he die?" Cassie asked.

"He was clearin' some brush, hit a bad spot and the tractor rolled over on him. It was gettin' late, right at dark, but he felt he needed to finish the job, so he kept goin', and—" She looked away, remembering.

Cassie fingered through more snapshots, some older, many newer. A younger Sylvia with her Johnny, Will in a football uniform, Will graduating from high school, one or two Will had obviously taken at college and sent back home…. Photographs to mark the life of a family.

Bonnie hadn't taken any photos of her as a baby. Or if she had, they were destroyed along with those of her father. There were none from her growing years either since Bonnie had refused to buy any of her school photos.

She touched one or two more of Sylvia's pictures as a sense of melancholy settled over her.

"I got these out," Sylvia said, breaking into her abstraction, "because I thought I remembered havin' somethin' you'll be interested in. Here—" she pushed a photograph over to Cassie "—take a look at this."

Cassie lifted it to examine. It was an official type of photograph taken at some kind of groundbreaking ceremony in town. A crowd of people huddled around a man—Ray Taylor—who stood, smiling widely and at the ready with a pair of scissors to cut a ribbon draped across the opening to a park play area. Brand-new children's swings and slides, a roundabout and an intricate wood climbing structure were in the background. "It's the park in town," Cassie murmured.

"See the man two down from Ray on his left?" Sylvia asked.

Cassie followed the direction…and her body became very still as unconscious memory surged forward to whisper who he was. "Is this—?" she breathed.

"It's your daddy—Patrick Edwards. He built the fort and put the rest together, too."

Cassie's eyes were riveted on the man. He had long dark hair, as Sylvia had said, and was handsome in an eternally boyish way, with a smile that invited everyone else to drop what they were doing and join him in having fun. She remembered the "fort" too, dubbed that name by all the children who played in and on it.

"He built the fort?" she echoed. Her mother had *never* taken her there. Cassie had gone on her own, of course, when few others were about, never knowing that her father—

She touched his face with a wondrous finger, unconsciously mimicking Sylvia's earlier action. She'd been so young when she'd lost him. She had snatches of memory—the two of them playing together, him making her laugh. Up to now, though, she'd not had a fully realized face. Her father…

Anger and resentment against her mother bubbled up and over, catching Cassie unawares. "Why would Bonnie throw all his pictures away? Why?" she demanded. "What harm could it possibly do for me to remember him? She stole *him* from me! She—" Tears welled up in her eyes and began to slide down over her cheeks. Embarrassed, she wiped at them. "I'm sorry. I didn't mean to—"

"You don't need to be sorry, Cassie," Sylvia said softly. "I'm the one who should apologize for springin' this on you. I should've warned you a little better."

Cassie sniffed. She'd teared up more in the last couple of days than she had in…well, since she was a teenager. "I just don't understand," she murmured.

"People have a lot of reasons for doin' what they do. Have you ever asked her?"

"Sane people, yes."

"Have you ever asked her?" Sylvia repeated.

Cassie lifted her eyes away from her father's face. "No, but she's not—"

"Ask her," Sylvia urged. "Your mother's not crazy, Cassie. She does some odd things and has some odd beliefs, but I've watched her for years, talked to her a number of times over those years, too, and she's just as sane as I am, as you are."

Cassie gave Sylvia a long searching look of her own. "There're so many things—"

"Ask her about them, too. At the very least, you'll have tried. But I think you'll be surprised." She covered Cassie's hand. "It's not good to go through life bein' angry and upset with somebody…look at Robbie and Ray. Look at the mess they've gotten themselves into. And us." Sylvia gathered the photo that had fallen to the table and passed it over to Cassie. "Here, you take it. It's yours."

Cassie's gaze was again drawn to her father as she held the photo in her hand. What would her life have been like if he hadn't died so young? Then again, likewise, what would Will's and Sylvia's and Robbie's lives be like if Johnny Taylor hadn't died early? Then she realized she was leaving someone out—her mother. What would *Bonnie's* life have

been like if she'd had a husband to share her life with? She'd
never remarried. Cassie had always dismissed the idea, considering her mother too weird to attract another man. Yet that
was a child's view, not an adult's. An adult would wonder, and
then would try to find the answer.

She met Sylvia's gaze. "Thank you," she said quietly.

Sylvia nodded and seemed to understand that Cassie's expression of gratitude went beyond the gift of her father's picture.

CASSIE SPENT THE AFTERNOON helping Sylvia with the flower-
beds, weeding and mulching and snipping old blooms. Sylvia had resisted at first, but relented at Cassie's insistence.

Cassie told her about the plants she had in her apartment,
their dilapidated state; Sylvia either praised or lamented the
progress of her roses and zinnias, marigolds and petunias and
lantana. The hours passed pleasantly, deep thoughts ignored
by both women. The Duchess watched from the porch for a
time, then joined them to inspect their work and get in the way.

Echoes of a time when she had worked in another garden,
her tiny hands doing what they could to help but mostly getting in the way as the Duchess was doing, reverberated in Cassie's mind. A woman—Bonnie—young and pretty, laughing
in delight as a man—Cassie's father—swooped her small
self up into his arms and, turning with her in rhythmic circles, danced his way over to Bonnie's side, where, despite the
mud smeared on Cassie's cheeks, both parents kissed first her
and then each other.

That memory had never come to her before. It was a time
when she had a real family…. They'd been happy! And she'd
felt safe, protected.

She hadn't realized that she'd stopped working until Sylvia nudged her elbow and teased, "Penny for 'em."

"Oh…no…it was nothing," she murmured and snipped

off another withered bloom. But it was very much more than nothing. It was a memory she'd hold close to her heart for the rest of her life.

SUPPER WAS MOSTLY LEFTOVERS from the days before when Sylvia had cooked for the ravenous Warrens. But even they had reached their limits and the family, including Cassie, tucked into what remained.

Robbie, though quiet, did justice to his meal. It was Will who seemed distracted and ate only a little of what was on his plate.

Ever since he'd come into the house a short time after six, Cassie had been highly aware of him.

"What's wrong, son?" Robbie asked, sitting back in his chair while Sylvia poured their after-dinner coffee.

"Traveler's limpin'."

"Limpin'? Limpin' bad?" Sylvia asked, the carafe held suspended over Cassie's cup.

"Bad enough I've put a call in to Frank."

Both Sylvia and Robbie frowned. Then Sylvia, glancing at Cassie, said, "Traveler's one of our bulls. He's our best bull, matter of fact. We paid a lotta money for him about six or seven years ago. Frank Wilkins is the new vet. He's taken over old Doc Jones's practice." Her attention returned to her son. "What do you think it might be?"

Will shrugged.

"Back leg? Front leg?" Robbie asked.

"Right rear. I can't see or feel anything that might be causin' it."

"When's Frank gonna be able to get out here?"

"He says he'll stop by after he's finished at the Maynards. It could be late."

Sylvia, back at the table, spooned sugar into her cup. "Well, let's hope it's nothin' bad."

"Yeah, could be him just gettin' too frisky with the ladies," Robbie agreed.

Will fiddled with his cup handle, glanced at Cassie, then stood up. "Well, I better get back out there. I hauled him up to the pens, so best see how he's doin'."

"Hold on," Robbie called out, "I'll come with ya."

Sylvia and Cassie sat in silence for a moment after the men left the house. Then Sylvia, disinclined to drink her coffee as well, took it to the sink and poured it out.

"What would happen if it's not caused by him…being frisky?" Cassie asked.

"I don't even want to *think* about it," Sylvia replied and started on the dishes. When Cassie joined her at the counter to help, Sylvia added, "Vets cost money. So does havin' your best bull out of commission. So does buyin' a new bull—particularly one like Traveler. That's why I don't want to think about it."

"Then let's don't," Cassie suggested and smiled as she said it.

As they continued to work together, the subject never came up again.

CASSIE WENT TO HER ROOM EARLY that evening. A lot had happened that day and she was tired, but she wasn't ready for sleep yet. She curled up on the quilt, thinking to read, but the book remained unopened on the bed next to her.

Sylvia was still downstairs; Robbie and Will had yet to come inside. All were concerned about what possibly could be their latest misfortune. Cassie knew next to nothing about the actual ins and outs of raising cattle, but she had absorbed enough while living in Love to know that a prize bull was considered a great asset, and its loss—as Sylvia had intimated—could be devastating to a ranch already in financial difficulties. Hopefully, that wouldn't be the case. But that the family was worried... Cassie found herself worried along with them. She shouldn't be, but she was.

She was letting herself get far too close to their situation. Somehow, when she hadn't been aware of it, something inside her had altered, and she now wanted the sale to go through as much—maybe more—for their sake as for her own and for Jimmy's. Was it possible to fall in love with a man's family as well as the man himself?

She shook those thoughts away, unable to deal with them at that moment.

In order not to repeat the cycle, she made herself think about Ray. Earlier, she'd thought she'd found the rationale behind his refusal, but he'd made it more than obvious that she hadn't. There was still something holding him back. What could it be? He'd seemed genuinely startled by her questioning his affection for his twin. So even though anger and resentment for old hurts could have played a part, that wasn't all. But how to find the answer?

Anger and resentment—the words brought back Sylvia's admonition that she not live her life harboring such destructive emotions. She swung her legs over the side and reached for the photograph she'd hidden away in the narrow drawer of the writing desk.

Her father...Patrick Edwards...so young. He looked years younger than she was now. Barely into his twenties. From what Sylvia had told her, he and Bonnie had come to Love when she was still an infant. And she knew he'd died when she was three. How old had he been then? When and where had he and Bonnie met? Where had they lived before moving to Love? Bonnie had always said that they were alone in the world. Were they really? Could she possibly have family that she had never met?

Questions tumbled into her mind, questions that she'd

never let herself contemplate before. And there was only one person who could answer them—Bonnie.

She touched her father's face. When she got back to Houston she'd scan the photo and make some prints of her father alone.

Her father.

Then instead of tucking the photo back in the drawer, Cassie propped it on the desktop where it could be seen.

Chapter Eleven

"Ain't lookin' so good," Will's granddad muttered as the two men stood with their arms folded on the top metal rail of the holding pen, watching the huge black bull stand on only three legs.

"Let's don't borrow trouble."

"Might as well get ourselves prepared for the worst."

"I'm not ready to put him down yet, Granddad. You're goin' to extremes."

"Don't tell me you haven't considered it could happen."

"I'm tryin' to stay positive. Frank'll come, give him a look-see and in a day or two he'll be fine."

"An' next Sunday mornin' Jessie Orric's pigs'll fly!"

Will's patience was running out. He was having a hard enough time dealing with the situation. He didn't need his granddad to… He looked at the old man. The strain was starting to tell on him, too. The financial trouble the ranch faced, the continuing trouble between him and his brother. Worry had deepened the already weathered lines on his face, giving him an almost haggard appearance. He also seemed to move slower, to be quieter. Normally, it was Robbie who put an optimistic face on things. He was rarely ever negative.

"We're gonna get through this, Granddad. One way or another," Will stated firmly.

A muscle twitched in Robbie's cheek. "I hope so, son. I sure hope so."

They were silent for a time, watching the bull.

Then, out of nowhere, Robbie said, "I wish you had you a wife. And a kid or two."

Will laughed, ill at ease because his thoughts had automatically jumped to Cassie. "Just what I need," he quipped, "more mouths to worry about feedin'."

"You can always feed 'em, son. A wife who loves ya and the babies ya make together help smooth the harsh edges from life's hard times." His grandfather lifted a bushy eyebrow. "If our people had let the bad times get in the way of them gettin' married and havin' babies, none of us'd be here!"

Will let himself be carried along with his grandfather's lightening of spirit. "You're forgettin' somethin'. First there has to be a lady."

"No, son," his grandfather replied, "first ya hafta start lookin'! And sometimes that lady can be right under your nose."

Will pushed away from the rails. His grandfather, astute as always, had picked up on something. But he didn't want to talk about his feelings for Cassie right now. He wasn't sure enough what they were.

"Hope Frank Wilkins won't be too late gettin' here," he said.

Just after the words left his mouth, the vet rolled up in his SUV.

FOR THE FIRST TIME in what had to be more than a week, Cassie slept the whole night through. She'd gone to sleep the moment her head touched the pillow, and when she awakened to the crowing rooster, she didn't greet the new day with a groan.

Her first act was to reach over to the writing desk for the

photo of her father. To see again that young, happy face and, this time, note the small resemblances to herself. She'd inherited his coloring, the line of his brow and her nose could be the same as his—only smaller.

Did she sleep better because he was watching over her?

She propped the photo back in place and quickly got ready for the day. If she accomplished nothing else before sunset, she was going to talk to her mother. Sylvia was right. It was something she had to do.

As soon as she entered the kitchen, though, she knew that something was wrong. Sylvia and Robbie sat at the table, while Will faced them, arms crossed over his chest as he leaned back against the counter. Each expression was sober.

Upon seeing her, Sylvia stood up to get her a cup of coffee, but Cassie quickly refused. Sylvia sank back down.

"What's happened?" she asked, her eyes fixed on Will.

"We didn't get good news about Traveler. Vet wants to do some tests."

"He's not sure if somethin' broke or if it's somethin' else," Robbie added flatly.

"Either way, it's not somethin' we need right now," Will said.

"I'm sorry," she said softly as she slipped into a chair, and she truly meant it.

"Lord knows what it could end up costin'," Robbie said.

"More'n we got, that's for sure," Will replied.

Everyone was silent.

Cassie looked from one to the other. "What will you do?" she asked.

Will rubbed his neck. He didn't look as if he'd slept at all last night, and it was everything Cassie could do not to go over and offer comfort, just as he had comforted her when she'd needed it. But with Sylvia and Robbie there, she couldn't do it.

"We'll sell some cows," Will said. "Do whatever it takes."

Robbie winced.

"Whatever happens, we'll be fine," Sylvia murmured. Then more aggressively, "We will!"

A wounded look passed over Will's face that he instantly schooled away. If Cassie's eyes hadn't already been on him, she wouldn't have noticed. But she did. His mother's brave words seemed somehow to have pained him.

"Well, I'd better get out there," Will said, straightening. "Granddad, you up to helpin' me load him up?"

"Try'n stop me!" Robbie returned grimly.

"THINGS HAVE A WAY of pilin' up, don't they?" Sylvia said after the two women were alone. "I keep thinkin' we're goin' to be able to battle our way out of this, then…somethin' like this happens."

Cassie wanted to make her feel better, but didn't know how. The land sale was still too distant a possibility. She could only offer what Will had given as a solution. "Will said you could sell some cows."

Sylvia grimaced. "Oh, we can do that, all right. But if we do, we're cuttin' into the heart of the herd. Will's already culled down almost to the bone. Sell many more and we won't be able to break even, much less make a profit. And there's no guarantee what the pairs will bring at auction—the cow and calf. Can't sell one without the other at this stage. It just breaks my heart. He's been workin' so hard to improve the herd. A bull like Traveler was his daddy's dream, and Will made it come true. And now this."

"Maybe Traveler won't be as bad as you think."

Sylvia gave a disheartened little laugh. "Way things have been goin' for us…it'll be worse. Can't change what you can't change, though," she pronounced and stood up. "Want to come out to the pens to see Traveler for yourself?"

"I wouldn't be in the way?" Cassie asked.

"I don't think Will would think so."

Cassie caught her breath. But when she looked quickly at Sylvia, to see if she'd meant what she'd said in the way she seemed to have said it, the woman had already started for the door.

THE BULL WAS ENORMOUS to Cassie's eyes. Solid, strong, almost glossy black, with a thick neck, deep chest…and noticeably lame.

"This is Traveler," Sylvia said as they reached the pens off to the side of the outbuildings. "He's a beauty, isn't he?"

"He's huge!" Cassie exclaimed.

"Big, but mostly sweet tempered. I hope for his sake his problem is somethin' we can get cleared up quick. He's just everythin' my Johnny always wanted. Top quality, great lineage, all the right traits. And he's a machine when it comes to makin' fine babies."

Cassie noticed Will at work a short distance away, doing something to what had to be the trailer hitch at the back of his battered blue pickup truck. When Robbie came to stand beside Sylvia and the two of them began talking about the vet, she crossed over to Will.

If he was surprised to see her, he didn't show it. He finished what he was doing and then stood up slowly.

"I came to see Traveler," she explained.

He nodded.

She was still driven by the need to offer him comfort. "And to see you. I—I wanted to tell you how sorry I am, and—"

"You said that in the house," he broke in, his sky-blue eyes unreadable.

"—and to tell you that I hope everything will go well."

He nodded again.

"And—and…to tell you that—that I…"

He watched her steadily for a moment before stilling her stumbling words by placing the tip of his finger on her mouth, then, ever so slowly, tracing the outline of her lips.

Cassie couldn't move. She felt incapable of taking any but the shallowest of breaths. She wasn't sure where this was going; she only knew she needed to be with him.

Then he bent forward and kissed her. A kiss that rocked her to her core. So much so that when he pulled away, she felt…incomplete.

"One day I'm gonna get tired of doin' that," he warned softly, his voice barely above a husky whisper.

At first she didn't understand what he meant, till she realized it was the pulling away part. He wanted more. And so did she.

Her gaze was held locked by his when she remembered. They were totally in view of Sylvia and Robbie!

Springing back, she jerked her head around. Both mother and grandfather were looking at them with pleased smiles creasing their faces.

"If you're lookin' for help in those quarters, don't," Will advised.

"I…" She could say no more.

"They'd be more apt to help me keep you than to help you get away." He glanced toward the pen, then in a conspiratorial whisper said, "They're not lookin' anymore if you want to make your escape."

"Yes. Yes, I think I should," Cassie murmured and, flustered, turned back toward the house.

"Cassie?"

His voice stopped her, drew her around.

"Thanks," he said quietly, "for carin' about Traveler."

In a slight daze, she nodded.

CASSIE DIDN'T BOTHER to change into a suit when she left the ranch to go into town. For this talk with her mother, dressing up wasn't necessary. She wore what she'd had on since showering earlier that morning—a pair of jeans, a T-shirt and the athletic shoes that she'd taken to wearing around the ranch. Now, instead of sticking out like a sore thumb on the streets of Love, she looked as if she belonged. She'd given up the battle of holding herself separate. She might not like her history in the town, but it was a part of her. And that was a fact she was starting to accept.

She had no idea where her mother might be. Bonnie could be anywhere. As she drove away from the house where she'd grown up—having checked there first—she watched the sides of the streets and alongside houses for shortcuts, but saw nothing. She looked all over, circling blocks, cruising down Main, passing the Four Corners…and all along, the majority of the people she encountered smiled and waved, a few even called their hellos. There was no hostility, no derision, no scorn directed against her. And there was precious little curiosity remaining that she could detect. Her presence was just…accepted.

She'd felt so isolated growing up. But was it possible she had had a part in isolating herself? In her immature mind, had she magnified the townspeople's responses? Had her own embarrassment about her mother's strange behavior enhanced her negative perceptions?

Some of it had been real. The bullies, the rolled eyes, the scattered groans when her mother espoused some of her more odd ideas. Real, too, was her shame at having a mother like Bonnie. She'd pulled in, hidden herself away as she'd suffered humiliation after humiliation.

The worst had come during her teenage years. A time, she

now knew, when most teens were humiliated by their parents—even the normal ones. She'd envied them their normal complaints…because she had had Bonnie and hers had been so much worse. Everything was *Bonnie's* fault! But was it?

As Cassie continued her search, she had an idea. She drove back to her mother's house, parked the car, tried the door yet again, then set off on foot to the creek where her mother used to take her to play.

The sun was warm on her shoulders as she covered the half mile to where the ground started a gentle descent to the slowly moving stream where water gurgled over the rocky creekbed. At this point the stream was maybe eight feet across and mostly shallow. Cassie walked along the edge, remembering a time when the width had seemed vast and the depth far greater.

She reached her mother's favorite tree—one her mother had claimed had a gentle spirit—and found her there, asleep on a child's quilt. Cassie recognized the quilt. It had been hers.

Her mother's henna-red hair had been caught in a scarf and tied at the nape of her neck; her dress was another variation of multihued crinkled voile. Her frame so thin she looked breakable.

"Bonnie," Cassie called softly. "Bonnie, wake up." She touched the cool skin of her mother's arm.

Her mother stirred, focused her eyes and pushed upright. "Cassie?" she breathed wondrously. "I was just dreaming of you. You were—"

"We need to talk," Cassie inserted before her mother could veer off into fantasy.

Bonnie smiled. "We can talk here." She untied the scarf from around her hair and spread it out as a ground cover for Cassie.

Cassie accepted the gesture, folding her legs and sitting down.

"It's beautiful here," Bonnie murmured, dreamily content as she looked around. Then her gaze settled on her. "You're beautiful, Cassie."

"Bonnie—"

"I always knew you would be."

"*Bonnie*." She said the name sharply to break through.

Her mother recoiled, her smile faltering.

Cassie felt as if she'd slapped a kitten. Never before had she seen her mother react in such a way. Bonnie had always seemed oblivious. Or was it that before, she had never looked?

"I need to talk to you," Cassie said, almost defensively. "About—about my father."

Bonnie vigorously shook her head, denying Cassie's request. "No…no."

Cassie brought the photo from her purse. She pointed him out. "Do you realize this is the first time I've known for sure what my father looked like? The first time I've seen him since—"

Her mother, still shaking her head, started keening. "No…no…no…"

"Why did you throw all his pictures away? Why did you stop talking about him? You never mentioned him! You never said anything! All those years—"

Bonnie pushed the photo away, her expression stricken. "Take it away…put it away…I don't—"

"Why? Why did you do it?" she demanded. All guilt about upsetting her mother had vanished. She was determined to have the answer. "Didn't you love him? Didn't you want me to remember him? I was so little when he died. I barely—"

"Of course I love him!" her mother wailed. "My life…everything I do…" She dropped her face into her hands, her curls in wild disarray. "He's *not* gone," she said, looking up, pushing the curls away as she pressed a hand to her chest.

"He's in here! In here with me, with you—" She looked at Cassie, her eyes pleading. "You *have* to feel him inside you, Cassie. You *have* to." Her gaze fell again on the photo. "You don't need something like that to remember him."

"But I do, Bonnie. I did!"

Her mother folded her arms and started rocking. "It hurt *so* much," she moaned. "Every time I looked. He was so much more. That's paper! He's not paper. He's not *alive* in them."

As she watched her mother continue to rock back and forth, Cassie's anger began to dissipate. It *was* like punishing a kitten. "But I wanted one," she said huskily. "The one I used to have by my bed. It was of you and me and him. I remember it being there when I woke up in the morning….until you took it away."

Her mother began keening softly again.

Cassie leaned across to catch her thin shoulders, making her stop. "How did he die, Bonnie?" she asked quietly. "I've never known."

"No…" Her mother's expression was stricken.

"Bonnie…Mom…please tell me."

Bonnie groaned, but through her pain she seemed to hear the determination in Cassie's voice. After a moment, she said, "He fell. He fell from the tower. I told him not to go to work that day. I told him clocks were funny things and didn't always like to be corrected. But he laughed and told me that clocks were friends, that he always scratched them under their chins and made them chime. And I let him go—and he fell."

Clocks. The clock on the courthouse. Sylvia had said he'd been working at the courthouse. Suddenly, her mother's refusal to have a clock, a watch or any other timepiece about, made a kind of sense.

Bonnie must have always been a little fey, but her mother

loved her father…deeply, Cassie knew now. And after she had
lost him, maybe she'd pulled into herself, created her own
world, where possibly, somehow, her husband seemed nearby.
But Cassie hadn't been a part of that world. She'd always stood
outside. Wanting her mother to love her as other mothers did
their children. Was it that Bonnie didn't know how to reach out
to her? Was she afraid? Had she, Cassie, held her away? Blam-
ing Bonnie for something that she had little power to change?

Tears rolled down her mother's cheeks, her gaze still pleading for Cassie to…to what? To absolve her? To make everything right?

Cassie struggled with her emotions. With her remaining
anger over years of pent-up frustrations and pain. Then she
looked again at her mother, and she folded her into her arms.

A sigh that seemed to come from somewhere deep in Bonnie's soul escaped her lips as she relaxed into Cassie's embrace, her arms reaching out, tentatively at first, to encircle
Cassie's back.

For a long time, neither mother nor daughter moved. Then,
both sniffing and wiping their cheeks, they pulled back.

Cassie's throat was tight as she asked lightly, "Do you
have any honey cakes left?"

Bonnie's bottom lip quivered into a smile. "I made some
fresh ones last night. I saw an owl, so I knew something special would happen today."

It wasn't in Cassie anymore to be irritated with her mother's flights of fancy. Bonnie wasn't going to change; she
couldn't change.

Cassie smiled, changing herself. "I'd certainly love to
have one."

Her mother's face brightened. "And some of my special tea?"

"And some of your special tea," Cassie confirmed.

Together they left the creek for her mother's house.

CASSIE WAS IN HER CAR, on her way back to the ranch, when she saw Ray Taylor pull out onto Main Street in front of her in his late model Buick. She was sitting at a red light, he was turning with a green. Once her light changed, she didn't have any trouble catching up to him. He was driving very slowly. She followed him all the way to the Four Corners, and then into the parking lot at Handys.

He hadn't seemed to notice her until she called his name. When he looked around, Cassie was already striding toward him.

"I have nothing to say to you," he said coldly, and started for the store.

"That's all right," she said, catching up with him, "you can just listen."

He halted outside the automatic door. "I can call the police."

"Go ahead. I'll be happy to say this in front of them. In front of everyone."

A customer came up behind them, stopped, frowned at the blockage into the store, then cleared her throat impatiently. "Excuse me," she said.

Another customer was coming out. Ray Taylor looked at Cassie, looked at them, apologized profusely, then hustled her into the store and up to his office.

"*You* are starting to make me angry," he said tightly as he dropped into his chair.

"The feeling is mutual!" Cassie retorted.

She hadn't thought to do this today. She hadn't formed any plan of attack. She knew there was something beyond the old hurt Ray felt Robbie had inflicted upon him, but she had no idea how to prize it out of him. It was seeing him in his car, carrying on so blithely with his life, while Robbie and Will and Sylvia were facing possible ruination.

Hands outspread, she leaned forward on the desk. "You're

a very proud man. You're proud of your businesses, you're proud of your wife and your son and daughters." She glanced at the framed photos on his desk. "You're proud of your grandchildren. Are there any great-grandchildren yet?"

He didn't answer.

"You want to leave them something they'll be proud to say you built." She crossed over to the long windows that gave a view of the store. "You want them to be proud of you." She turned to face him. "How can they be proud of you when you're turning your back on the Taylor name? On your brother—your twin. Robbie told me that the Circle Bar-T goes back a hundred and twenty-two years. A hundred and twenty-two years! That's a long time in one family. And you're ready to watch it crumble. It's one thing when you can't do anything about it. When you don't have the money like Robbie didn't. It's something else entirely when all it takes is the stroke of a pen. For something you don't even care about!"

Ray Jr., who must have been standing outside the door for several moments, cracked it open and cautiously came inside. He didn't ask what was going on; he knew.

Ray glanced at him, not seeming to be pleased that he was there, but not ready to make an issue of it, before he looked back at Cassie. "Are you through?" His voice was flat.

"The situation is getting worse at the ranch. One of their bulls—their prize bull—has a problem with his leg. It's bad enough that the vet wants to do some tests."

"And why should I be interested in that?" Ray asked archly.

Ray Jr. came forward. "You know why, Dad. And you know what this means to them. You may be stubborn, but you're not a fool."

Ray's head jerked up.

Before his father could speak, Ray Jr. continued, "I don't

know what it is that you're holdin' out for. I don't know what you think you're going to gain…but it's not respect. People around town like Robbie and Will and Sylvia. And when they hear what you've been doing, about the way you won't lift a finger to help them—particularly if they end up losing the ranch—" He shook his head. "It's not gonna be a pretty sight."

Color rose in Ray's face. Because of what Ray Jr. had said? Or because his son at last had the courage to stand up to him?

Ray Jr. hurried on, as if unsure how much longer his courage would last. "I don't want it to be that way. You've given so much of yourself to this town, helping it to grow at a time when other small towns are dying. It's—it's *beneath* you, Dad. You're not the kind of person to be so petty. Even with all your disagreements with Uncle Robbie you don't want to watch him have to sell the ranch and them move…where to? Where would they go? What would they do? Will would find something, but—"

Cassie couldn't pull her eyes away from Ray. Each word that his son uttered seemed to strike some chord deep inside him. His color continued to heighten. His breathing became audible. Until finally, he slapped a hand down on top of the desk, the sharp sound echoing through the room, stopping the deluge of hard truths as it made both Cassie and Ray Jr. jump.

"That's enough!" Ray thundered. "That's…more than enough." He looked from one to the other. "All right, you've had your turns, now it's mine. Miss Edwards, yes, I want my family to be proud of me, to be proud of what I've built. And you—" he fixed his son with a sharp appraisal "—do you think it would make me happy to see Robbie lose the place? Because if you do—"

"I don't, Dad. I told you that."

Ray sat silently, his only continuing show of emotion the rapid twitching of his hands.

Cassie glanced at Ray Jr. The younger man looked physically ill.

"I love this town," Ray admitted, his voice rough. "I've watched it grow from having only one stop sign to what it is today. From having only a one-room schoolhouse, to having an elementary school and a middle school and a high school. I helped us get a library and a playground and a movie theater. God help me, I do love it. And I love Robbie, too—in my own way—and Sylvia and Will. I don't want bad things to happen to them. But I can't—I can't sign that damned contract!"

"Why not?" Ray Jr. pleaded. "Just tell us why, Dad. Don't make us think…" He stopped, unable to go on.

The answer seemed torn from Ray. "Because if I do, I'll be signing Love's death knell!"

Cassie almost rocked back on her heels at the unexpectedness of Ray's answer. Ray Jr. looked just as shocked.

"I don't…understand," Ray Jr. said, groping for a chair. Once in it, he pushed one over for Cassie as well.

Cassie sank onto the seat. "I don't either," she breathed.

"It's happening all over," Ray explained. "Big discount chain stores move in on little spits of land and next thing you know, all the small businesses in the town closest to it have to close up. All the money goes to the big store because they can afford to cut their prices. And they do, knowing that the town businesses can't compete. They don't care. And they don't care about the town either. Or the people." He looked pointedly at Cassie. "Neither does your boss. He's just out to make a buck."

"Handy's wouldn't close, Dad."

"It could. Places like that sell groceries and hardware.

They also sell *greeting cards,*" he said meaningfully, "and clothes and shoes and…you name it, they sell it. All at prices we can't begin to compete with. And if the businesses go, so goes the town. We'll turn into one of those bedroom communities that folks just come to sleep in. The town'll die. It won't be Love anymore. I *won't* let that happen!"

Ray rubbed the back of his neck, just as Will did when harried.

Cassie's mind was humming, trying to put together something that would make this all work. Something that would allay the deep-seated fear Ray was at last lowering his guard enough to divulge. Then she had it. "I don't know what Mr. Michaels's plans are at present. As far as I know, he's not thinking of selling the land right away. But…what if he would be willing to add a clause to the contract that would bind him from selling it to any kind of large discount-store operation?"

Both men looked at her.

"Would he do that?" Ray Jr. asked.

"I'll talk to him. See if we can work it out."

"*You'd* do that?" Ray asked. "After everything—"

Cassie smiled in relief. Her idea seemed to appeal to Ray. The first thing she'd come up with that he'd liked! "Of course I would," she said.

Ray pushed away from the desk and stood to offer her his hand. "If you can, we'll talk money next."

"I'll call him right away. I'm not sure he'll be available, but I'll try."

Also a first, Ray gave her a genuine smile. "Does that boss of yours know what a fighter he's got working for him? If you ever decide you'd like to move back to Love, you just let me know and I'll have a job waiting for you. Isn't that right, Junior? We'd hire her in a second."

"You're right, Dad. In a second," Ray Jr. agreed.

From where Cassie sat, she could see that Ray was looking at Ray Jr. with different eyes. In a strange way, it seemed to have reassured him that his son had stood up to him. That he hadn't backed down.

"Why don't we let Cassie have the office for a few minutes to make her call?" Ray suggested, and on the way to the door, father placed his arm companionably around son's shoulders, and son seemed to hold himself straighter.

Chapter Twelve

Cassie couldn't connect with Jimmy. He was out of the office at a meeting and Diane didn't know when to expect him back except "some time later this afternoon." Knowing that Jimmy always switched off his cell phone when he was conducting business, she left a message for him to call her ASAP. Then she went downstairs, gave the news to the two Taylor men and promised to get back to them as soon as she heard anything. While assuring them, she instilled in her voice as much positive confidence as she could muster. More than she actually felt.

Still, as she drove back to the ranch, it was difficult to contain a burgeoning excitement. With Ray Jr.'s help she had found the key. Now if she could just talk Jimmy around... But she couldn't say anything to Will or Robbie or Sylvia. Not yet. She didn't want to get their hopes up when the deal was still fluid.

As she passed through the Circle Bar-T's gate, conscientiously closing it as she'd always done after that first day, she tamped down any feelings of elation. She would have to pretend that nothing out of the ordinary had happened.

Once again, she found the Taylors in the kitchen, positioned much as they had been that morning. Robbie and Sylvia at the table, and Will leaning back against the counter.

She looked from face to face and still saw deep concern. "How's Traveler?" she asked quickly.

"Well," Robbie said, "it's good and bad. Good because it's not as bad as it coulda been, and bad because Traveler's gonna be out of commission for a coupl'a months. Got a broken bone in his foot."

"He was supposed to have another month out with the ladies, so we'll be missin' a good number of his babies next spring," Sylvia said.

"Traveler's calves mean a lot to us," Will explained to Cassie. "They bring higher prices at auction because of their bloodline."

"But at least he'll be back in tip-top shape on down the road," Sylvia said, trying to look on the brighter side.

"That's true," Will agreed.

"If we're still here." Robbie spoke aloud what the others must have been thinking.

They all looked so downcast. It was everything Cassie could do not to spill her secret.

Then Will helped her by saying, "I saw Tim Hassat today. He says he might know someone who might be interested in talkin' to us about a lease this fall. He kept sayin' might a lot, though. So I'm not holdin' my breath."

"Tim Hassat?" Sylvia's head lifted. "Tim wouldn't say anything he didn't think was pretty close to fact."

"He said he'd call if he heard anythin' more."

A musical theme played enthusiastically inside Cassie's purse, making them all start. She quickly reached for her cell phone, hopeful that the caller was Jimmy. His voice cut in and out and, excusing herself, she moved swiftly onto the porch and the spot that she'd previously found best for reception.

Mindful to keep her voice down, she greeted him. "Jimmy! I think I've done it! Ray Taylor's coming around. There's just one thing, though. He's worried about the land being sold to some kind of big discount chain-store operation. Terrified, is more accurate. That's what's been holding him back. He's concerned for his business interests, but even more so for all the town's other small businesses."

"And?"

"And I've told him I thought something could be done about that. In the contract."

She sensed Jimmy's quick frown. "What kind of something?"

"A stipulation that you won't sell the land to any corporate entity with that kind of intention."

"Ever?" Jimmy asked.

"Well…yes."

"That's tyin' my hands, Cassie. I'm not sure I'm willing to agree to it."

Cassie was silent. She let Jimmy think. As the moments stretched, her nerves stretched right along with them.

"All right, I'll do it," he said at last. "I never had that kind of thing in mind for the future anyway. That strip has a lot goin' for it. Direct access by both highway and rail. Close proximity to a growing employee base. There'll be somethin' nice come along on down the line. Something that will make Ray Taylor very happy."

Cassie released a silent breath. "If you overnight the amended contracts to me, I can have it all sewn up by tomorrow evening."

"Where are you at on the price?"

"The second level, but I'm pretty sure I'll have to go to the third."

"Then do it. Let me know and I'll amend that as well."

"And you'll overnight it to me at the ranch?"

"I can do better than that. I'll bring 'em to you! I've been itchin' to get out of Houston, and I think I'd like to meet these two stubborn old goats face-to-face."

"I'll tell Sylvia Taylor you're coming. She'll probably want to fix a big meal."

"You do that! It's been a long time since I've had some good home cookin'."

After Cassie clicked off, she instantly dialed Ray Taylor's number.

"Mr. Michaels has accepted the stipulation," she said as soon as he answered the phone. "When would you like to talk money?"

CASSIE HURRIED BACK into the house. "I, uh, I need to go back into town. I'll see you all…later?"

She did her best to control her mounting exhilaration, but some of it must have slipped through. Sylvia looked at her with questioning eyes and Will, pushing away from the counter, said, "I'll walk you to your car."

Cassie wanted to sprint to the car, but held herself back. She didn't want to add to Will's suspicions.

Before she could slip behind the wheel, he asked, "What's up, Cassie?" His eyes were serious.

"I just…need to go back into town."

"Why? Who are you goin' to see?"

She couldn't tell him. It would be too cruel to hold out salvation for the ranch and then snatch it away if Ray had a sudden change of heart. "It's something I need to do."

"Does it involve Uncle Ray?"

"Will—"

"It's just a simple question."

Will was four or five inches taller than his mother, which made the difference between his height and Cassie's height striking. She couldn't just reach up and do the only thing she could think of to deflect his attention from his questions. So she stepped up onto the car chassis, using the steel frame as

a stool, then tipping up onto her toes, put her hand on his neck
and pulled his lips across to meet hers. To say that he was surprised was an understatement. But it was a surprise he instantly accepted. His arms came around her, pulling her close.

Cassie hadn't meant for this kiss to be anything more than
a quick peck. But it went on, and on, and soon the reason for
her return to town began to fade from her mind. His hard-mus-
cled body against hers, his arms straining her closer. The
taste of him, the scent of him. All awakened a desire in her
that she had never felt so deeply before.

But she had to break away. She had to.

She struggled to be free, stopping herself as much as she
was stopping him.

When he drew back, his breaths were unsteady, his eyes
alive with his need of her.

"I have to go," she whispered, her knees threatening to
buckle.

Somehow she managed to settle into the driver's seat in a
smooth motion that gave no hint of her inherent weakness.

He bent with her, his eyes searching, as if to peer into her
soul. "Don't be long," he said.

His low husky voice rippled along her nerve endings.

"I won't," she breathed.

He stepped away and shut the door.

Cassie was trembling so much she could scarcely start the
car. She didn't want to leave him. She didn't want to put even
so much as an inch of space between them. It was as if he was
the soul mate she had been searching for her entire life.

Finally, she got the car started and put it into reverse. This
was something she could do for Will, and for Sylvia and Robbie. She could ease their lives. She'd come to the ranch a vir-
tual stranger, looking upon the negotiation for the land sale
as a task to be accomplished as quickly as possible so she

could hurry away. And now the ranch and the people who called it home mattered to her.

She was unaware that Will had jogged out to the gate, but by the time her car approached it, he'd swung it open for her to drive through.

Her bottom lip trembled as she rolled past him. His long, lean body braced against the metal, his right hand lifted in an abbreviated wave, his sky-blue eyes following her.

CASSIE HAD TO PULL HERSELF together yet again as she repeated the oft-driven ride into town. By the time she reached the store, she wanted no one to be able to tell that she hadn't just taken a relaxing drive into the countryside, and then a relaxing drive back.

She found Ray alone in his office. Ray Jr., he said, was at work in his greeting card shop. In a return to gentlemanly manners, Ray saw her into a chair, offered her a refreshment that she refused, and then got down to business.

The process didn't take long. After a little dickering back and forth, Ray, much to her relief, seemed pleased to settle at her third authorized level. When she told him Jimmy himself would be bringing the contracts tomorrow, he was even more pleased by the personal attention. Afterward, he shook hands with her—like Robbie, a man of his word.

Cassie called Jimmy from the parking lot, gave him the agreed-upon number and clicked off after he told her he would see her at the ranch tomorrow at around eleven o'clock. Then again, she set off for the ranch.

Her car, she thought whimsically, would know the way on its own. She giggled at the thought, only to end up laughing outright. Then reality hit her…tomorrow she would be going back to Houston.

Her laughter stopped. What had seemed the most important goal in her life five days ago now seemed a punishment. She would be leaving Will. And Sylvia. And Robbie. And the ranch. And her mother…

The joy she had expected to feel upon her return to the ranch was muted by her jumbled feelings. She didn't want to go back to Houston. But she couldn't stay. She had no reason to stay, not now that she'd accomplished her purpose.

She opened the car door, stepped outside, and did her best to appear gratified.

FROM THE CLANKING SOUND Cassie heard coming from the outbuildings, she knew to bypass the house in order to find Will. She wanted to tell the family the good news together, not one by one.

He was in the workshop, doing something with a strip of metal that involved the vise and a hammer. The clanking was much sharper as she drew near him.

He looked up, the hammer raised.

"I have some news," she said quietly. "Would you come into the house?"

Will set the hammer aside, his task suspended.

They walked up the path together in silence. Cassie was so aware of him it hurt. But since her position beyond tomorrow was unclear, she held herself under rigid control.

Robbie was deep into his afternoon siesta when Cassie and Will entered the kitchen, but upon hearing that Cassie wanted to talk to them as a group, Sylvia hurried off to wake him.

"What's doin'?" Robbie asked, still blinking sleep from his eyes as he lowered himself gingerly into a chair. Upon awakening, his stiffness seemed to be more pronounced.

Sylvia, sensing that something important was about to happen, caught hold of Will's sleeve.

Cassie looked at each of them and smiled. "Ray has agreed to sign the contract."

"Whoopee!" Robbie exclaimed, waving his arms, his stiffness and sleepiness forgotten.

"At a dollar amount that's higher than the one you agreed to," Cassie continued, "so your amount will be higher as well."

Robbie couldn't contain himself. He jumped up, his face beaming, as he grabbed a tearful Sylvia and spun her about in celebration.

"He did it! He's doin' it!" he cried jubilantly. Then he sobered for a quick check. "He shook hands with ya, did he?"

"He did," Cassie confirmed.

Robbie released Sylvia to do a little jig on his own, then he fell back into his chair, slightly winded but still grinning.

"I can't believe it," Sylvia said, tears of joy still flowing. She hugged Will, then drew Cassie into the hug as well. "Thank you," she said close to Cassie's ear. "Thank you. I kept hopin', but I didn't believe it was goin' to happen. I thought— I thought—" Overcome with emotion, she couldn't finish.

In the three-way hug Cassie's side was pressed against Will. She held herself stiffly until Sylvia released her. Then she stepped away, avoiding Will's gaze.

"What caused him to change his mind?" Will asked.

"Yes," Sylvia agreed, looking at Cassie, "what?"

"Ray Jr.," Cassie answered simply.

WILL COULDN'T GET HER to look at him. It was as if, for whatever reason, Cassie had pulled back into herself. Barely an hour earlier, she'd been anything but distant, reaching out to kiss him when it was the last thing he'd expected, and then responding in a way that had convinced him the two of them had a future together. But just now there'd been no yield in her taut flesh.

Cassie continued, "Ray Jr. said some things that got his father thinking, made him realize—" Her eyes flitted to Will's momentarily, silently acknowledging the correctness of his conjecture that Ray Jr. could help. "In the end, Ray agreed to sign as long as Mr. Michaels would be willing to add a stipulation that prohibits him from selling the land to any kind of large discount-store operation in the future. Mr. Michaels agreed." She shrugged, minimizing her part in the negotiation, then addressed his mother. "Sylvia? I hope it's all right…Jimmy—Mr. Michaels—is bringing the contracts himself tomorrow morning and I mentioned that you might be willing to cook dinner for him. He's looking forward to it. He'll be arriving around eleven."

Sylvia's expression brightened even more, if that was possible. "I'll cook him a meal he won't forget in a long time, that's for sure! Maybe barbecue some steaks. What do you think, Will?"

Will's mother was so happy, so was his granddad. It was inconceivable for him to take away from their joy because he was unsettled in his love life.

His love life…was that what it was? He'd had quite a few "in likes" in his younger years and one or two "in likes a lot," but never… He hadn't found—

"Will?" his mother repeated, looking at him oddly, as if she couldn't understand why he wasn't as happy and enthusiastic about the good news as she and his granddad were.

He was happy. He was enthusiastic. The money from the sale would all the difference in the world for them. It was just—with her job finished, Cassie would be leaving.

His mother continued to look at him and, for a moment, he couldn't call to mind what she'd asked. He ran it down. Cassie's boss was coming with the contracts…Cassie had said something about dinner—

"Sure, yeah, steaks sound fine," he said. And was relieved when his mother seemed satisfied with his answer.

"I'll call Ray and Ray Jr. and tell them to bring along June and Lisa Ann, too," his mother continued, delighted to make the meal a family occasion with the wives included as well. "Might as well sign everythin' at one time, don't you think?" Then, obviously not wanting to rock any boats, Sylvia asked Cassie, "That should be all right, shouldn't it? It won't cause any problems?"

Cassie seemed to force a smile. "No." Then she made her lips curl up a little more. "But I'm thinking we should sign first and eat after. That'll help everyone's digestion."

"Good idea." Sylvia grinned.

"An' *I'm* thinkin' I'd like a little coffee right now to celebrate!" Robbie proposed. "How 'bout the rest 'a ya? And it's all because 'a you, little lady." He winked at Will. "I told ya this little gal would keep after 'im till he changed his mind!"

"Are we gonna need to put a muzzle on you tomorrow, Dad?" Sylvia asked, half teasing, half serious.

"Naw, I'll be good. I'll put on my Sunday manners and ev-erythin'." Then the reality behind the reason for celebrating hit him and he lost his good cheer. "Can't say it won't be hard to sign on that dotted line, though. Hope ol' Nelson and Ida won't be too mad at me for doin' what I'm gonna do." He started to smile again. "Like you said before, Will—they could be cheering me on!"

Will nodded his agreement. "I'm passin' on the coffee. To-morrow's shapin' up to be a big day, so I'd better get some extra chores done while I can."

"Me, too," Cassie said quickly. "I'm…a little tired."

Sylvia swirled the coffee remaining in the carafe. "Want me to make some fresh, Dad? Or will this do? Seems I'm goin' to be the only one drinkin' it with you."

Cassie glanced at Will before stepping into the hall. Will debated following her, but decided against it. What could he do? Ask her not to go? Yeah, and then watch her disappear in a cloud of dust as soon as she could after dinner tomorrow. Maybe it was all just in his mind. As he'd said to her once— he was male, she was female. It was natural that there'd be an attraction. It didn't have to mean anything.

He went back to the workshop and beat on the replacement metal strap for the trailer a lot longer than he really needed to. He was still beating on it when his mother came up beside him.

Once he became aware of her presence, he set the hammer down sheepishly and released the strap from the vise's grip.

His mother watched him in some concern. "Is somethin' wrong, Will? Earlier, you seemed—"

"Nothin's wrong, Mom."

Her eyes searched his face. She knew he wasn't telling the truth. "Is it Cassie?" she asked.

Since his mother had seen them kiss earlier in the day, how could he deny it? "Yeah."

"You have…feelings for her?"

He tossed the metal strap onto the workbench. "Yeah."

"I always thought she was a sweet little thing even when no one could get a word out of her. She seems to have grown into a good woman, too." When he said nothing, she continued, "Some people say it takes a long time for a person to decide if another person's the right one for 'em. I knew I was goin' to marry your daddy the first time I laid eyes on him. He came out to our farm in Watson County, visitin' with a friend of your Uncle Dan's—" she named her brother "—and I knew. Right then and there, I knew. Took him longer to decide. But he kept comin' around a lot more than he needed to, probably neglectin' his work around here, and after a while—" she smiled in memory "—he came around to my way of thinkin', too."

"Did you ever think he might not?"

Sylvia laughed easily. "I had a few bad moments—days, actually. Times when he didn't come by like I thought he was goin' to." She shook her head. "*A fine torture,* I think I heard somebody describe it once. And it was…and it is."

She reached out to hug him. "Don't push too hard, but don't stop pushin'," she advised as she stepped back. Then, grinning like the girl his father had fallen in love with, she said, "I wouldn't mind havin' grandbabies with dark hair and dark eyes."

CASSIE DIDN'T VENTURE downstairs until it was time for supper. She didn't want to chance running into Will. In the kitchen she could be safe, at least as safe as she could be when it was herself she was battling. But for all her worry, Will and Robbie were both absent from the meal, leaving only Sylvia and herself to share the table and the big terrine of hearty vegetable soup that Sylvia had prepared.

"I packed 'em off with some sandwiches," Sylvia said. "So much has been goin' on— Thanks to you, it'll all be a lot easier, at least pressure-wise. I'm still havin' to pinch myself sometimes to make sure I'm not dreamin'." She demonstrated by giving her arm a light pinch. "I know it's not what some folks consider a fortune, but to us, it is. The bank's gonna get most of it, but the ranch needs a few things. And—" she grinned "—I might get that dishwasher. Dad says he wants a new recliner chair, too." Sylvia smiled. "And it's all thanks to you."

Cassie was warmed by the words, but she had to keep the record straight. "It wasn't just me. Ray Jr.'s the one who made it happen."

"Junior," Sylvia mused. "I know you told us he stood up to his daddy, but I'm still havin' a hard time picturin' it. Good for him that he did, though. He's needed to do it for a long time. Let his daddy know he has a spine. He's a good man. He's just been a little too soft where his daddy's concerned." She eyed Cassie as Cassie took another spoonful of the delicious soup. "Did you have a chance to talk with your mother today?"

Cassie nodded.

"And did she answer your questions?"

At Cassie's second nod, Sylvia said, "Good," and took another spoonful of soup herself.

They finished the meal in companionable silence. It was only when Cassie took her bowl and utensils to the sink that Sylvia asked quietly, "Are you happy to be goin' back to Houston tomorrow?"

The question pierced her heart. "Mmm. I—I suppose," Cassie managed to answer. Then, hearing the uncertainty in her voice, added more forcefully, "But I've certainly enjoyed my stay at the Circle Bar-T. I'll—I'll tell my friends about it. Some of them might want to come. That is, if you're still going to be catering to guests?"

"Oh, I think I am. At least for the time being I will. I kinda enjoy meetin' all the new folks, hearin' what their lives are like, watchin' 'em enjoy the ranch." She gave Cassie a long look. "We'll miss you, you know. You can come back whenever you want. And not as a payin' guest. You're one of us now, Cassie, even if you're off in Houston."

Cassie's throat grew tight. She had spent her life wanting to belong. On the outside wanting in. Looking through that window, with her nose pressed to the glass, desperate for what others had and took for granted. "Sylvia—" she murmured.

"No strings attached," Sylvia inserted. "You're one of us."

Cassie lowered her chin. She didn't want the other woman to see the moisture that had sprung into her eyes. "Thank you," she whispered tightly. "I'll always remember that. And you."

Sylvia took the bowl and utensils out of Cassie's hands and placed them on the counter. Then, arms wide, she invited, "C'mere, give me a hug."

And Cassie went willingly into her motherly embrace.

SINCE THIS WAS GOING TO BE her last evening on the ranch, probably forever, Cassie spent it on the wide front porch, sitting in one of the rockers, with the Duchess hopping on and off her lap according to feline whim. Sylvia kept her company for a long period, the two women talking about general things of interest, but nothing of the personal. It was as if both wanted to avoid tender spots.

Then just before dusk Sylvia announced, "I'm gonna go look in a few of those catalogues those stores keep sendin' us in the mail and start gettin' an idea of what sort of dishwasher I want. I still can't believe it!" She grinned. Then she stooped to give the top of Cassie's head a quick peck before she went inside.

The Duchess disappeared as well, off to enjoy a night's hunt for small prey, but Cassie couldn't make herself go indoors. The sun had set behind the house a short time before, but a few of the light, fluffy clouds scattered overhead were still tinged with pinks and violets. She watched their colors slowly fade.

Boots clumped through the house, stopped at the screen door, and then pushed on through to the porch. Cassie didn't need to turn to know it was Will.

Chapter Thirteen

Without saying a word, Will walked to the railing, propped a raised arm against the support and squinted off into the deepening gloom.

Cassie sat frozen in the chair. She could get up and walk away, she probably *should* walk away, but she couldn't do it. Secretly, she let her gaze absorb everything about him from the top of his golden head down to the scuffed and worn boots that encased his feet. His long, lean muscles had been hardened and sculpted by the work he did. His profile honed by nature to be arresting. But it wasn't just the way he looked. It was Will himself, the kind of man he was—devoted to his family and the land they loved, a kind man, strong on the inside.

He'd been so quiet when she'd told everyone about the sale. She'd expected him to be as exultant as his mother and grandfather…but he hadn't been.

She moved uneasily in the rocking chair, unintentionally making it squeak, and the sound drew his attention.

"Nice evenin'," he said easily.

"Yes…I've been enjoying it."

His gaze moved slowly over her. "So you did it. Congratulations."

Cassie wanted to squirm again, but made herself sit still. "The congratulations go to you, too."

"Yeah, the money's gonna help." He moved to one of the cane chairs, lowered his weight onto it and rocked it back against the wood siding of the house, balancing the chair on its two rear legs. The toe of one boot kept him steady. "How'd you finally end up doin' it?" he asked.

"Like I said, Ray Jr. did most of it. He told his dad that people in town weren't going to like it when they heard he had a part in y'all losing the ranch. Then he told him the way he's been acting was beneath him." She paused, remembering the tension-filled moments. "It was pretty strong. Ray got upset."

Will laughed grimly. "I bet he did."

"Then he told us what's been behind it all along. I'm sure part of it was getting back at Robbie, but the biggest part was his fear that Jimmy—Mr. Michaels—would sell the land to one of those big discount chain-type stores. He was worried about Love and its small businesses...what a big discount store moving in so close by would do to them."

"He has a few of those small businesses himself."

"Yes, but he's really worried more for the town. It's almost as if he thinks of Love as one of his children. That he has to take care of it, protect it. To his mind, one of those chain stores would kill it."

"Hmm."

"I guess he feels about Love the way you and your grand-dad and your mom feel about the Circle Bar-T. I'm not sure he truly understood how bad things were for you all until after Ray Jr. got him to see it."

"Sounds as if Junior's finally found his feet."

"Your mom said he's found his spine."

Will smiled dryly. "I could think of a couple other parts of the male anatomy that would fit even better."

Cassie smiled but quickly lost it. She looked away from Will, out into the newly fallen darkness. The safe topic concerning the day's events had been exhausted.

This was her last night here. By tomorrow night she would be back in the heat and humidity of Houston. In her own bed, in her own apartment, with her few scraggly plants… She closed her eyes. It didn't compare to this.

"So you'll be leavin' us tomorrow," he said, again as if privy to her thoughts.

"Yes."

There was a slight pause. "What if I was to ask you not to go?" In the silence that followed he brought the chair back down on four feet and bent forward to look at her. "Or do you have someone back there who's waitin' for you?"

Cassie cast about for the right thing to say. Was he actually asking her not to go? Why? For what reason? Attraction? "No. I—"

"Then why not stay for another couple of days? Let us have a chance to say thanks properly?"

Now he was asking for himself *and* his family. Maybe it was simple gratitude. She was glad she hadn't answered earlier with her heart.

"I—no, I should go back. Jimmy will probably have something else he wants me to do. Another…negotiation." She stood up. She needed to break this off. Kisses were one thing. So, even, might be a deeper dalliance. But she wanted more. She wanted—

"Cassie."

The way he said her name, softly in his husky baritone, curled like smoke through her body. "Yes?"

"I'd like you to stay."

To hear him say that…! But—suddenly she was afraid. Too much had happened over too short a time. She'd learned things about herself, her mother, her father, the town. Big things. Important things. Things that were going to change her life. Things that *had* changed her life. And for her to have fallen in love with Will—if that was what this was—had the most life-changing potential of all. He was asking her to stay another couple of days. She couldn't do that. She couldn't get closer to him and then leave.

"I—no. No, I—" She stumbled to the door, where she paused to whisper, "I'm sorry," her throat so tight she could barely get the words out.

He came slowly to his feet, but he didn't move toward her.

She forced herself to go inside.

CASSIE CRIED HERSELF to sleep that night, careful to keep her misery silent. But she didn't sleep soundly. Her rest was disturbed by dreams in which she was both running to and running away from the same being. A being that she never saw, only felt. And when she awakened the next morning, having missed the rooster, it was already after nine. She felt like death warmed over, yet she couldn't stay in bed. Jimmy would be arriving with the contracts in less than two hours.

She dragged herself out from beneath the covers, wobbled her way down the hall to the bathroom and finally came alive in the shower.

When she presented herself downstairs, Sylvia was already getting things ready for the big barbecue. The sauce was finished on the stove and various vegetables had been cleaned and readied for cutting.

Without a word, Sylvia filled a cup with coffee and held it out to her. Accepting it, Cassie sat at the table.

After she'd taken a few sips, Sylvia asked, "Had a hard night?"

"I didn't sleep very well."

"I don't think Will did either. He was off his feed this mornin', then he sorta stomped out to see to the horses."

As soon as Will's name was mentioned, Cassie's nerves tightened. She took another sip of coffee, then to divert Sylvia from the subject, asked with forced brightness, "What can I do to help?"

THE NEXT HOUR AND A HALF flew by and before Cassie knew it, it was almost eleven. She debated changing into one of her business suits for the signing, but decided against it. This was a ranch, they were having a barbecue. Everyone would expect her to dress casually. Her only concession was to change into a crisper shirt that dressed the jeans up a little.

When she arrived back downstairs, Will was in the kitchen ready to help his mother move the table outside under the shade tree. Cassie quickly went to assist Sylvia while Robbie held the door open.

"Can't have your boss sittin' on a stump," Sylvia declared, laughing.

They heard a car in the driveway.

"It's Ray," Robbie reported after checking.

Cassie and Will were left to bring out the chairs in addition to an extra folding chair or two that Sylvia had unearthed, while Sylvia and Robbie went to greet their guests. Cassie did her best to avoid physical contact, and for his part, Will seemed intent on the job.

The living room was crowded with people as Cassie entered it from the hall. Will had been following directly behind her, but had gone upstairs…she supposed to change, since he'd been out working earlier.

June, Ray's wife, remembered Cassie from the years before; Lisa Ann, Ray Jr.'s wife, had only lived in Love for a few years, having married Ray Jr. after his first wife died. The older woman matched her husband in roundness, her hair fully silver, its short length tightly curled. The younger woman, barely ten or so years older than Cassie, was pretty in a fussy way but with soft doe eyes. Both greeted Cassie warmly. Ray Jr., at his wife's side, nodded to Cassie with a small satisfied smile.

The twins stood on different sides of the room, but as the minutes ticked by, with everyone seeming to ignore them, they made their way over to each other and soon were talking.

Cassie caught Sylvia's conspiratorial wink and knew that the two men had been ignored on purpose.

Jimmy was the next to arrive. As his huge white Cadillac rolled down the drive, Cassie stepped out on the porch to meet him. Glancing at the gate, she saw that he'd closed it. An East Texas farm boy knows the rules about gates.

Jimmy was dressed to the hilt in one of his tan custom western suits with a black bolo tie and a matching Stetson. His silver-gray hair was newly cut, his nails recently manicured, his shave, typically, barbershop fresh. Cassie had never learned his true age. He could be anywhere from forty-five to sixty, but he moved like a much younger man as he bounded up the stairs onto the porch. He was only a few inches taller than Cassie, and slim everywhere but the belly, but because of the way he filled his space he seemed a much larger man.

"Howdy, Cassie," he boomed cheerfully, removing his hat. "Looks like the fresh air's been doing you just fine! I have those contracts right here." He patted his inner suit pocket. Then he lifted his nose and sniffed the tangy scent of barbecue sauce. "Mmm-mmm! That sure smells good. Smells like somebody's gonna burn some meat today. Hope it's us!"

Cassie couldn't help but smile. Jimmy was irresistible.

"Come inside and meet everyone," she invited, then said in a quick aside, "I think we should do the signing first."

"My thinkin' exactly," he murmured in return as he held the door open for her to enter.

Introductions were made all around. Everyone seemed fascinated by Jimmy, and he quickly made himself at home. Talking with Robbie and Ray and then consulting Sylvia about her thoughts on what he could do to make his own homemade barbecue sauce taste better.

From her position at Jimmy's side, Cassie felt her heart give an enormous flip the instant Will entered the room. Not only had he changed into clean clothes, he was wearing a newer pair of jeans, a colorful plaid shirt with shiny pearlized snap buttons, and his scuffed boots had been given new life with a little leather cleaner. He'd also showered and freshly shaved. All for the occasion. Cassie couldn't take her eyes off him. No matter what he was dressed in, he would always be an attractive man. Wearing skins in a cave, he'd make his mate's temperature rise. But this was the first time she'd seen him take special care all week and the result was devastating.

To her relief, Sylvia handled his introduction to Jimmy.

Then Will's eyes settled on her…and Cassie forgot to breathe. Voices in the room faded. There was just him…and her. The two of them.

"Cassie," a faraway voice called her name. "Cassie?" It came again, only closer. When Jimmy touched her arm, she was surprised that an electric spark didn't jump into his fingers, shocking him. There seemed to be so much charged energy surrounding her.

"Yes?" She quickly dragged her eyes away from Will, and tried to ignore that he continued to watch her.

Jimmy handed her a long envelope. Then he addressed the crowd, "Might as well get the business part over with first. If you two gentleman would like to look over the contracts—" He held out a document to each man. "Feel free to take your time."

Robbie motioned Will to his side and Ray Jr. moved closer to his father. The room waited as each word was read.

"You'll see I've added the stipulation you requested, Ray." Jimmy directed their attention to a clause. "And since the property has been in your family for a number of generations, you'll see that you're retaining the mineral rights. I enjoy turning a profit, but I don't want to rob people. I like to sleep at night."

Cassie smothered a smile. Jimmy had told her once that he'd cheated a man early on in his career as a land speculator and had felt so bad about it afterward that he'd tracked the man down over three states and five years in order to give him his money back. He *did* like to sleep at night.

"Looks all right to me," Robbie said.

"Me, too," Ray agreed.

"All right, gentlemen. Now if you'd care to sign on the appropriate line." He pulled two pens from his pocket.

Sylvia moved a bowl of flowers off the center of the coffee table and both men sat down to sign.

"And now we need two witnesses," Jimmy said.

Ray handed the pen to Ray Jr. and Robbie gave his to Will.

"Now for the best part!" Jimmy grinned. And he motioned Cassie forward. "Cassie, why don't you do the honors."

Cassie opened the envelope and gave each brother his check.

Robbie looked at his for a long time, then, eyes moist, he held it up for Will and Sylvia to see. He soon had to wipe his nose on a tissue.

Ray seemed surprised at the show of emotion. If nothing else up to now had driven home to him how important the sale was to his brother, that one small act did. He moved uncomfortably, cleared his throat, then offered his brother his hand. Robbie, equally surprised, looked hard at Ray's face. Then he reached out to clasp it.

"I think this calls for somethin' nice to drink," Sylvia said happily. "Lemonade anyone? I made some fresh this mornin'. And there's tea for those of you who want somethin' different. And I can always put on some coffee."

THE MINUTES WERE counting down. Cassie could almost feel them speeding by. She ate alongside everyone else at the table under the shade tree, but she couldn't have said how the meal tasted if her life depended on it. Jimmy raved, but she'd expected him to. And the others added their compliments to Sylvia, Cassie included.

After the meal, the men went off to inspect the outbuildings—Jimmy gathering Ray and Ray Jr. into the tour even if they might rather not have come. Jimmy was so friendly, so enthusiastic, he could persuade even the most resistant soul.

The women, left behind, cleared the table. After the dishes were washed and put away, Sylvia showed them the dishwasher she was thinking of purchasing. Then she suggested that they have their refreshments on the front porch.

Cassie couldn't do it. Last night, with Will, was too freshly seared in her memory. She pleaded a headache, which wasn't far from the truth, and went to her bedroom…to pack. The process was simple. The removal of a few things from the narrow closet and the emptying of several drawers. She made everything—including the additional clothes she'd purchased—fit into her single suitcase.

When she was done, she looked around the room. It had seemed so small when she'd first seen it…now it was just right.

She crossed to the writing desk to retrieve the photo of her father. That boyish face, that playful smile. What advice would he give her?

Jimmy's characteristic laugh, full and uninhibited, floated upstairs and into her bedroom. The men had returned to the house.

She looked again at the image of her father, wished that he could speak and slipped the cherished picture into her briefcase.

Then she went downstairs. Her place, at the moment, was at Jimmy's side.

THE MEN WERE SEATED at the kitchen table that they must have moved back inside. They'd helped themselves to coffee and some of the peach cobbler left over from the meal.

Jimmy looked up, saw her and said, "I wondered where you'd disappeared to."

"I was packing."

"Here—" he said, pushing an empty chair out for her with his foot "—have a sit for a while. You aren't in a hurry to leave, are you?"

"No," Cassie said, knowing the answer to be both truth and lie.

The seating arrangements were different at the table. Jimmy and Ray occupied the two chairs at the ends, while Robbie, Ray Jr. and Will were seated along the sides. The chair Jimmy had readied for her was directly across from Will. She pretended to concentrate on settling in the chair rather than meet Will's gaze.

"We were just talkin' about Love," Jimmy said. "About how it's growing, and a little of its history." He paused for a second. "I didn't know you came from Love, Cassie."

"My family moved here when I was a baby."

"So this trip was a homecoming for you." He beamed a pleased smile.

"You could say that," she murmured.

"You still have family here?" he asked.

"My mother."

Jimmy had never asked her about her past. He tended to take people as they were. But he was an astute enough man to know that she had faced difficulties in her earlier life. Difficulties that had encased her in an emotional shell. Picking up on her hesitancy to talk about it even now, he stopped that line of pursuit to instead tease, "So I'm thinkin' that maybe I shouldn't have to pay you for it!"

"You better," Ray warned, smiling. "If you don't, Junior and I will hire her away from you."

"You folks allow poachin' in this part of Texas?" Jimmy demanded archly.

The question elicited a laugh as Jimmy had meant for it to, then he switched the conversation to the various business interests in the town, asking Ray and Ray Jr. to tell him about the different ones as well as their own.

He heard them out, then said, "You realize, as your town grows—as your county grows—you're not goin' to be able to keep a big discount store out forever. There'll be one built somewhere, whether it's in or near your town or in a town farther down the road. People will drive to wherever it is and shop there. Everybody wants a bargain. May not happen for some years. Won't happen on that strip I just bought off you. But it's comin'. My advice is for you to start makin' some plans. Do you have any?"

Ray stiffened in his seat, but Ray Jr. sat forward. "I was thinking what we need is to specialize more. No one knows our customers like we do. We can offer them items that they can't get in one of those big places. And we can start doing more to get tourists to stop in Love instead of passin' on through. Start sellin' the local's arts and crafts—like those quilts and those rag dolls your mother and the church ladies make, Will. And those funny mailboxes Jenny Martinez makes. We can even come up with some kind of festival— call it somethin' with a clever take on the town name, like The Love Bug Festival. Have beetle races and cookin' contests…that kind of thing." He sat back on the last words, as if realizing that he'd maybe let his tongue get away from him. "Well," he said, slightly embarrassed. "Not that name necessarily, but something like it." He glanced at his father, who continued to sit stiffly.

"That's exactly the kind of thinkin' I'm talkin' about!" Jimmy approved enthusiastically. "Other towns have done it, you can, too!"

"I don't mean right away," Ray Jr. said to his father. "Just maybe…start planning."

Ray shifted in his chair, rubbed his neck, and said, "Sounds like a good idea. Why don't you bring it up at the next chamber meeting?"

Ray Jr. nodded agreement.

"Looks like Junior's a chip off the ol' block, after all, Ray," Robbie said, grinning.

As the others talked, Cassie felt Will's eyes burning into her. Finally, she could stand it no longer. She turned to Jimmy. "If you don't need me anymore, I think I would like to leave early so I can stop by and see my mother."

Jimmy frowned slightly as he looked back at her, but he said, "No, I don't need you. Go ahead."

Cassie did her best to leave the room without seeming to hurry. But as she reached the kitchen door, a second chair scraped back and she knew Will was intent on following her.

She quickened her pace in the hall, but Will's long legs allowed him to pass her and block her way onto the stairs.

Keeping his voice low to prevent both the men in the kitchen and the women on the porch from hearing, he said, "We need to deal with this, Cassie. You know there's somethin'. I know there's somethin'. If you go back to Houston—"

"I can't stay," she said tautly, her reply equally muted.

"Tell me that when you're lookin' at me, and then I'll believe you."

Cassie slowly lifted her eyes, saw the muscle that twitched along the side of his jaw and knew she couldn't do it. "All right," she admitted. "There's…something. But it's only been a week."

"We've known each other most of our lives."

She shook her head. "No. We haven't *known* each other. I knew who you were. You knew who I was. Me…Bonnie Edwards's daughter. I know now that my mother can't help being who she is. And that the town…and the people…aren't as bad as I remember. But I can't—I don't—everything's so—" In distress, she pushed the short feathery hairs curving onto her cheeks back behind her ears.

"It's only as complicated as we make it, Cassie."

"I need time, Will."

Conflicting emotions passed over his face as he struggled with her assertion. Finally, he said huskily, "Then take it." And after a pause, "Can I come see you?"

She was already shaking her head no before he finished speaking.

He stared out the screen door over her head. A moment later he stepped out of her way. "Tell me when you're ready and I'll take your suitcase to the car."

Cassie wanted more than anything at that moment to throw herself into his arms, uncaring if it was only for a moment, an hour, a few days. But, hard as it was, she knew she was doing the right thing. Here, her emotions were in too much of a jumble. She couldn't…sort things out. Especially with Will so close by.

"I'm ready now," she said. "I'll—I'll bring it downstairs." She didn't want to be alone with him in such a private place as her room. She couldn't trust herself.

"I'll be here," he said and looked at her in such a way that she knew he meant not only when she came downstairs, but also whenever she wanted to contact him again.

THE GOODBYES TO THE OTHERS were harrowing. When a few minutes later Cassie was handing her suitcase over to Will, Sylvia came inside from the front porch. She'd been smiling at something the women were talking about, but her smile vanished instantly as soon as she saw what was taking place.

"You're leaving so soon?" she asked, surprised.

Cassie nodded. "I'm going to stop by and see Bonnie first and then go."

"But—" Her eyes moved to Will, searching his taut features before switching back.

Cassie set her briefcase down and collected the woman's hands in both of hers. "I'm so glad everything worked out for your family, Sylvia. Thank you. Thank you for everything."

Sylvia caught her bottom lip. "You remember what I told you yesterday."

"I will," Cassie promised.

Robbie hobbled in from the kitchen, followed by the other men. Cassie went to shake his hand, but he quickly turned it into a hug. "You don't be a stranger, little gal," he said gruffly.

Ray, leaning past his brother, held his hand out. "Good doing business with you, Cassie."

Then Ray Jr. shook her hand, but said nothing. His smile and nod were sufficient.

"See ya back in Houston Monday mornin'!" Jimmy called, having fallen into a deeper accent after visiting on the ranch for a couple of hours.

"You're not going to give her a little time off?" Ray demanded.

"She can come in a half hour late, if she wants," Jimmy teased.

Cassie knew that after a long negotiation she could take as much time off as she wanted, but she had a feeling that she was going to need the activity of work. To keep herself from thinking of Will, and the ranch….

"I'll take this on out," Will said quietly and she dug in her purse for the keys.

It was a little like tearing part of her heart out to walk through the front door onto the porch—where she said good-bye to the two other Taylor women—then, after another hug for Sylvia and another for Robbie, too, she walked to her car.

Everyone, except Will, had clustered onto the porch to see her off. Even the Duchess was there, gray tail flicking annoyance on the lower step because her favorite rocking chair had a stranger in it.

In a haze of tears, Cassie turned one last time to wave.

Will, already having deposited her case in the trunk, held the driver's door open.

Cassie leaned in, deposited her purse and briefcase on the passenger seat and straightened. Her heart was thumping like mad, her throat so tight it was painful. When she looked up at him, his face was a study in fortitude.

"Don't be long," he said. Then he stepped back.

Cassie's dark eyes were swimming by the time she started the car. Even dabbing at them with a tissue didn't seem to do any good because fresh moisture only reappeared.

Once again, she wasn't aware that Will had jogged out to the gate until she rolled near and saw him swinging it open. In the rearview mirror, she saw the family still gathered on the porch.

It was all she could do to give an abbreviated wave to all

of them as she turned onto the blacktop road and headed for the highway.

Her leave-taking was so different from her arrival. *She* was different.

If she was going to do this, though, she had to put the afternoon's emotions out of her mind. She had another stop to make, and then she would be off for Houston. Where she could think.

Chapter Fourteen

Exhausted in every way it was possible to be exhausted, Cassie let herself into her apartment. The drive from Love to Houston had seemed endless. She was glad to have it over. But the emptiness of the place was so pronounced after the conviviality of the past week that she felt no welcome. And there was a staleness to the air-conditioned air that she had never noticed before.

She left the cases by the door and after turning on a couple of lamps to chase away the evening gloom, slumped into the nearest chair. Frequently on the way home she'd wondered if she was doing the right thing. Or if she only *thought* it was right. Will had said he wanted her to stay. He'd asked her more than once. He'd said there was something between them, which meant he felt something too. *Something.*

The word made Cassie moan.

Bonnie had been impossible to find, not at home, not out by the creek. Cassie had searched for her for about a half hour and then had ended up leaving a note. In it, she promised her mother that she would be back to see her and that she should call whenever she had the opportunity. Bonnie didn't have a telephone in her house, but she didn't object to using a pay phone.

Cassie's thoughts returned to Will. By now the company would have left, and he would probably be hard at work again, trying to make up for the lost time. Sylvia would likely be sitting on the front porch resting with the cat and Robbie either with her or out with Will, helping where he could.

Her gaze traveled around the open room. She'd worked really hard to make the apartment attractive and comfortable and reflective of her personality. But now, she wasn't the same person she used to be. She no longer had need of a brittle shell, or to pretend that she wasn't who she truly was. Many of the things she saw here she might no longer have chosen.

She looked down at her jeans and the, by now, somewhat rumpled shirt. She'd never worn jeans, not before her stay at the ranch. Now they felt a part of her.

She thought of her father and dragged herself out of the chair to retrieve his photo from the briefcase. Tomorrow, she would scan it into her computer, use her limited photo-enhancing skills, and create as many photos of him as she wanted. She could have a framed picture of him in every room.

For tonight, though, his picture would come with her as it was and she'd prop it on her bedside table.

And try not to dream of Will.

OVER THE NEXT FEW DAYS she did her best to fit back into her life in Houston. On Sunday she talked to a couple of friends, catching up on their lives, but careful not to let the conversation touch on hers. Then she did her laundry, stopped by the cleaners, shopped to put a few things back in the refrigerator and, after working on the computer for a short time, made the set of photos that she wanted. But she still felt incomplete. All too often her thoughts went back to the ranch.

Monday and Tuesday she spent at work. Jimmy hadn't returned yet from his day in the country, having extended his travels to other small towns in the area. Refreshing his sense of the area, as he'd termed it. Scouting for other prospects, was another way to put it.

With Jimmy away, though, the office was quiet and Cassie busied herself by catching up with paperwork. It was the hours after work that were the most difficult, when time seemed to drag and the loneliness of her apartment became almost painful and even meeting a friend for a meal in the evening was unfulfilling.

By Wednesday, Cassie looked forward to Jimmy's return with pent-up nervous tension. She'd run out of things to occupy her time. But Jimmy was late coming in that morning and Diane, who during the previous two days had provided an avenue for conversation, secretly confided that she had partied a little too hardy the night before and all she wanted was to hold her head in her hands, in hope that the monster headache would lessen before Jimmy finally did arrive. And the other member of the staff, Louise, who'd worked with Jimmy almost since he'd started out—first as his one-woman office support, now acting as his office manager/second-in-command, and though well past retirement age, still trundled in every day to keep them on the straight and narrow—was in a grumpy mood and didn't want to be disturbed. Leaving Cassie to invent something to do.

Organizing and updating her e-mail contacts list and address book wasn't enough, though.

Will and the ranch continued to exert a pull that she was finding more and more difficult to resist. Maybe she'd been in love with him all along and hadn't known it. Maybe that was why she'd been reluctant to let her other romantic relationships progress. Maybe—

Was she in love with Will?

At the ranch she'd been afraid that what she felt for him was caught up in all the other emotions swirling around her in that week. That her schoolgirl crush had somehow taken over and she was no longer thinking clearly. Instinctively, she'd known that as long as she was in his and the ranch's spell, the reality of her feelings was questionable. But she was back in Houston…and those same feelings still existed.

And Will…what did *he* feel? She knew beyond a doubt that he was attracted to her. But—

"Cassie!" Jimmy swept into her small office space, making it feel even smaller. "You know I was only kiddin' when I said you had to come in. You could've taken a few days off." He looked at her closely. "Did you go to that same party Diane did? Musta been a *hum*dinger! Both of you look like somethin' the cat drug in!"

Cassie smiled and shook her head. "No, no party."

"Humph," he grunted and dropping into her only spare chair, leaned back and clasped his hands behind his head. "Gotta tell you. I sure enjoyed myself on Saturday. Those Taylors are *nice* people. All of 'em. And can that Sylvia cook! I ate so much I thought I was gonna pop!"

Cassie nodded. "She's good."

"And that Will, he seems to be a fine young man. What'd you think of him?"

Cassie felt heat rise into her cheeks. She averted her eyes, but knew Jimmy had seen. "He's…what you said."

Jimmy made no reply. Cassie waited, and waited, and finally looked at him.

He smiled impishly. "So what are you waitin' for?"

Her discomfort increased. "I—I don't know—"

He sat forward. "Yes, you do. I saw the way you two were eyein' each other. I also saw the way you left—the way you looked before you went and the way he looked after."

Cassie moved pens and papers around on her desk. "You have an active imagination."

"Not when it comes to love, I don't. And I'm talkin' about the emotion, not the town. You know me, Cassie. Been married to the same woman for twenty-two years and I still thank my lucky stars every day that she came into my life. Now, what's holdin' you back?"

"I…" She thought to stall, but could come up with nothing to say. Anyone else and she might have been able to bluff her way through. But Jimmy was immune to bluffs. She took a breath and admitted miserably, "Jimmy, I don't know what to do. Everything's so…jumbled up. When I went back to Love to negotiate the contracts, I didn't go there willingly. I— I never wanted to see the place again. Or my mother, if I could avoid it." She looked down, struggling for a way to say what needed to be said. "My mother's…different, and I blamed her for a lot of things I shouldn't have. And I blamed the town. But I know better now. I understand that a lot of it was in me." She lifted her gaze. "You remember how I was."

"You're not that way now."

A smile touched her lips as she thought of how much he'd helped her. "No."

"I still don't see what the problem is," he said.

"I think—I *know* that I love him. But…it's all so soon. So on top of everything else. And I got scared."

"Are you still scared?"

"Not as much."

"So when are you gonna put that young man out of his misery? And yours."

"I don't know how *he* feels. I know—" She stopped. There were some things she just wasn't going to talk about to Jimmy. "He says there's somethin', but—"

"Did he ask you not to leave?"

Her eyes widened. Had he had one of his talks with Will, too?

He smiled. "It's what I'd of done. I probably would've locked Kate in a room and kept her there till she told me what I wanted to hear!"

"I told him I needed time."

"Do you still need it?"

"Well, uh, no."

"Then get to it, girl!"

"But he—"

"Go get to it. Find out how he feels! It's something you need to know. And you can't do that sittin' here!"

She motioned around the room, to the outer office. "But, my work."

He stood up. "You've earned some time off. Just give me a call on down the road and let me know what's happenin'." Then he swept out of the office as grandly as he'd swept in.

For a moment Cassie could only sit there, blinking. Then she did as he advised.

She got to it.

"YA THINK THAT BOY'S GONNA LAST out the week?" Robbie asked as he and Sylvia watched Will load up the bed of the old red pickup with the supplies he needed to replace a section of pasture fence.

"Not if he keeps goin' the way he's been goin'," Sylvia replied.

Robbie shook his woolly head. "Seems to think he's Superman or somethin'. 'At fence might need replacin', but it could wait. Originally, he wasn't plannin' on doin' it until after we work the calves next week. Now, it's gotta be done right away."

"It all comes down to Cassie."

"Tryin' not to think about her," Robbie muttered.

Sylvia nodded agreement.

"What's he gonna do if she don't come back?" Robbie asked.

"What he's doin' now, most likely."

"Ain't right."

"He told me Cassie asked for some time and he's tryin' to give it to her."

"Time for what?" Robbie snapped. "In my day, ya found the person you wanted and ya got married. As simple as that. There was none 'a this nonsense 'bout *thinkin'* about it."

Sylvia looked at him, and with a small smile said, "In your day, you smacked 'em over the head and drug 'em back to the cave, did ya?"

"Naw," Robbie retorted, grinning, "I was more *so*phisticated. I asked 'em out to supper first."

Sylvia laughed, then slowly sobered. "I hope she doesn't take too long. One way or the other, she needs to tell him."

ON HER OTHER TRIPS to and from Central Texas, Cassie hadn't noticed the wildflowers that, though late in the spring, still grew along the sides of the highways and in the fields and pastures. Bluebonnets and Indian paintbrush, their royal-blue and red-orange colors striking both because of their beauty and their sheer numbers. People came from far and wide to see them...and she had been too turned inward to appreciate the display.

Her mother would claim it as an omen. As if nature was cheering her on, encouraging her return. And in this instance, Cassie wanted to believe it. Wanted to believe that this journey back to the town, to the ranch and to the man she loved was preordained. Wanted desperately to ignore the reality that nothing was preset. That she could go to the ranch, go to Will...and have it not work.

Her grip tightened apprehensively on the steering wheel. As Jimmy had said, she needed to find out.

"AT LEAST COME IN and have a hot supper with us," Sylvia pleaded from the saddle, having ridden Polly out to where Will was working. "All this rushin' around isn't good for you. Neither's existin' on sandwiches. You need to take a little time and relax."

Will lifted his hat to let a little air in, then positioned it back in place. "I got a lot to do, Mom."

"This fence'll wait! I want you in for a meal."

He looked down the line of posts he'd already set in place a short space from the existing fence, in effect doubling it, and looked the other way at the much greater distance he had yet to cover. "Can't wait too long," he said, hedging.

"It can wait an hour!" she insisted.

His mother was determined. And Will knew from past experience that there was no stopping her, or denying her, once she got the bit between her teeth.

He rubbed a sore shoulder and caved in. "All right. I'll come in."

"Good. Don't be late!" And with a click of encouragement, she wheeled the horse around and, at a leisurely pace, headed back to the house.

Will checked the time, saw that he had a half hour before he needed to start in and began to work on another hole. At the rate he was going, he could get the new fence finished by the end of the week and the old fence pulled down. It was a job he'd been needing to do for a while but never got around to. But after Cassie left…

What kind of a fool was he to have let her walk out like that? What sort of a man? Short of tying her down, though, what else could he have done? She'd asked for some time. He could have refused, he could have pressured her—but that wouldn't be right. He wanted her to *want* to be here. To *want* to be with him. She shouldn't feel forced. She'd spent so

much of her life hiding from the people of Love, hiding from
herself even, according to her own words. She shouldn't be
made to feel the need to hide from him.

So he'd agreed to give her time. But he wasn't an easy
waiter. He was accustomed to seeing a problem and solving
it. And her not being here was a problem.

Once the hole was dug, he checked the time again, then
leaving his tools where they were for later use, he hopped
back into the truck and started home.

He'd give her through the weekend, he decided. After that,
he was going to Houston.

CASSIE DROVE ALONG Main Street and past the Four Corners,
this time experiencing none of her previous anxiety. And
no matter that she told herself yet again that this could all
be for naught, her heart rate increased from growing excitement as she took the turnoff to the ranch. It increased
even more as she bumped over the railroad tracks, and by
the time she reached the ranch's front gate, her heart
seemed to be beating so hard that her chest could barely
contain it.

The first time she'd come here she'd wondered how the
Taylors would react to Jimmy's offer to buy the land. Now
she wondered how they'd react to her. Robbie seemed to like
her, Sylvia did for sure, and Will—

She swallowed. It was Will she was here to find out about.

Cassie heard the family in the kitchen as she stepped onto
the porch. It was a little after six…supper time. The Duchess
looked up sleepily from her spot on the rocking chair and Cassie bent to scratch her ears. Then she moved to the screen door
and knocked on the frame. The voices instantly stopped.

She'd not made much noise coming up the drive or parking, and since they probably weren't expecting anyone at this hour, they couldn't help but wonder at the caller.

Cassie nervously brushed a hand down the front of her black jeans and smoothed the collar on her cream-colored blouse. She heard footsteps in the hall and Sylvia soon appeared, walking toward her.

There was a moment's pause when Sylvia recognized who she was, and then her pace quickened.

"Cassie! You're back!" she proclaimed as she opened the door and drew Cassie inside and into a hug. "Oh, I'm so glad to see you!"

From the warmth of the greeting, it could have been a year and not four days since Cassie had left. But to Cassie it felt like a year, and she clung to Sylvia as tightly as Sylvia did to her.

"Are you hungry?" Sylvia asked, pulling back. "We're just finishin' supper, but there's still plenty."

"I—well—"

"C'mon," she said and pulled her down the hall.

Will was already standing as Sylvia and Cassie entered the room. He looked thunderstruck. Cassie's eyes moved over him and then away. But her heart had started thumping madly again.

What she wanted was to run straight into his arms. Only she wasn't sure enough of her standing. Or if, after her brief absence, the action would even be welcome. She thought it would. But… She put a halt to her runaway speculation. Her heart wasn't the only thing racing overtime.

"Hi, Robbie," she murmured to the older man who had suddenly begun to grin.

"Why look who's back. Our little gal! Look, Will," he directed his grandson, who didn't need any directing.

Cassie nodded in general as she slipped into her usual chair. It felt so right to be at this table, in this room, in this house, on this ranch…with these people.

Sylvia hurriedly set Cassie's place and started passing her food. Cassie took a little of this and a little of that, but doubted she'd eat even a small portion. She could feel Will's eyes burning into her and after a moment, forced herself to meet his gaze.

Robbie said something, but Cassie wasn't sure what. Then there was some kind of movement and, a space of time later—she had no idea how long—she came to the awareness that Sylvia and Robbie had slipped away, leaving her and Will alone.

"You don't have to eat any of that if you don't want." Will flicked a finger to her plate.

"No." She glanced at his plate. He hadn't finished his meal, but he no longer seemed interested in what remained.

She wished she could think of something to say. Something that would ease their way into the conversation that needed to be exchanged. But she could come up with nothing. For a second, a whisper of panic made her wonder what she was doing here, but the feeling quickly went away.

He pushed back from the table. "Wanna take a walk?"

"Yes," she said, and stood up just as he did.

Outside, they fell into step together as they walked slowly toward the outbuildings.

The temperature was starting to heat up a little, the sun warmer on her skin than it had been the week before. It was nice, though, the higher heat of summer still in the future.

"Wanna go out to the creek?" he asked.

Cassie nodded.

She was very aware of him. Aware of the easy way he moved. Aware that he'd matched his longer gait to hers. Aware of the golden hair that his hat didn't cover. Aware that as tension-filled as the situation was between them, they could walk together in amiable silence. In the distance, a cow bawled.

"Am I taking you away from your work?" she asked, able at last to venture a question.

"There's always work."

At last they reached a cluster of trees and brush and the creek that flowed through their midst. Love Creek. But it looked very different here from the area where Cassie had played as a child. This part of the creek flowed from a higher level and down along cracks worn deep into several large limestone boulders. Each crack created a little waterfall that collected into a good-sized pool before the stream narrowed again to meander through the ranchland and on past the outskirts of town.

"It's beautiful here," Cassie murmured. "I can see why the Warrens came so often."

"It's spring-fed," Will said. "But you probably already know that. The source is a mile or so northwest of here."

"Did you swim here when you were a boy?" she asked.

"Still do sometimes," he said.

"I used to wade around in it farther down by town."

She moved to the pool's edge and bent to wiggle her fingers in the cool water.

"You could've come to swim here, too," Will said. "A lot of my friends did."

"I wasn't your friend then," she replied, straightening. She took the few steps to the closest miniature waterfall and let the flow of water run playfully over her fingertips.

"Are you my friend now?" Will asked.

Cassie's body stilled, but not her heart. Once again, it was starting to pound. "Do you want me to be?"

"Why'd you come back, Cassie?" He cut directly to the chase.

She wiped her fingers with her other hand as she turned to face him, letting the warm dry air take care of the rest. "Because—because I need to find out what that *something* you talked about between us really is."

Will hesitated, his expression serious, then he said simply,

"I wasn't sure at first what it was. You came back here so different—I couldn't stop thinkin' about you. I tried, but I couldn't. And now I don't want to. You're the one, Cassie."

"The one…what?" Cassie breathed.

"The woman I want to make my life with."

Cassie felt her knees give way a little. "Why?" she breathed again. She was waiting for that one word….

He closed the distance between them, reached down and tipped up her chin. "Because I love you," he said huskily.

He'd said it! And if he said it, he meant it. That was the way it was with Taylor men. Cassie wanted so badly to kiss him. She let her eyes flutter shut and waited with building excitement for his lips to touch hers…but they didn't.

Instead, he repeated his earlier question. "Why'd you come back, Cassie? I need to know."

Cassie's eyes fluttered open again, surprised that he had to ask. Her gaze searched his rugged, clean-cut features and found only sincerity. He, too, needed to hear.

"Because I love you, too," she said softly.

Will waited no longer. With a low groan, he pulled her against him, holding her as if he'd never let her go.

"Ah, Cassie," he said, his voice thick with emotion. "I thought I'd lost you. When you left—the way you left—these past days have been *hell!*"

Her arms wrapped tightly around his waist, she laughed shakily. "For me, too. I started wondering if I was doing the wrong thing shortly after I left. But…I had to be sure, Will. Last week I'd been through so much."

"But you're sure now," he said, a statement of fact yet with a lingering question.

"I'm sure," she said. She drew away enough so that she could see his face and gaze into those wonderful blue eyes. "I think I've loved you for a long, long time, Will."

Then she stretched up and Will bent low, until their lips finally met in a kiss that left absolutely no room for future doubt.

"HOTDIGGITY!" Robbie exclaimed as he and Sylvia hurried out into the backyard to greet the pair upon their return.

"Will! Cassie!" Sylvia looked from one grinning face to the other. "Is this meanin' what I'm thinkin' it's meanin'?"

Will tightened his arm around Cassie's shoulders. "It's meanin' it," he confirmed.

"Oh! I'm so *happy!*" she cried, and hugged both of them at the same time, while Robbie did a little jig similar to the one he'd performed upon hearing that Ray had agreed to sign the contract.

"Awright!" he cheered at the end of it and hurried over to pump Will's hand and kiss Cassie's cheek. "'Bout time!" he added gruffly as he stepped back.

Her face beaming, Sylvia hurried into speech. "I saw you comin' from the window and just couldn't be sure—but then you got closer and I called Dad and—oh, this is just so wonderful! Let me get us some iced tea!"

"I'll help," Cassie quickly volunteered. She didn't want to part from Will, but thought a moment alone with his mother was a good idea.

Sylvia continued to smile hugely as she gathered glasses, filled them with ice and set them on a round serving tray. Cassie poured the refrigerated tea.

"I'm so happy for both of you," Sylvia said, watching as Cassie completed her chore.

"I am, too." Cassie grinned. Then she sobered, thinking she already knew the answer to the question she was about to ask, but feeling that it should be asked anyway. "And you don't mind...Bonnie?" She hurried on to explain, "It's one thing to know someone and not mind that their mother is different. It's another thing entirely when that someone is…close to someone in your family."

Sylvia reached for her hand. "Do you love Will?" she asked solemnly.

"I love him," Cassie replied, her answer resonant with feeling.

"Then that's all that matters," Sylvia said, and began to smile again.

"SO YOU FINALLY DECIDED to listen to what I been tellin' ya all along." Robbie clapped his grandson on the back.

"I just had to find the right one."

"Well, you got a good'un in that little gal in there. She sure saved our bacon talkin' Ray around. When's the weddin'?"

"We're gonna give it a bit of time, Granddad. Not rush into things." Will grinned as he added, "I'm hopin' sometime next month."

"Wanna get your brand on her quick, huh?"

"Don't let her hear you say that."

"Let *who* hear you say *what?*" Sylvia teased as she and Cassie rejoined them under the shade tree. She winked at Cassie before passing the tray around. "I wonder if they're talkin' about you or me?"

"We were talkin' about somethin' that's none 'a your business, woman," Robbie declared, taking a glass. "It's man stuff."

"Ooo!" Sylvia retorted. "Cassie and I will remember that the next time you two want to know what we're talkin' about."

Will watched Cassie take a glass. His heart gave a little leap as she then moved over to his side and, smiling at him, slipped close in under his arm as he automatically lifted it. The action was so natural, yet so significant. He couldn't believe his good fortune.

Considering his earlier desolation, everything that had happened since their interrupted supper had a surreal, dream-like quality to it. Yet he knew he wasn't dreaming. He could feel the warmth of Cassie's body close to his. Could still feel the wonderous sensations of being even closer to her. His body stirred and he took a quick gulp of tea.

"No, Will," his mother scolded. "You're supposed to wait for the toast."

Cassie giggled. The first time he'd heard her do that. He grinned down at her like an idiot.

"To Cassie and Will!" Sylvia said, lifting her glass.

"To the Old Home Place," Robbie added, lifting his as well. When Sylvia looked at him slightly askance, he explained, "If it weren't for that, Cassie wouldn'ta come back."

"To the Old Home Place!" Will echoed, hoisting his glass.

"To the Home Place," Cassie agreed.

And they all took a long drink to happiness.

CASSIE WAS BACK in the upstairs guest room, the clothes she'd brought with her at last hung up and put away. She hadn't brought all that much again this time because she hadn't been sure of the outcome. But it had taken a while before she'd been able to get up here. Sylvia and Robbie were so happy. She and Will had sat with them, first under the shade tree out back, and then on the porch. Only when dusk began to fall did she get upstairs.

Parting from Will had been difficult again. But he'd walked her upstairs and they'd shared a long, passionate kiss outside the bedroom door, after which he'd told her he had to go see to a few things out back. On a ranch, something always seemed to need doing. Cassie didn't mind, though. She was here. And Will very much wanted her here.

As she set one of the framed photos she'd made of her father on the writing desk, she thought of what she and Will had talked about on the way back from the creek. A wedding date. He wouldn't rush her, he'd said. But Cassie no longer felt rushed. What he'd said about her being the one…he was her *one* also. And he'd been the one, she now knew, since the afternoon he'd rescued her outside the post office when she was twelve. She'd fallen in love with him then. She loved him now. She'd always love him.

A LIGHT TAP SOUNDED on her door a half hour later, and delight washed through Cassie's body that it could be Will.

It was.

"Mom and Granddad have called it a night. Wanna come sit on the porch with me?" he asked.

Cassie nodded. She would go anywhere with him.

There was only one place for them to sit close together on the porch and that was on the steps.

"Gonna have to get us one of those porch swings put up," Will commented as he settled his arm around her back and she rested her head against the crook of his shoulder.

"That would be nice," she murmured, "but this is nice, too."

"Darn right, it's nice."

"I expected you to be longer."

"I had a good reason to take a few shortcuts." He kissed the tip of her nose, then seemingly unable to resist, found the lips that were waiting for his.

A few moments later, they were back where they'd started, his arm curled around her and her head resting on his shoulder.

"I've been thinking," she said into the silence. "How does a fall wedding sound?"

"Too far away."

She chuckled. "What about late summer?"

"Still too far away."

"There's things to be done, Will, even for a small wedding." She jerked forward in remembrance. "Oh my gosh! Jimmy! What am I going to do about Jimmy? I'm going to have to go back. I can't just walk out on my job. Not after—" She'd yet to tell Will the part Jimmy had played in her transformation.

Will drew her back to his side. "Your boss looked like a reasonable man to me. I'm bettin' he'll understand."

She frowned. "I'll have to talk to him tomorrow. See what I can work out. Oh!" She started to jerk forward again as another thought struck her, but she stopped herself, staying put. "I just thought about my mother," she explained. Her lips curved into a smile. "She's not going to be surprised, though." She paused. "Do you remember when we ate the honey cakes out by the creek where we'd stopped after we visited her? *Eat them when the moon is starting to rise, and you'll be together for the rest of your lives*—something like that. Do you remember when she said that?" When she felt his nod, she continued, "And do you remember when we thought we were safe to eat them because it was broad daylight?"

"Are you tellin' me we weren't?"

The dry amusement in his question made her giggle. "After I got back into the truck, I looked up…and there it was. The moon in the daytime, rising!"

Will shook his head, chuckling. "So your mom was right after all."

"Seems like."

They were silent again for a time, content to be together. Then contentedness took a back seat to mutual attraction and need.

Finally, Will held himself away from her.

"How 'bout next week for that weddin'?" he proposed huskily. "Mom's not goin' to put up with any cohabitatin' in her house until after."

"A month, Will. Your mom would want us to take a month so she can plan out what she'll feed all the guests. I can have a meal catered, but I don't think she'd be happy with that. And I need to find a dress. There's lots to do."

"All right," he agreed. "A month. That'll give me time to get the calves worked and the pasture fence I started puttin' up finished, along with a few other things. And then maybe we can take a little time off, go somewhere for a honeymoon."

Of all people, Cassie knew the financial realities of the ranch. Even with the sale, every penny had a place to go. "Being here with you is good enough, Will," she murmured. "I don't need anything else."

"What about our own house one day?" He motioned past the windmill toward the state highway that led to Love. "We could build it over there. Close enough to this house to be a part of the compound, but far enough away to give us a little privacy."

"Maybe one day. But right now, this is fine. I love your family, Will. I like being a part of it."

"Maybe we could build another room or two on the back. For us. I want us to have our own space, Cassie. I think that's important."

"Our own set of rooms it is," Cassie agreed. She teased, "That'll give your mom another spare room upstairs for visitors."

Will groaned and looked heavenward.

Then his gaze came back to her, studying her face in the fledgling starlight as he brushed back the short dark hairs that fell over her forehead and cheeks.

Looking long and deep into her equally dark eyes, he said huskily, "I don't need anything else, either, Cassie. Just you."

And once again he set about to prove it.

Epilogue

"That boss 'a yours sure does know how to give a weddin' present," Will declared with a light laugh as he settled into the first-class airline seat next to Cassie's. They both glanced at the other passengers around them—men and women on business trips, a few who must be celebrities because of the way they talked and dressed, others who had to be high-ranking executives in one field or another.

"I told him a trip like this was too much," Cassie said, "and that was when I thought the tickets were in economy!"

"I get the feelin' he thinks a lot of you."

"I think a lot of him."

"He sure was proud to walk you down the aisle."

A flight attendant paused on her way by. "Would you like a pair of slippers?" she asked them.

Will smiled at her. "Sure. Why not?"

"I'll bring them right away," she trilled, obviously having to make an effort to pull her eyes away from the ruggedly good-looking golden-haired cowboy who still wore jeans and boots and had only recently parted with his hat so it could be stored safely away in a compartment.

Only Cassie knew that the boots were new, as was the hat, and that—courtesy of Sylvia—the jeans and the striped shirt were like new as well because they'd been put back over the past year for special occasions.

Another thing she knew was that their flight to Hawaii wasn't going to seem as long as they'd first thought. Not judging from the flight attendant's interest in Will. She'd probably be back as often as she could, just to look into those striking blue eyes.

Will brought Cassie's hand up to his lips and kissed the golden band that he'd placed there only the day before. Then he compared it to his.

"Looks right," he said softly and gave her one of his slow smiles.

The flight attendant arrived with their slippers, handing them to Will. Then she asked him sweetly, "Would you like something to drink?"

"You know, I'd really like to have some water," Will replied. "How 'bout you, Cassie?" He raised Cassie's left hand to proudly show off the ring. "She's my wife."

The attendant didn't miss a beat. "Congratulations."

"I'll have water as well, thank you," Cassie said.

"How long have you been married?" the attendant asked.

"One whole day," Will replied.

"And you're going to Hawaii on your honeymoon. I envy you," she said with more real warmth than she'd showed up to that point and included Cassie in the conversation. "Let me bring you some champagne. You should celebrate!"

Then she was off again, only to be stopped by one of the celebrity-types who made a request sound like a demand.

Will shook his head. "Like I said, your boss sure knows how to give a gift."

"Setting me up at the ranch so that I can keep working for him from there is a pretty nice gift, too."

"Better to use the guest room for an office than to have more strangers in it."

"I was a stranger."

"You were never a stranger. But you sure bothered the heck outta me from the very first."

"Do I bother you now?" she asked with mock innocence.

His mouth curved wryly. "If we weren't in an airplane, I'd show you how much you bother me."

"It won't be easy, but I can wait," she teased. "You have an entire week to show me."

"No cows, no horses, no fences to mend—" He gave a quick little frown. "I wonder how it's all goin' back there."

"Just fine. Your mom and granddad are there, and Tim Hassat and his boys won't let you down. Your mom told me to tell you that, if you asked."

His frown turned into a rueful smile. "Won't mention it again," he promised.

They were laughing softly together when the attendant arrived with the champagne and two glasses.

As they sipped the bubbling liquid a moment later, Will said, "You know? I could get used to this." And wiggled his toes in the soft slippers.

Cassie wiggled hers as well. "Me, too," she agreed.

He lowered the back of his seat to match Cassie's, who'd already settled hers into a comfortable position. Then he rolled his head to look at her, his eyes warm with his love.

"Mrs. Will Taylor," he whispered.

"Mr. Will Taylor," she whispered back.

And when the flight attendant paused again to offer them something else, she quelled what she'd been about to say, and smiling almost enviously to herself, backed off to leave them alone.

Neither Will nor Cassie noticed.

* * * * *

Welcome to the world of American Romance!
Turn the page for excerpts from our May 2005 titles.

THE RICH BOY by Leah Vale

HIS FAMILY by Muriel Jensen

THE SERGEANT'S BABY by Bonnie Gardner

HOMETOWN HONEY by Kara Lennox

We're sure you'll enjoy every one of these books!

The Rich Boy (#1065) is the fourth and final book in Leah Vale's popular series THE LOST MILLIONAIRES. The previous titles are *The Bad Boy, The Cowboy* and *The Marine*. In this book, you'll read about Alexander McCoy. He's just found out that the mighty McCoy family, one of the richest in the nation, has a skeleton in its closet. When reporter Madeline Monroe discovers the secret, she will do anything she can to prove that she's more than just a pretty face. This is a story about two people from very different walks of life, who both want to be loved for *who* they are—not *what* they are.

I, Marcus Malcolm McCoy, being of sound mind, yadda yadda yadda, do hereby acknowledge as my biological progeny the firstborn to Helen Metzger, Ann Branigan, Bonnie Larson and Nadine Anders et al, who were paid a million dollars each for their silence. Upon my death and subsequent reading of this addendum to my last will and testament, their children shall inherit equal portions of my estate and, excepting Helen's child, Alexander, who already has the privilege, shall immediately take their rightful places in the family and family business, whatever it may be at that time.

Marcus M. McCoy

Tuning out the chatter from the party going on the other side of the study's locked doors, Alexander McCoy slumped back in the big desk chair. Staring at the scrawled signature at the bottom of the hand-written page, he tugged loose his black tuxedo's traditional bow tie. If only he could tune out the burn of betrayal as easily.

For what seemed to be the hundredth time, he had to admit to himself that he was definitely looking at the signature of the man he'd spent his life believing to be his brother. The brother he'd initially admired, then set out to be as different from as possible. And only Marcus would have had the nerve to belittle legalities by actually writing *yadda, yadda, yadda* especially on something as important as an addendum to his last will and testament.

Even if Alex could harbor any doubts, he would have had a hard time dismissing the word of David Weidman. The McCoys' longtime family lawyer had witnessed Marcus writing the addendum—though David claimed to have not read the document before sealing it in the heavy cream envelope that bore his signature and noting the existence of the unorthodox addendum in the actual will.

A will that had been read nearly a month ago. Four days after Marcus had been killed on June 8 while fly-fishing in Alaska by a grizzly bear that hadn't appreciated the competition. Before the reading of the will, Alex had grieved for the relationship he'd hoped to one day finally develop with his much older brother. Now…

Muriel Jensen's *His Family* (#1066) is the third book in her series THE ABBOTTS, about three brothers whose sister was kidnapped when she was fourteen months old. At the end of the second book, *His Wife,* we met China Grant, a woman who thought that she might have been that kidnapped daughter, but as it turns out, she's not. No one is happier about that than Campbell Abbott—who never believed she could be a relation.

Campbell Abbott put an arm around China Grant's shoulders and walked her away from the fairground's picnic table and into the trees. She was sobbing and he didn't know what to do. He wasn't good with women. Well, he was, but not when they were crying.

"I was so *sure!*" she said in a fractured voice.

He squeezed her shoulders. "I know. I'm sorry."

She sobbed, sniffed, then speculated. "I don't suppose DNA tests are ever wrong?"

"I'm certain that's possible," he replied, "but I'm also fairly certain they were particularly careful with this case. Everyone on Long Island is aware that the Abbott's little girl was kidnapped as a toddler. That you might be her returned after twenty-five years had everyone hoping the test would be positive."

"Except you." She'd said it without rancor, and that surprised him. In the month since she'd turned up at Shepherd's Knoll, looking for her family, he'd done his best to make things difficult for her. In the beginning he'd simply doubted her claims, certain any enterprising young woman could buy a toddler's blue corduroy rompers at a used-clothing store and claim she was an Abbott Mills heiress because she had an outfit similar to what the child was wearing when she'd been taken. As he'd told his elder brothers repeatedly, Abbott Mills had made thousands, possibly millions, of those corduroy rompers.

Campbell had wanted her to submit to a DNA test then and there. If she was Abigail, he was her full sibling, and therefore would be a match.

But Chloe, his mother, had been in Paris at the time, caring for a sick aunt, and Killian, his eldest brother, hadn't wanted to upset her further. He'd suggested they wait until Chloe returned home.

Sawyer, his second brother, had agreed. Accustomed to being outvoted by them most of his life, Campbell had accepted his fate when Killian further suggested that China stay on to help Campbell manage the Abbotts' estate until Chloe came home. Killian was CEO of Abbott Mills, and Sawyer headed the Abbott Mills Foundation.

Killian and Sawyer were the products of their father's first marriage to a Texas oil heiress. Campbell and the missing Abigail were born to his second wife, Chloe, a former designer for Abbott Mills.

When Chloe had come back from Paris two weeks ago, the test had been taken immediately. The results had been couriered to the house that afternoon. China had been there alone while everyone else had been preparing for the hospital fundraiser that had just taken place this afternoon and evening. She'd brought the sealed envelope with her and opened it just moments ago, when the family had been all together at the picnic table.

They'd all expected a very different result.

After spending most of her life as either an army brat or a military wife, Bonnie Gardner knows about men in uniform, and knows their wives, their girlfriends and their mothers. She's been all of them! In her latest book, *The Sergeant's Baby* (#1067), Air Force Technical Sergeant Danny Murphey is in for a big surprise—Allison Raneea Carter is pregnant. With more than a little past history together, Danny has to wonder—is the woman who refused to marry him because she wanted her independence carrying his child? Find out what it's going to take for her to change her mind about marrying him *this* time!

Danny Murphey lay quietly in bed in the darkened hotel room and listened to the soft, rhythmic breathing of the woman beside him. He reached over and caressed the velvety smooth, olive skin of her cheek and was rewarded with a sleepy smile and a soft moan of pleasure. It was music to him after two endless years apart.

He found it hard to believe, after so much time, but Allison Raneea Carter was really here, lying beside him, in this bed. She had responded to him—they had responded to each other as if they were designed to be the other's perfect match. It seemed almost as if the past two years had never happened.

Technical Sergeant Daniel Murphey had dedicated that time to emptying out the dating pools of Hurlburt Field, Eglin

Air Force Base, Fort Walton Beach and Okaloosa County, and had been ready to start working on the rest of northern Florida, when Allison had suddenly reappeared in his life.

He might have told his buddies back on Silver Team of Hurlburt Field's elite special operations combat control squadron that he liked playing the field, but he knew better. He had been trying to forget. Now that he and Allison had reconnected, Danny was ready to chuck it all and do the church and the little redbrick-house-and-white-picket-fence thing.

He'd been certain that he was ready to settle down two years ago, but Allison hadn't been. She'd wanted a career, and he, as a special ops combat control operator, could not envision his wife working. Men were supposed to provide for their families, and their wives were supposed to care for the home and their children. What better way to demonstrate his love than by wanting to provide for the woman he loved.

Allison hadn't seen it that way then, and it had caused a rift they had been unable to close.

They had never been able to compromise, and that one thing, for Allison, had been a deal breaker. She'd walked out on him, accepted a transfer and a promotion, and had not looked back.

Danny was sure that now, after two years apart, two years where he'd sown all the wild oats he'd wanted to and gained the reputation of ladies' man extraordinaire among the other members of his squadron, he and Allison would be able to compromise. He was okay with her working until the kids came along, and maybe when the kids were older and in school, she could go back. What woman wouldn't agree to that?

Allison shifted positions, giving Danny a tantalizing view of her ripe, full breasts. He could imagine his child, his son, suckling at her breasts, and the thought made his heart swell, as well as another part of his anatomy. He brushed a strand of her long, jet-black hair away from her face so he could gaze at her beauty. God, he could watch her all night and never be bored.

He'd always known that Allison was "the one." And this time, he was certain that she knew it, too.

As much as he wanted to wake her, to get down on bended knee right now to propose, he'd wait. He wanted everything to be perfect.

He'd ask her first thing in the morning.

This time he was going to do it right. And this time he was certain she'd say yes. "Allison Carter, I want you so much," Danny whispered into the darkness. "I know you're gonna give in and let me take care of you."

He leaned over and dropped a light kiss on her soft, full lips, then he lay back against the pillows and drifted off into contented sleep to dream of what would be.

But, when he woke up…he was alone.

With *Hometown Honey* (#1068), Kara Lennox launches a new three-book series called BLOND JUSTICE about three women who were duped by the same con man and vow to get even. But many things can get in the way of a woman's revenge, and for Cindy Lefler, it's a gorgeous sheriff's deputy named Luke Rheems—a man who's more than willing to help her get back on her feet again. Watch for the other books in the series, *Downtown Debutante* (coming September 2005) and *Out of Town Bride* (December 2005). We know you're going to love these fast-paced, humorous stories!

"Only twelve thousand biscuits left to bake," Cindy Lefler said cheerfully as she popped a baking sheet into the industrial oven at the Miracle Café. Though she loved the smell of fresh-baked biscuits, she had grown weary of the actual baking. One time, she'd tried to figure out how many biscuits she'd baked in her twenty-eight years. It had numbered well into the millions.

"I wish you'd stop counting them down," grumbled Tonya Dewhurst, who was folding silverware into paper napkins. She was the café's newest waitress, but Cindy had grown to depend on her very quickly. "You're the only one who's happy you're leaving."

"I'll come back to visit."

"You'll be too busy being Mrs. Dex Shalimar, lady of leisure," Tonya said dreamily. "You sure know how to pick husbands." Then she straightened. "Oh, gosh, I didn't mean that the way it sounded."

Cindy patted Tonya's shoulder. "It's okay, I know what you mean."

She still felt a pang over losing Jim, which was only natural, she told herself. The disagreement between her husband's truck and a freight train had happened only a year ago. But she *had* picked a good one when she'd married him. And she'd gotten just plain lucky finding Dex.

"It's almost six," Cindy said. "Would you unlock the front door and turn on the Open sign, please?" A couple of the other waitresses, Iris and Kate, had arrived and were going through their morning routines. Iris had worked at the café for more than twenty years, Kate almost as long.

Tonya smiled. "Sure. Um, Cindy, do you have a buyer for the café yet?"

"Dex says he has some serious nibbles."

"I just hope the new owner will let me bring Micton to work with me."

Cindy cringed every time she heard that name. Tonya had thought it was so cute, naming her baby with a combination of hers and her husband's names—Mick and Tonya. Micton. Yikes! It was the type of back-woods logic that made Cindy want to leave Cottonwood.

Customers were actually waiting in line when Tonya opened the door—farmers and ranchers, mostly, in jeans and overalls, Stetsons and gimme hats, here to get a hearty breakfast and exchange gossip. Cindy went to work on the Daily Specials chalkboard that was suspended high above the cash register.

"Morning, Ms. Cindy."

She very nearly fell off her stepladder. Still, she managed

to very pleasantly say, "Morning, Luke." The handsome sheriff's deputy always unnerved her. He showed up at 6:10, like clockwork, five days a week, and ordered the same thing—one biscuit with honey and black coffee. But every single time she saw him sitting there at the counter, that knowing grin on his face, she felt a flutter of surprise.

Kate rushed over from clearing a table to pour Luke his coffee and take his order. The woman was in her sixties at least, but Cindy could swear Kate blushed as she served Luke. He just had that effect on women, herself included. Even now, when she was engaged—hell, even when she'd been *married* to a man she'd loved fiercely—just looking at Luke made her pulse quicken and her face warm.

HARLEQUIN®

AMERICAN *Romance*®

Blond Justice

Betrayed…and betting on each other.

Coming in May 2005, don't miss the first book in

Kara Lennox's

brand-new miniseries.

HOMETOWN HONEY

Harlequin American Romance #1067

Cindy Lefler gets the shock of her life when her groom-to-be leaves her just days before their pending nuptials. But rather than get mad, Cindy plans to get even. And thanks to two other jilted brides and one very sexy local sheriff named Luke Rheemes, Cindy soon smells victory for her and her little boy. And maybe even her own happily-ever-after?

DOWNTOWN DEBUTANTE
(September 2005)

OUT OF TOWN BRIDE
(December 2005)

Available wherever Harlequin books are sold.

www.eHarlequin.com　　　　　HARHH0505

If you enjoyed what you just read,
then we've got an offer you can't resist!

Take 2 bestselling love stories FREE!

Plus get a FREE surprise gift!

Clip this page and mail it to Harlequin Reader Service®

IN U.S.A.	IN CANADA
3010 Walden Ave.	P.O. Box 609
P.O. Box 1867	Fort Erie, Ontario
Buffalo, N.Y. 14240-1867	L2A 5X3

YES! Please send me 2 free Harlequin American Romance® novels and my free surprise gift. After receiving them, if I don't wish to receive anymore, I can return the shipping statement marked cancel. If I don't cancel, I will receive 4 brand-new novels every month, before they're available in stores! In the U.S.A., bill me at the bargain price of $4.24 plus 25¢ shipping & handling per book and applicable sales tax, if any*. In Canada, bill me at the bargain price of $4.99 plus 25¢ shipping & handling per book and applicable taxes**. That's the complete price and a savings of at least 10% off the cover prices—what a great deal! I understand that accepting the 2 free books and gift places me under no obligation ever to buy any books. I can always return a shipment and cancel at any time. Even if I never buy another book from Harlequin, the 2 free books and gift are mine to keep forever.

154 HDN DZ7S
354 HDN DZ7T

Name	(PLEASE PRINT)	
Address		Apt.#
City	State/Prov.	Zip/Postal Code

Not valid to current Harlequin American Romance® subscribers.

Want to try two free books from another series?
Call 1-800-873-8635 or visit www.morefreebooks.com.

* Terms and prices subject to change without notice. Sales tax applicable in N.Y.
** Canadian residents will be charged applicable provincial taxes and GST.
All orders subject to approval. Offer limited to one per household.
® are registered trademarks owned and used by the trademark owner and or its licensee.

AMER04R   ©2004 Harlequin Enterprises Limited

eHARLEQUIN.com

The Ultimate Destination for Women's Fiction

Becoming an eHarlequin.com member is easy,
fun and **FREE!** Join today to enjoy great benefits:

- **Super savings** on all our books, including
  members-only discounts and offers!

- Enjoy **exclusive online reads**—FREE!

- Info, tips and **expert advice** on writing
  your own romance novel.

- FREE romance **newsletters,**
  customized by you!

- Find out the latest on your
  favorite authors.

- Enter to win exciting **contests
  and promotions!**

- Chat with other members in our
  community message boards!

To become a member,
visit www.eHarlequin.com today!

INTMEMB04R

HARLEQUIN®

AMERICAN *Romance*®

A new miniseries from

Leah Vale

The McCoys of Dependable, Missouri, have built an astounding fortune and national reputation of trustworthiness for their chain of general retail stores with the corporate motto, "Don't Trust It If It's Not The Real McCoy." Only problem is, the lone son and heir to the corporate dynasty has never been trustworthy where the ladies are concerned.

After he's killed by a grizzly bear while fly-fishing in Alaska and his will is read, the truth comes out: Marcus McCoy loved 'em and left 'em wherever he went. And now he's acknowledging the offspring of his illicit liaisons!

THE BAD BOY (July 2004)
THE COWBOY (September 2004)
THE MARINE (March 2005)
THE RICH BOY (May 2005)

The only way to do the right thing and quell any scandal that would destroy the McCoy empire is to bring these lost millionaires into the fold....

Available wherever Harlequin Books are sold.

www.eHarlequin.com   HARTLM

HARLEQUIN®

AMERICAN *Romance*®

THE ABBOTTS
A Dynasty in the Making

A series by

Muriel Jensen

The Abbotts of Losthampton, Long Island, first settled
in New York back in the days of the *Mayflower*.

Now they're a power family, owning one of the
largest business conglomerates in the country.

But…appearances can be deceiving.

HIS FAMILY
May 2005

Campbell Abbott should have been thrilled when his
little sister, abducted at the age of fourteen months,
returns to the Abbott family home. Instead, he finds
her…annoying. After a DNA test proves she isn't his
long-lost sister, he suddenly realizes where his prickly
attitude toward her comes from—and admits he'll do
anything to ensure she stays in his family now.

Read about the Abbotts:

HIS BABY (May 2004)
HIS WIFE (August 2004)
HIS FAMILY (May 2005)
HIS WEDDING (September 2005)

Available wherever Harlequin books are sold.

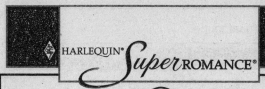

HARLEQUIN® *Super*ROMANCE®

On sale May 2005

With Child by Janice Kay Johnson
(SR #1273)

All was right in Mindy Fenton's world when she went to bed one night. But before it was over everything had changed—and not for the better. She was awakened by Brendan Quinn with the news that her husband had been shot and killed. Now Mindy is alone and pregnant…and Quinn is the only one she can turn to.

On sale June 2005

Pregnant Protector by Anne Marie Duquette
(SR #1283)

Lara Nelson is a good cop, which is why she and her partner—a German shepherd named Sadie—are assigned to protect a fellow officer whose life is in danger. But as Lara and Nick Cantello attempt to discover who wants Nick dead, attraction gets the better of judgment, and in nine months there will be someone else to consider.

On sale July 2005

The Pregnancy Test by Susan Gable
(SR #1285)

Sloan Thompson has good reason to worry about his daughter once she enters her "rebellious" phase. And that's before she tells him she's pregnant. Then he discovers his own actions have consequences. This about-to-be grandfather is also going to be a father again.

Available wherever Harlequin books are sold.

www.eHarlequin.com

HSR9ML0405

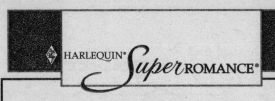

HARLEQUIN *Super*ROMANCE®

Come to Shelter Valley, Arizona, with
Tara Taylor Quinn...

...and with Caroline Prater, who's new to town. Caroline, from rural Kentucky, is a widow and a single mother.

She's also pregnant—after a brief affair with John Strickland, who lives in Shelter Valley.

And although she's always known she was adopted, Caroline's just discovered she has a twin sister she didn't know about. A twin who doesn't know about her. A twin who lives in Shelter Valley...and is a friend of John Strickland's.

Shelter Valley. Read the books. Live the life.

"Quinn writes touching stories about real people that transcend plot type or genre."
—Rachel Potter, *All About Romance*

www.eHarlequin.com   HSRSB0405